THE
DEFENDANT

Book **Eight** in the
Munro Family Series

CHRIS TAYLOR

LCT Productions Pty Ltd
18364 Kamilaroi Highway, Narrabri NSW 2390

ISBN. 978-1-925119-16-9

The Defendant is a work of fiction. Names, characters, places, brands, media and incidents either are the product of the author's imagination or are used fictitiously. Any resemblance to actual persons, living or dead, events, or locales, is entirely coincidental.

Published in the United States of America

Home is where the heart is...

Detective Sergeant Chase Barrington has never forgotten his high school sweetheart. He and Josie Munro planned to marry as soon as she graduated, but fate stepped in and Chase made the painful decision to end it. Unable to find the courage to tell her the truth, he left town without a word of explanation.

A decade after graduating high school, Doctor Josie Munro, Child Psychologist, has recently returned to her hometown. When she's appointed by the court to provide a report on a child's capacity to stand trial for murder, it's inevitable that she runs into the lead detective on the case. Unaware of the real reason why Chase ended their relationship, her anger and grief from all those years ago immediately rise to the surface.

Being a consummate professional, she has no choice but to complete the task she's been given, but she's determined to keep Chase at a distance and to get the job over with as quickly as possible.

As Josie gets to know the child through therapy sessions, she's torn between doing what the law requires of her against what her heart knows is right. She's also conflicted over her feelings for Chase. She wants to hate him, but she can't.

Will she follow her head or her heart?

THE MUNRO FAMILY SERIES

THE PROFILER
(Book One—Clayton and Ellie)

THE INVESTIGATOR
(Book Two—Riley and Kate)

THE PREDATOR
(Book Three—Brandon and Alex)

THE BETRAYAL
(Book Four—Declan and Chloe)

THE DECEPTION
(Book Five—Will and Savannah)

THE NEGOTIATOR
(Book Six—Andy and Cally)

THE CHRISTMAS VIGIL
(A Munro Family Series Novella)

THE RANSOM
(Book Seven—Lane and Zara)

THE DEFENDANT
(Book Eight—Chase and Josie)

THE SHOOTING
(Book Nine—Tom and Lily)

THE MAKER
(Book Ten—Bryce and Chanel)

Dedication

ACKNOWLEDGMENTS

As usual, no book comes into being without a lot of help and support by my friends and family. A world of thanks must go to my friend and fellow author Angela Bissell, critique partner extraordinaire, and a girl who loves the Munro family as much as I do.

To Pat Thomas, the best editor in the world. I love working with you. You turn my humble offerings into something truly amazing. I couldn't do it without you.

To Alisha of damonza.com, thank you for yet another fantastic cover. To my sister, Nicole Guihot, thank you for your excellent editorial comments and suggestions. Nic, I hope you like the final result.

To Grace Anselmo, a quirk of fate has brought us together and I now can't imagine writing a Munro Family story without your input. Thank you for all of your suggestions. They are highly valued. I look forward to working with you again.

To Detective Superintendent Michael Kilfoyle, thank you once again for all of your technical expertise. Any mistakes are wholly my own.

To Amy Atwell and her dedicated staff of miracle workers at Author EMS who are so much more than book formatters. Amy, once again, heartfelt thanks for working your magic.

To the fantastic writer organizations such as Romance Writers of Australia, Romance Writers of America and Romance Writers of New Zealand for all the help, support and encouragement they offer all authors, including me.

To my readers, thank you for your support and love for the Munro family. Your encouragement and enjoyment make this journey all worthwhile.

And lastly, to my friends and family, especially my husband and children. Thank you for putting up with late dinners and even later conversations as I've emerged day after day from the sometimes scary but always enthralling world I've created on my computer.

PROLOGUE

Neil Whitcomb felt around for the flask of cheap whiskey wedged between his thighs. In the pitch darkness, he couldn't make it out, but his fingers finally closed around it. With a sigh, he brought it to his lips and gulped greedily. With one hand, he pulled the steering wheel hard as far as it would go and stamped on the accelerator pedal.

The car fishtailed across the two-lane highway and into a tight corner. He cackled with delight. Adrenaline surged through him. Spinning the wheel in the opposite direction, he floored the accelerator pedal again. This time, the car shot forward, tires squealing on the asphalt. Whiskey sloshed out of the flask, spilling onto his rough gabardine pants. He cursed and emptied what remained of the alcohol down his throat.

Scratching the bristle of his prison-short hair, he dug around in the ash tray for a pill he might have overlooked amongst the cigarette butts. His meth high had worn off long ago and if it weren't for the whiskey, he'd be disgustingly sober. His fingers latched onto the smooth roundness of an ecstasy tablet and he crowed with relief.

How lucky was that? He swallowed the pill dry, anticipating the waves of euphoria that soon would come over him and make everything right with the world. The very thought of the impending rush was like a powerful stimulant and his mood changed considerably.

He relaxed against his seat and the constant urge to look over his shoulder eased. He continued to drive along the darkened highway with a renewed sense of purpose, putting considerable distance between him and the jail that had been his home for a decade.

As the pill began to work its magic, lights buzzed behind his eyes and excitement filled his veins. Now he could focus on taking care of other matters, like the throbbing between his legs.

He couldn't remember the last time he'd had a woman. He'd never succumbed to the pressure to fuck one of his fellow inmates. The very thought of it repulsed him. Desperate or not, he refused to stoop to the level of an animal.

The ecstasy tingled in his gut and warmed him throughout. Confidence filled him, flooding every pore. He'd never felt more alive. He turned the car into another tight corner and kept the accelerator pedal flat. The cheap sedan his cousin loaned him might have looked like a piece of crap, but it could get up and go when he wanted it to.

The highway worked its way through an almost deserted agricultural area. The sporadic lights from farmhouses were few and far between. He couldn't remember the last vehicle he'd seen, but it was way past late. Most people were probably in bed.

Neil scoffed. Sleep was for losers. With an E on board, he could drive all night. Ecstasy was good like that. He might even make it over the Queensland border by dawn. New South Wales and Sydney's Long Bay Jail in particular, would be far behind him, along with the hellish nightmares of the past ten years.

He took another corner at high speed, enjoying the rush low in his gut. A light glimmered up ahead. In the distance, he glimpsed the hulking silhouette of a farmhouse, visible through a stand of gum trees that grew a little way off the road. A vast area of vacant field surrounded the solitary, lonely building.

A thought took hold in his mind. With a lascivious grin, he

moved his hand with purpose toward his crotch. Within moments, his cock swelled beneath his fingers and the pressure in his balls became painful. A couple of more miles up the road, he spied a graveled driveway that led in the direction of the house.

His hand strayed toward the knife he had sheathed in a leather pouch on his belt. With sudden clarity, he swerved off the road and bumped along the rough dirt track. The light came closer. Anticipation surged through him…

CHAPTER 1

Daniel Logan rolled over in his bunk bed and hoped the squeak of the bed frame didn't wake his little brother Jason, asleep below him. He sat up and rubbed his eyes, unsure what had woken him. A glance out the window on the opposite side of the room assured him it was still night, the darkness broken by only the slightest sliver of a moon.

A noise from his mother's room snagged his attention. She always left the door open on the nights his father was away. The noise came again and he realized it was the sound of voices: The deeper voice of a man, followed by his mother's.

His heart leaped with excitement. *Had his father come home early? Had he finished his truck run ahead of time?* Daniel eased out of bed and padded across the room. The floorboards were cold beneath his bare feet, a reminder that winter was on its way. Stepping into the corridor, he tiptoed toward the faint gleam of light that came from his parents' room.

The sound of his mother's fearful cry stopped him cold. His heart thudded. *Something was wrong.* A man's voice rumbled again, the words not quite distinguishable. Daniel's palms went damp. He could barely hear anything over the rush of blood that pulsed through his ears, but one thing was for sure: The voice did not belong to his father.

Confusion and uncertainty warred in his head. His pulse thumped double time. He stood, stranded in the hall, unsure what to do. His mother cried out again and then he heard what sounded like a slap. Every nerve in his body screamed at him to run.

Another gasp. Another sob. He could tell his mother was crying. He drew in a deep breath and squared his shoulders. He was twelve years old, nearly thirteen. With his father away, he was the man of the house. It was his responsibility to look out for her; it was his job to keep her safe.

With his heart in his throat, he crept forward, inching closer toward his mother's bedroom. Finally, he came to a halt outside the open door. The lamp on her nightstand illuminated the darkness with a soft and gentle glow, in stark contrast to the terror that glinted in the whites of his mother's eyes.

She lay spread eagled on the bed, her nightgown hitched up around her hips. The dark, bulky shape of an unfamiliar man loomed above her. His hands dug into the pale skin of her thighs.

Fear like Daniel had never known kept him frozen to the spot, mere feet from her doorway. As the reality of the scene unfolding before him became clear, shock pulsed through him. He stared at the two of them, stunned.

His mother turned her head and saw him and her eyes widened in surprise. Panic and fear etched themselves on her face, a sight he would later remember in vivid detail. Daniel stepped forward with clenched fists and opened his mouth to yell.

His mother shook her head violently...once, twice, her wild gaze now frantic. He hesitated, all of a sudden horribly uncertain of what to do.

What was going on? The man loosened his belt and tugged down his dirty pants. Terror surged through Daniel's veins. His head moved back and forth between his mother and the man. Fear and indecision paralyzed him and kept him rooted to the spot.

Once again, his mother caught his eye and motioned him to leave. Torn between his need to help her and his fear of the large man who kneeled over her, he hesitated again.

For a third time, his mother signaled for him to leave, her expression increasingly desperate.

Coming to a decision, Daniel spun on his bare heel and ran back the way he'd come, his feet barely disturbing the air. He sped past his room, relieved to see his brother was still asleep. Barely able to hear over the thudding of his heart, he ran into the kitchen and made his way across the room with the aid of nothing more than memory and the slice of moonlight. He avoided the squeaky floorboard near the stove and eased open the back door.

The shed seemed a lifetime away, but he tore down the steps and across the patchy back lawn. Determination surged through him. Within minutes, he reached the steel shed door and heaved it open. Grabbing the flashlight from its hook on the wall, he switched it on and aimed the thin beam at the gun safe that stood tall and foreboding against the far wall. With hands that trembled, he punched in the security code, beyond relieved that he'd taken notice every time his father had unlocked it.

Reaching inside, he ignored the Ruger double barrel shotgun and the Winchester .243 for the .22 caliber Browning rifle. He pulled it out and laid it on the shed floor. Shining the flashlight into the bottom of the safe, he tugged the locked ammunition case toward him and felt for the key underneath. His heart pounded and his breath came hard and fast in the silence.

His fingers closed around the key and he breathed a sigh of relief. A second later, he fit it into the lock and pulled out a handful of .22 caliber hollow point bullets. He picked up the gun off the floor and pulled out the magazine. He plugged in the bullets as quickly as he could, the urgency in his fingers making them clumsy. He swore under his breath and then bit his lip. His mom disapproved of him cursing.

At the thought of his mother, another surge of panic went through him and he prayed she was all right. It felt like hours since he'd left her.

Grateful for the times his father had taken him to the rifle range and shown him how to shoot, he thrust the last bullet home and slid the magazine back into place. It locked inside the gun with a decisive click. He tore out of the shed, the flashlight now abandoned on the floor.

He raced across the yard, his heart still pumping hard. The sound of his mother's cries froze his blood. The scene in the bedroom replayed itself in slow motion and he moved across the lawn with increased urgency, his breath harsh in his ears.

His mother's room materialized in front of him and his vision was filled with the shadow of the stranger as he leaned over Daniel's mother. The man's bare buttocks clenched and flexed in a regular rhythm while his mother lay still and whimpered.

Fury raged through him, consuming him in its white-hot heat. A red haze clouded his eyes. The weight of the gun was heavy in his hands, but he lifted it and looked through the scope, aiming the crosshairs at the back of the man's head.

Time stood still. All noise receded—his mother's harsh cries, the man's guttural grunts—all of it melted away. Nothing existed but the gun and its target. He increased the pressure on the trigger. Slowly, slowly he pulled it toward him.

He barely heard the sound of the gunfire. It was the slightest little *pop*. The target dissolved into a mass of blood and brain matter. He lowered the gun slowly, numb, his body limp and exhausted. A second later, he was overcome by his mother's relentless, bloodcurdling screams.

CHAPTER 2

The strident ringtone of his cell woke Detective Sergeant Chase Barrington from a dead sleep. The ringing cycled three more times before he managed to locate the phone amongst the clutter on his nightstand.

"Barrington," he muttered, still half asleep.

"Detective Barrington, it's Sergeant Haynes from the Watervale Police Station. We've received an emergency call from a farmhouse out on Bruxner Road. There's been a shooting. The boss is already on his way. He needs you out there."

Chase cursed under his breath. He should have known better than to indulge in alcohol while he was on call. A few drinks after work with his boss and friend, the Local Area Commander, Riley Munro and Riley's wife and kids, had put him in a melancholy mood. He'd come home later than he'd planned and then spent a few more hours polishing off the bottle of Jack Daniels he had on the shelf of his liquor cabinet.

He was twenty-nine years old and had no family to speak of. As an only child with both of his parents deceased, lately he'd found himself yearning for something more permanent than the occasional fling with a girl he met on a Friday night at Watervale's popular drinking establishment. The night out with Riley and his family only served to underscore his loneliness.

He sighed quietly. It wasn't like he was playing hard to

get. He was a regular at The Bullet and quite often went there in the hope of finding someone special. The problem was none of the girls he got friendly with were Josie Munro. It was a problem he had no idea how to solve.

He grimaced and pushed the thought of her out of his mind. After getting directions to the crime scene and reassuring his colleague that he was on his way, Chase ended the call. Hoisting himself out of bed, he padded naked to the bathroom, flicking on the light as he entered. He stared at himself in the mirror and winced at what he saw.

His eyes were bloodshot. His hair was askew. He looked like he'd been on a bender. He shook his head in disgust. *He was getting too old for this shit.*

Leaning over the sink, he splashed cold water over his face and scrubbed at the whiskers on his chin. He shaved before he'd left for Riley's house, but the stubble never remained hidden for long—a result of his Italian heritage. His surname, 'Barrington,' sounded like it had come from a long line of British descendants, and it did, but his mother had been born in Florence.

He reached for the towel that hung on the bath rail and swiped it across his face. Running his hands through his unruly hair, he did his best to return order to the thick tangle of curls. It was too early in the morning to worry about a hairbrush. Besides, he'd had way too little sleep to care.

Returning to the bedroom, he glanced at the clock on his nightstand. *Three forty-six.* He threw a wistful glance toward his rumpled king-sized bed and then resolutely headed for his closet and began to dress.

Chase spied the small, non-descript mailbox on the side of Bruxner Road and turned his unmarked police vehicle into the dirt driveway. A few minutes later, a tired weatherboard farmhouse, in dire need of a coat of paint, came into view.

A tidy yard and garden in stark contrast to the dilapidated state of the house, was visible through the criss-crossing red, blue and white light beams of the emergency vehicles at the scene.

He came to a halt next to an ambulance which was parked right outside the front door. At least three other squad cars crammed into the front yard. As if they'd watched for his arrival, two of his colleagues appeared from inside the house and met him on the porch.

"What have we got?" he said by way of greeting.

Sergeant Ian Crowne shook his head. "It's not good."

Probationary Constable Luke Dawson looked chalky, his lips matching the pallor of his skin. A second later, he pushed past Chase and vomited all over the lawn. Chase grimaced. It didn't bode well for what he was about to find. Shouldering his way through the front doorway, he made his way down a hall of bare floorboards polished to a dull gleam and headed in the direction of the low murmur of voices.

A row of family photos on the wall in the corridor caught his eye. Pictures of two smiling young boys were proudly displayed in heavy wooden frames. A wedding photo of a youthful couple gazing at each other with love hung on the opposite wall. The innocence of the photographs was in stark contrast to the violence that had recently occurred in the home. Swallowing a sigh, Chase continued down the hall and came to a halt outside the bedroom at the very end.

The male victim lay face down on the unmade bed, a bullet hole in the back of his head. Blood and brain matter seeped onto the pale bedspread in an elongated stain beneath his head. His pants and underwear were around his knees, but he was otherwise clothed. His boots had left dirty marks on the pale pink-and-white bedspread.

Chase shifted his gaze to the woman who stood crying quietly in the far corner of the room. Blood and body tissue were splattered over the front of her white cotton nightgown. More blood was smeared across her face. A blanket was draped around her shoulders and a paramedic talked to her in tones too low for Chase to hear.

A flash of light snagged Chase's attention. He glanced around and caught sight of the police photographer. The man snapped off another shot of the crime scene and then changed his position. Chase's boss stood behind the photographer. Chase sidled up to him.

"What happened, Riley?"

Riley turned away from the scene of carnage and acknowledged him. "Chase, thanks for coming. It's a messy one. There's a young kid involved. I've called in Forensics. They're on their way over from Grafton. They'll be here in a couple of hours. We're going to need all the help we can get." He offered a half-hearted smile. "Lucky we didn't have a late one last night or we'd both be in a world of pain."

Chase pressed his lips together and nodded. No need to tell his boss he'd been awake for most of the night—not when the woman who'd kept him sleepless was his boss's sister. Forcing his thoughts away from Josie Munro, Chase focused on the scene before him. "So, what do we have? A domestic?"

Riley grimaced. "I wish."

"Who is he, then?"

"The driver's license we recovered from the wallet in the victim's back pocket says it's Neil Whitcomb. We ran him through the database. He got out of Long Bay late yesterday afternoon. He must have hightailed it straight out of Sydney and headed north."

Chase's gaze shifted to the woman who still huddled in the corner, her blue eyes wide with shock. Her hair was a soft brown color that now lay tangled around her face. She looked like she was in her late thirties. Shivering and dazed, she barely resembled the pretty, young woman he'd seen in the wedding photo down the hall. His gaze returned to his boss and he pitched his voice low. "Who is she?"

"Kelly Logan. Thirty-seven years old. Moved north from Melbourne a few months ago."

"Is she the shooter?"

Riley's lips tightened and his expression turned grim. "No, that would be Daniel Logan, her twelve-year-old son."

Chase reared back in surprise. "Fuck."

"Yep."

The tragedy that had unfolded in the house became more and more apparent. Chase ran a hand through his hair. Cold dread weighed heavily in his gut. What had started out bad had just become a whole lot worse. Nothing about this night was going to end well.

"Where's the boy?" he asked.

"I told Jake to take him out of here. I think they're waiting in the kitchen."

CHAPTER 3

The boy's tousled head glinted like gold under the soft lighting in the kitchen. The resemblance to his mother was plain to see. Dark shadows haunted his eyes, but Chase guessed sleep was the last thing on the boy's mind. He sat in a worn pine chair near the kitchen table and stared at the cracked linoleum floor, his body as still as if he'd been nailed to the spot.

Chase approached him quietly, his heart heavy. He caught the eye of Jake Simons, the constable who had removed the boy from the scene and gave the officer a brief nod of acknowledgement. Hunkering low, he brought himself down to eye level with the boy.

"Hey, buddy. I'm Chase, one of the detectives from Watervale. What's your name?" The boy continued to stare at the floor. Chase tried again.

"I've just come from your mom's bedroom. Something happened here tonight, buddy. I really need you to tell me about it."

Still, the boy remained silent and immobile. Chase glanced up at Jake, who shrugged. He swallowed a sigh. He hated to manipulate the boy's emotions, but he was left with no choice.

"Listen, buddy, if you don't talk to me, I'm going to have to go back in and question your mom. She's pretty upset in there. You don't want me to upset her any further, do you?"

The needling had its desired effect. The boy's head

snapped up, his eyes fierce. "*No!*" Just as quickly, his head dropped back down until his chin almost touched his chest. He rocked back and forth on his chair. Fat tears slid down his cheeks.

Chase felt like a prick. He was harassing a child, a boy who had suffered through the worst kind of horror and torment way too early in his life. If it wasn't so necessary to know what had happened, Chase would have offered comfort, like he wanted to, rather than threats. He stood and met Jake's gaze. The constable's expression was also tortured.

"I'm going to confer with the boss," Chase murmured. Jake merely nodded.

Retracing his footsteps, Chase returned to the bedroom. Riley now stood near Daniel's mother, talking quietly to her. She responded through gasps and sobs, her words disjointed.

Chase cleared his throat to gain Riley's attention.

Riley glanced up at him and then eased himself away from the woman. "What is it?" he asked when he reached Chase, his voice pitched low.

"It's the boy. He's in a bad way. Shocked almost to the point of muteness. Can barely spit out a syllable. We're not going to get anything out of him while he's in that state. What did you get out of the mother?"

Riley's lips compressed into a thin line. "A little, but she's still in shock. She lives here with her husband, Trevor Logan and their two sons. Trevor's a truck driver for New England Transport. Right now, he's out on the road. We've tried to contact him, but he hasn't answered his phone. Probably asleep."

Chase closed his eyes and shook his head. "Poor bastard."

"Yeah. Anyway, Kelly said she was in bed asleep when she was woken by a noise. The next thing she knew, Whitcomb was standing over her, threatening her with a knife. She didn't want him to discover her sons, so she did her best to stay quiet. Unfortunately, Daniel woke and came upon them.

"Hell."

Riley drew in a deep breath and released it on a heavy sigh. "Yeah. By that time, Whitcomb had his pants down. Daniel saw everything. She tried to warn him away. He left, but a few minutes later he returned, this time with a gun. He put a bullet through the back of Whitcomb's head."

"Did you find the knife?"

"Yeah, a four-and-a-half-inch Bowie. It had fallen down the side of the bed. Whitcomb's got a scabbard on his belt."

Dread cemented in Chase's gut. Knowing he would have done the same thing if he'd been in Daniel's position didn't make it any easier.

"Christ," he breathed, shaking his head slowly. "No wonder the poor kid isn't talking."

"Yeah. No wonder." Riley sighed again. "What do you want to do?"

"I'm not going to hound him any further. He'll talk when he's ready. We need to get someone in to see him, a professional trained to deal with children and trauma."

Riley nodded. "My sister Josie's just returned home. She took up a private position through Rural and Regional Health in Watervale about a month ago. She's a child psychologist. I could call her and see if she can meet us at the station."

Chase stared at Riley in surprise and his heart pumped double time. *Josie.* The sweet sound of her name rolled silently off his tongue. He didn't realize she'd left Brisbane and was so close by.

Nervousness surged through him, coupled with an underlying feeling of anticipation. He'd been in love with Josie Munro all of his life. The last time he'd seen her was the night of her high school graduation. It had been the most beautiful night of his life.

Then the memories of what happened afterwards crashed in on him and he had to turn away. The pain of it, as raw and fresh as if it had happened yesterday, battered him from all sides.

He'd promised her a future and he'd reneged. He hadn't even told her why. She'd loved him; she'd trusted him, she'd believed in him...and he'd let her down. The hurt he'd caused was ingrained in his memory. It would be naïve for him to think she could ever recover from it, let alone forgive him, no matter how much he yearned that things could be different.

"Chase? Are you okay?"

The concern in Riley's voice reached him through the plethora of decade-old memories. With a determined effort, Chase shut down the personal thoughts and concentrated on his boss.

"I-I'm fine. I was just thinking about...all of this."

"Yeah, it's a fucking tragedy all round." Riley's gaze fell on the body and his eyes hardened. "Except for this piece of shit. He got exactly what he deserved."

"Yeah, when word gets out, there won't be too many around who'll sympathize with the son of a bitch." Chase glanced at Kelly Logan who remained standing in the corner of the room, quietly sobbing, the paramedic still by her side. "I hate to think what this will do to their family."

Riley followed his gaze and his face darkened. "She needs to get to the hospital where they can do up a rape kit. We'll talk to her again a little later. I'll call Josie. It's early, but when I explain to her what's happened, she'll be more than happy to help. That poor boy needs her."

The thought of seeing Josie again after all this time, let alone being in the same room as her, made him feel a mixture of emotions. He pressed his lips together and nodded. Silently, he sent a prayer heavenwards that he'd have the courage to handle it.

CHAPTER 4

Josie blinked hard and wiped the sleep from her eyes with her fist. She glanced at the clock mounted on the dashboard of the forest green Boss 351 Mustang she'd borrowed from her father and stifled a groan. *Four-thirty*. It was way too early in the morning to be out.

When Riley had called her, waking her from a deep and dreamless sleep, she'd immediately thought something had happened to one of their parents. They were both elderly and while they still enjoyed good health, that kind of thing could change in an instant. She had only to remember what had happened the previous Christmas.

It had only been four months since her father had been lying in the ICU, unconscious, after a brain hemorrhage. The scar that ran from the base of his skull to just below his ear was still puckered and pink. Seeing him so still and pale against the white sheets of the hospital bed, with tubes and monitors and other medical paraphernalia surrounding him, she'd been rudely reminded of the fragility of his existence and how tenuous one's grip on life could be.

After forcing herself to ask the question, she'd been beyond relieved when Riley assured her he wasn't calling about their parents. He'd gone on to explain in the briefest of detail why she was needed at the station. She'd immediately agreed to come in and it only took a few minutes for her to throw on her clothes.

Now, she peered through her windscreen, grateful for the

extra powerful driving lights her brother Riley had insisted she install now that she was back living in the country. The bright beams cut a wide swathe through the darkness and illuminated the road in front of her. She'd been warned by her neighbors to watch out for kangaroos while driving at night and she now had her eyes peeled to the shoulders and ribbon of asphalt unfurling before her.

She was thankful she didn't live too far out of town. She'd accepted the job before making enquires about the availability of houses to rent. When the time came, she searched on the Internet and was a little concerned to discover decent rentals in Watervale were in short supply.

Her parents had insisted she could stay with them and while she loved them for making the generous offer, she'd come home to Grafton to take stock of her life. Standing on her own two feet, with her shoulders back and her head held high—finding a place to call her own was an important first step on the journey.

Not that she could call a rental house her own, but at twenty-eight, it would be better than moving back in with her parents, no matter how dearly she loved them. To move home would have been the easiest thing to do, but it would feel like she'd failed to make it if she took that route.

A week before she was due to start her new job, she'd stumbled across an advertisement in the local paper. The house had been listed privately and she'd immediately called the landlord. The cottage was small, but it was only a ten-minute drive from Watervale. When she'd taken a look at the place, she'd fallen in love with the serenity of the quiet green fields that surrounded it. She could imagine having a dog and a cat and she had just the right chair for the front porch. There was plenty of room for a veggie patch and maybe even a few chickens.

She smiled and turned to the landlord, who'd been waiting a little anxiously behind her. 'I'll take it,' she'd said and signed a six-month lease on the spot.

Now, the lights of Watervale showed up in the distance and Josie swallowed a sigh. In a very short time she'd be facing a boy who from all accounts had been traumatized to such a degree he was almost mute. She hadn't asked Riley what had caused it and he hadn't offered. He'd only asked for her help. She hoped she was up to the task.

Josie parked in the car park adjacent to the modest brick building that housed the Watervale Police Station. Collecting her briefcase, she stepped out of the Mustang and tugged her jacket closer around her. The night air had a definite chill to it, reminding her that winter wasn't far away. It came so much earlier in Watervale. The northern climes of Brisbane, not far from the coast, were almost immune to its effects. She'd never worn a winter coat while she'd lived there.

The lights of the station beckoned. Blinking away the last vestiges of sleep, she entered the building through the automatic glass sliding doors and made her way over to the counter. Her gaze focused on the man who stood behind it. A second later, her brain registered the all-too familiar face and her mouth dropped open.

Chase Barrington stared back at her. *How…?* Her heart stopped still and then took off at a pounding gallop. He was the last person she'd expected to see. She'd had no idea he was stationed here at Watervale. At least, she assumed he was an officer. He'd been in training to become one when they'd last met. He wasn't dressed in a uniform, but he stood behind the counter in such a manner that made her think he belonged there.

Against her will, her gaze ran over the broad shoulders that were only emphasized by his navy blue, tailored suit and pristine white business shirt. His hair was as dark and unruly as she remembered. *Boy, did she remember.* The longish curls wrapped intimately around his ears, like they used to around her fingers.

The memory sent a surge of anger flooding through her.

She hadn't seen him for a decade. For ten years, her questions had gone unanswered. For months, even years, after he'd left, she'd struggled with the injustice of it.

How he could love her one day, and ignore her the next? And not only ignore her—completely and utterly cut her off without a word of explanation. Not a phone call or text, not even an email.

It had taken her a long time, but she'd eventually managed to put it all behind her, refusing to dwell on the pain that had marred her youth. The only relief she'd found was that her single night in his arms hadn't resulted in a pregnancy. As close as she was to her family, she hadn't told a single soul about what had happened, preferring to bury the pain and humiliation in a deep dark place inside her. A teenage pregnancy would have made that impossible.

She closed her eyes briefly at the memory and steeled herself to acknowledge him. With more courage than she thought she could muster, she lifted her gaze to his and bit back a gasp. His eyes burned with an emotion so fierce she took a step back.

Confusion whirled inside her. Was he *angry?* What right did *he* have to be angry? No, she must be mistaken. It couldn't be anger. She was the one who had the monopoly on *that* emotion. After all, she'd been the one who was dumped.

Refusing to let him see how much his presence affected her, she arched her eyebrows in a casual show of surprise.

"Chase Barrington? Is it you? Are you working here, in Watervale?"

Chase stared at her. His jaw moved and then he swallowed. A flush crept up his neck. He opened his mouth and finally uttered a few words.

"Josie Munro. Fancy seeing you here? Riley only just told me you'd moved back from Brisbane. What have you been up to?"

Josie desperately looked around for her brother, praying silently for him to appear. When he failed to materialize, she stammered a reply.

"I-I'm a child psychologist. I'm privately contracted with Regional and Rural Health, but I suspect Riley's already told you that or else I wouldn't be here. What's the problem? Riley mentioned something about a boy."

Chase drew in a breath, as if relieved to have another topic to focus on. "Yes, Daniel Logan. Twelve years old. Tonight he shot and killed the man who was raping his mother."

"Oh, God." The hoarse words fell out of her mouth before she could stop them. Her mind flooded with visions of the poor child who was no doubt replaying the night's events in all its Technicolor detail and wondering how the hell it had happened.

"Where is he?" she asked, in a voice that wasn't quite steady.

Chase's lips compressed. He looked at her with sympathy and understanding and something else she wasn't brave enough to define.

Josie looked away. She didn't have time for distractions.

"He's in Interview Room Three. If you head over that way, I'll go and unlock the door and take you down to see him."

Josie turned and looked behind her at the door Chase indicated, relieved to put a little distance between them. A moment later, the door swung open, cutting her relief short. Chase met her on the other side. She stepped through the doorway and the sleeve of her jacket slid up against his. Emotion flared in the emerald-green depths of his eyes, halting her breath. A second later, it was gone.

"Come through here. I'll take you to him." With that, he spun on his heel and headed across the squad room. Josie stumbled after him, wishing his legs weren't so long. His strides ate up the distance and she struggled to keep up. As if sensing her predicament, he halted and turned to face her, his gaze running over her from top to bottom.

"I don't know how you manage to walk anywhere in those heels," he muttered.

Heat followed in the wake of his gaze, along with an increase in her pulse. She steadfastly ignored both and fixed her gaze at a spot somewhere below his neck.

"The boy's through here." He turned away and continued across the floor of the squad room. A closed doorway led to a corridor with rooms branching off from either side. Riley stepped out of a room about halfway down. He saw her and smiled briefly, though the expression in his eyes remained grim.

"Josie, thanks for coming. I'm sorry to drag you out of bed."

She waved away his apology. "No need to apologize, Riley. I'm happy to help."

"I take it Chase filled you in?"

She kept her gaze fixed on Riley and replied, "Yes, he did."

"Did he tell you the boy's not talking?"

She glanced at Chase and just as quickly looked away. "No, but from what I understand the child's been through, I'm not surprised."

"His mother's been taken to the hospital and we haven't yet been able to locate his father. Daniel has a younger brother who's been taken to emergency foster care. They have no other family living close."

"So, Daniel's in there alone?"

Riley's lips compressed and he nodded grimly. "Yes."

"Then he needs me." Ignoring both men, Josie pushed past them and stepped into the interview room Riley had exited moments before. A boy with tousled blond hair, who looked a little small for his age stared at the gray Formica table, his hands twisted in his lap. He wore a faded navy T-shirt with a white Nike emblem splashed across the front and a long pair of cotton pajama pants.

The room was small and sparsely furnished. Apart from a pair of hard plastic chairs, it was utterly devoid of comfort and seemed to engulf him in its starkness. Josie's heart went out to him.

"Hi, Daniel, my name's Josie," she said gently. "The police have asked me to come and talk to you. Is it okay if I sit down?"

She waited for a response, but none was forthcoming.

Stepping closer to the table, she pulled out the vacant chair and lowered herself onto it. Flipping open her briefcase, she tugged out the legal pad and a pen. Daniel's gaze remained fixed on the table. She busied herself for a few moments, recording the date and time and place of the interview. Without looking at him, she spoke again.

"So, Daniel. Let me tell you a little bit about myself. I was born in Grafton, a couple of hours from here. My dad was a judge and my mom was a nurse. I have five older brothers and a younger sister. Let me tell you, I had it pretty tough. My brothers still give me a hard time. You have a brother, don't you?"

She posed the casual question and was rewarded with the slightest of nods. She disguised her relief with another question. "What's his name?"

"Jason." The response was barely a whisper. Still, Josie took it as a good sign. At least the boy was talking.

"Are you older or younger?"

"Older." Again, the reply was soft and hesitant, but Josie didn't lose heart. Instead, she smiled. "Ah, so you're the one who gets to give *him* a hard time. How old is he?"

"Eight."

She nodded sagely. "I see. You must be...what...twelve? Thirteen?"

"Twelve. I'm nearly thirteen."

"It's hard to have much in common with an eight-year-old. You must be in high school, right?"

"Yeah..."

Josie nodded and returned to her notes. "So, tell me about your little brother. What's he like?"

Daniel shrugged again. "He's all right, I guess."

"How do you like school?"

"It's okay."

"What's your favorite subject?"

"Sport."

"Are you a runner or a swimmer?"

"I like to run. Cross country."

"I bet the hills around here make you work for it."

His lips tugged the tiniest bit upward and then his smile slowly faded. Once again, he stared at the table.

Josie drew in a breath and let it out slowly. A few moments passed in silence. "We need to talk about what happened tonight, Daniel."

His body tensed. His hands clenched into fists and his breath came faster. Josie waited patiently. Gradually, he relaxed again.

"Who lives with you at home, Daniel?"

"Mom. Dad. Jason."

"Were Dad and Jason there tonight?"

"Jason was. Dad's away. At work."

Josie made a few notes on her legal pad. "Where does Dad work?"

"He's a truckie. He's always on the road. He does the long hauls from Brisbane to Melbourne, up and down the coast."

"What about Jason? Where was he?"

Daniel paused and his voice lowered. "He was asleep."

"How do you know?"

"We share a room."

"What happened, Daniel?" Josie asked quietly.

The boy scrunched his eyes up tight and tears leaked down his cheeks. A moment later, he gasped on a heartrending sob.

"I-I was asleep. I woke up. I don't know why. I sat up in bed and kind of listened. I heard something. Voices—Mom's and the voice of a man. I thought it might be Dad. I thought he might have come home early. I wanted to see him. He's been away for more than a week."

He gasped on another sob and his shoulders shook. Josie ached to offer him comfort, but she needed him to finish while he still could. She'd seen case files where traumatized children would often speak straight after an event, but within a short time later, they refused to speak at all. They blocked the event out by shutting down and retreating within themselves. It was a simple, but effective coping mechanism and one that was entirely understandable.

It was important she discover what had happened from

Daniel's point of view, before he was beyond offering even the simplest of explanations. But try as she might, she couldn't ignore the shock and pain that flooded the young boy's face. Unable to help herself, she pushed away from the table and went around to where he sat.

She bent and put her arms around him, knowing her every word, her every action was being recorded. Riley and probably Chase too, were no doubt watching the interview from behind the two-way glass, but that knowledge didn't deter her. She couldn't sit by and watch a child fall apart. His life from now on would never be the same. He had no idea yet, but she did and she was going to ease him into the realization as gently as she could.

"*Shh*, honey. It's going to be okay. I'm here for you. I'm on your side. I promise it's going to be all right." She hated the murmured lies that fell so easily from her lips, but there was no way she was going to tell him the truth. If the police laid charges and the prosecutor proved Daniel knew that what he was doing was wrong, he'd be thrown into a whole new world of hurt and nothing she could do would help him. The reality of what might happen was a burden he didn't need to carry right now.

Daniel swiped at his eyes with the back of his hand and let his breath out on a shudder. Josie moved away and regained her seat. She gave him another few moments to collect himself and then quietly started again.

"Talk to me, Daniel. Tell me what happened."

He tensed. The expression on his face showed her how hard he fought to remain stoic. Her heart lurched at his bravery. "Start at the beginning," she added softly. "What happened after you heard your mother's voice?"

He drew in a deep breath. His slight body trembled when he breathed out.

"I climbed out of bed and started down the hall. I wanted to say hello to Dad. It was the middle of the night, but I didn't care. I knew Mom and Dad wouldn't either. Mom knows how much me and Jason miss Dad when he's away. She misses him, too."

Josie kept her gaze lowered to the paper in front of her and tried to concentrate on making her notes. "What happened next, honey?"

"I kept walking down the hall and I-I heard Mom cry out. I realized the voice didn't belong to Dad after all. It was someone else. Another man. Someone I didn't recognize." His breath came faster.

"Something was wrong. Dad wasn't home. There was a man in Mom's room. When she cried out again, I forced myself forward. She sounded really scared. I was scared, too, but Dad left me in charge. I'm the man of the house. It's my job to look after Mom and Jason when he's away. I had to make sure she was all right."

Josie blinked back the sudden surge of emotion that burned behind her eyes. Twelve was far too young to feel so responsible. Despite the unsettled feeling deep inside her at the knowledge of what was to come, she forced herself to ask the question, knowing it had to be done.

"What happened next, Daniel?"

"It was dark. I couldn't see much at all, but there was a light coming from Mom's bedroom. The door was open so I guess that's why I heard them. I inched along the hall. I didn't want to go in. I didn't! I was so scared. But then it came again—my mother's cry of pain—and I knew I had to. I'd promised Dad. I promised I'd keep her safe."

His breath was harsh in the silence. Josie wanted nothing more than to tell him to stop, that it was all right, that he didn't have to say any more, but she couldn't. She'd been called in for a purpose. As much as she hated it, she had a job to do.

"Keep going, Daniel. Honey, you're doing so well. I know how hard it is to think about it, but I need you to stay brave. You're the bravest boy I know."

He drew in another shaky breath and continued. "I-I got to the door. That's when I saw them."

"Who did you see?"

"M-my mom and...and *him*."

"When you say him, who do you mean, Daniel?"

"Him. The man who hurt my *mom*." His voice cracked on another sob.

Josie's heart broke. She glanced up at the two-way mirror, but the cold, dark glass offered no comfort. Daniel continued to sob, quieter than the first time, but heart wrenching just the same.

"Would you like a drink? A Coke or maybe a Fanta?"

"I want my mom," he whispered, his voice low and ragged.

"I know, honey. I know. The police will bring her here as soon as they can. How about I go and find something for you to drink? Would you like that?"

Fresh tears formed in his eyes, but he offered her a jerky nod. Josie stood and left the room, selfishly grateful for the short reprieve. Daniel's pain was hard to bear. She was close to losing her composure. It was only her years of training that kept her from falling apart.

She sensed Chase before she saw him. A moment later, he was there, his expression showing his annoyance.

"What are you doing?" he demanded. "You need to keep going. You need to get him to finish."

———————————

Chase tried to temper his tone, but it came out sounding like an order just the same. Josie's eyes flashed with anger and he cursed under his breath.

"Please don't tell me how to do my job." Her reply was all the more effective for its deadly calm delivery. He couldn't blame her for her reaction.

"Josie, I didn't mean—"

"No, of course you didn't. Just like you didn't mean to dump me the minute I had sex with you."

"No." Pain tore through him, but he resolutely forced it aside. "That's not true. I..." He stopped. Now wasn't the time and this certainly wasn't the place. She stared at him, hurt shadowing her beautiful blue eyes.

"Of course it's true and even now, after all these years, you can't offer me an explanation." She turned her back on him and strode away, down the hall toward the squad room. The door dividing the two areas closed quietly behind her.

"Damn." Chase scrubbed at his hair in frustration and fatigue. It had been too long since he'd strung more than a handful of hours of sleep together. Coupled with the shock of seeing Josie again, his manners were far from their best.

Impatience surged through him at the thought of the boy, his irritation made worse by the knowledge that Josie was right. The kid was as fragile as fine-blown glass and just as likely to disintegrate into a thousand pieces with the slightest pressure. She'd made the right decision by giving him some breathing space.

He could see her now, through the glass that separated them. She stood at the drink machine just inside the squad room, a frown marring the perfect smoothness of her face. His gaze tracked across her pale blue blouse. She'd removed her jacket and he couldn't help but notice the soft outline of her breasts. His gaze moved lower, cataloguing the slim hips encased in a tailored skirt that ended just above her knee. Her shapely calves were exposed to his appreciative gaze.

It was five in the morning and yet she looked as beautiful as she had a decade ago as an innocent, fresh-faced teenager. He wished he could say the same thing about himself.

A can of soda rattled into the bin and Josie reached in and collected it. He watched while she took a deep breath and squared her shoulders before heading back toward him. He wondered if it was the thought of passing by him again or what was waiting for her in the interview room that she braced herself against.

She stalked past him without a whisper of acknowledgement and re-entered the room where Daniel waited. Chase bit down hard on a sigh of longing and regret.

Chapter 5

Josie did her best to push thoughts of Chase Barrington to the back of her mind and focus on the boy in front of her. The fact that the man she'd been in love with for more than a decade still held the power to hurt her, stirred her anger. She was no longer an innocent young teenager, high on life and love. She'd grown and matured; she had a successful career. She didn't need a man in her life to make her feel worthy.

And yet, after a handful of moments in the company of her high school sweetheart, her confidence was shot to hell. She was once again the eighteen-year-old girl who had loved with all her heart; who foolishly and naïvely believed her love had been reciprocated; who had fallen for the good-looking, charming captain of the football team and had believed every one of his whispered promises.

She thought she'd let the hurt and disappointment go. She thought she was over him. She'd had ten years to make a life without him and it was a life with which she was content...most of the time. She hadn't realized until a moment ago how much she still yearned for an explanation for the way he'd treated her. Even now, when she'd asked him directly, he hadn't had the courage to give her one.

Fresh fury surged through her veins and she clenched her jaw until her teeth hurt. She didn't realize she'd voiced her anger until she saw Daniel lift his head, a frown of confusion on his face. The sight of it was like being doused in iced water. He was the one who'd been dealt the bad hand. This boy, the one hunched over the table, with fear and uncertainty obvious in every line of his young body, this boy was the one who had the right to complain. He was the needy one—and she was supposed to be there to help him.

With renewed determination to do everything she could to ease him through what was to come, she regained her seat and offered him the can of soda. He looked at it for a moment and then took it from her.

"Thanks."

"No problem. Take your time, we'll start again when you're ready."

He opened the soda and drank. A mouthful. Two. He set the can aside. Josie drew her notepad closer and picked up her pen. She chewed on the end of it and debated her next course of questioning in silence.

"I want to tell you what happened."

Her head jerked up in surprise and she stared at the boy in front of her. He stared back at her, his expression now earnest, his eyes shadowed with fear...and determination.

"Okay," she responded quietly.

Daniel filled his lungs and blew out his breath on a heavy sigh. He leaned over the table, his shoulders slumped.

"I saw that man with my mother. I saw the terror in her eyes. She was terrified and she was hurting. I couldn't make the man stop. He was so much bigger than me. As I watched what he was doing to her, all I could think about was getting a gun."

He paused and Josie saw the struggle on his face. She held her breath and silently willed him to continue. A moment later, he did.

"I ran to the shed, to the gun safe. I knew the code to open it."

"How did you know the code, Daniel?"

"I've watched Dad lots of times. We go to the shooting range together. I got my gun license the day after I turned twelve."

Josie made a few notes on her legal pad and then waited for him to speak again.

"It was dark. I found the flashlight in the spot Dad usually leaves it. I punched in the code and pulled out a gun."

"What kind of gun?"

"The .22 Browning rifle. Dad bought it for me after I got my license. I take it to the range."

Josie nodded. It wouldn't occur to a boy living in the city to apply for his gun license, but for many country kids, especially boys, it was a natural progression in their journey toward adulthood.

"What happened after you took the gun?" she asked quietly.

"I found the case that held the ammunition and unlocked it. Then I loaded the gun. I was hurrying. I was scared I wouldn't get back in time to help Mom. I was so glad I'd loaded bullets into the magazine enough times that I could do it without even thinking about it."

"How long did it take?"

Daniel shrugged. "I don't know. Twenty, maybe thirty seconds. I'm used to doing it quickly at the range. The sergeant-at-arms gets cranky if we hold up the shoot."

Josie raised an eyebrow in surprise. She was a kid born and raised in the country, but she'd never lived on a farm. Her father hadn't been interested in firearms and living in the city of Grafton, there hadn't been a need. Not like there was in the bush, where the eradication of wild pigs and kangaroos was often a necessity in order to protect precious crops.

"What did you do after you loaded the gun?"

"I took off back to the house. I had to get back there. I had to help my mom." His voice trembled. His gaze lowered to his lap where he picked at a loose thread on his pajamas. Josie said a silent prayer that he'd hold it together enough to finish.

"It's okay, Daniel. Take your time. The next part's going to be rough. When you're ready, you can tell me." She watched while he pulled more determinably at the thread around the waistband of his pants. He bit his lip and frowned and then sucked in a deep breath. He looked up and his gaze skittered over hers and then landed on the floor. Her heart lurched at the pain on his face.

"What happened when you got back to the house, honey? You went back to your mother's room?"

He gave her a jerky nod, his gaze still fixed on the industrial-strength linoleum that covered the interview room floor.

"Then what happened?"

Tears sprang to his eyes and he swiped at them with the back of his hand. He drew in a shuddering breath and let it out on a heavy sigh. Josie stayed quiet, giving him the time he needed. At last, he looked up at her with eyes so haunted, the picture would stay with her until the day she died.

"He was lying on top of my mom. He had his pants down. My mom wasn't moving. All I could see were her legs, spread wide. He was grunting like a boar on the run from pig dogs. Mom was still crying, but softly, not like before. I lifted the gun and looked through the scope. There was enough light from the lamp on the nightstand for me to take a good aim. I was more scared than I've ever been in my life, but I had to stop him. I had to stop him hurting my mom."

Daniel's breath came hard and fast and he rocked to and fro on the seat. It was almost like he'd left Josie and was back there, reliving the scene frame by frame. Her heart went out to him. She couldn't imagine the horror he felt.

"I took aim. I knew what I had to do. A moment later, I pulled the trigger." He bent over as if in agony and held his head in his hands. A howl of pain escaped him, followed quickly by another and another. He spoke through gasping sobs.

"It all happened in slow motion. His head exploded in front of me. It spattered the walls and the pillows and the headboard. There was blood everywhere. My mom wouldn't stop screaming..."

Josie drew in a shaky breath, feeling nearly as harried as

the boy. A coldness settled deep inside her and she was frightened it would never thaw. Daniel had witnessed a horror too awful to describe and yet, he'd managed to do just that. She couldn't imagine how he'd pick up the pieces and go on; come to terms with the reality of what had happened—to him and to his mom—and to overcome it enough to move on with his life and live as normally as possible.

How was he going to manage it? How would he ever feel normal again? She couldn't imagine how anyone would even take the first step toward accepting the night's events and putting them behind them. It would take years of therapy and even with that there was no guarantee. She wanted to help him, but what if she couldn't?

She'd been a practising psychologist for nearly six years, but she'd spent all of that time in a private practice in one of the wealthier, northern suburbs of Brisbane. Her patients of the past were mostly rich and spoiled teens who were giving their parents a headache. That was far removed from what she'd just experienced in the early hours of the morning in an interview room buried in the bowels of the Watervale Police Station.

In Brisbane, after a few sessions giving a child her undivided attention and listening, *really* listening to their problems, she always followed it with a family session where she bluntly told the parents the truth: Their children needed less of their money and more of their time; their children needed to feel that they mattered.

Most of the time, she was able to fix things and everyone went away happy. Well, maybe not everyone. More often than not, the parents were less than thrilled with her tactics, but no one complained about the results.

After six years where nothing much changed but the names of the children who filed through her office, she'd gotten to the point where she was disillusioned with her chosen profession. She'd started out in her first year of university with stars in her eyes and the world at her feet. There was nothing she couldn't achieve. She was young and so idealistic and determined that nothing would stand in her way. She was going to make a difference; she was going to save the world—one desperately sad and lonely child at a time.

But it hadn't turned out that way. It hadn't meshed with her ideals. Her initial excitement when she'd been offered the job in the exclusive private practice had waned over the years and she'd become more than a little jaded.

When her father suffered a brain hemorrhage last Christmas, she'd finally given voice to her dissatisfaction. Sitting by his hospital bed in the ICU, she'd found the courage to say it aloud, albeit to a man who was in a coma. It was then that she'd realized the truth: She hated her job.

The reality of it was nothing like what she'd imagined; nothing like the career she'd worked hard for and dreamed of. Disappointed and disillusioned, she decided to leave the city and come home. She needed time to regroup and to rethink the direction of her career. It had been a stroke of luck her mother had seen the job advertisement in the local newspaper for the position with Rural and Regional Health.

And here she was, dealing with a child who couldn't be further from the patients she had worked with in the city. A child who needed her so desperately, she was terrified she might let him down.

What if she didn't have the experience he needed? What if she said the wrong thing? He was broken inside. *What if she couldn't put him together again? What if he never healed?*

She swallowed a moan of despair, not wanting to alarm him. This was about *him*: Daniel. It had nothing to do with her. She had to pull herself together and believe in her abilities. She needed to employ whatever skills she had at her disposal to make him whole. Or as whole as he could be under the circumstances. She vowed with every fiber of her being to make that happen.

———

Chase stared at the woman and the child through the two-way glass and steeled himself against the emotion that tightened his chest. Dread weighed down his limbs. He glanced at Riley, who looked as grim as he felt. Chase closed his eyes at the thought of what he had to do.

"We have to charge him," Riley murmured tiredly.

Chase drew in a deep breath and released it slowly. His shoulders slumped on a sigh. "Yeah, we do. As soon as we get his confession on record."

"We need to call him a lawyer."

Chase grimaced. "We both know the public defender will be sleeping off another late-night bender. He won't even hear his phone. If we wait until we get someone from Grafton, it might be too late. The boy might clam up again. I say we do it now and the let lawyers argue over the rules."

Riley stared at him for a long moment and then gave a reluctant nod. "Yeah, I guess. Do you want to do it, or shall I?"

Chase scrunched his eyes closed and rubbed at the headache behind them. A moment later, he opened them. His gaze was steady on Riley's, even as his gut twisted into knots. "I will."

"You're sure?"

"Yeah, he knows me from the farmhouse. A formal interview might be better coming from someone who's a little familiar."

"I don't know if anything in this poor kid's life is ever going to be better again, but we have no choice. He admitted to blowing that son of a bitch's brains out. We have to let the courts take it from here."

"It's too bad."

"Hey, I don't like it any more than you do, but that's the way things are. We believe in a justice system that upholds the rules we all agree to abide by, even if you're only twelve."

"What are we going to do with him?"

"Charge him, fingerprint him. Do what you'd normally do."

"What about his mother? Should we wait for her?"

Riley shrugged. "She might well be admitted to the hospital overnight. She's probably been sedated. I say let's get it over with. Josie can stay with him. She seems to have built a rapport with him."

At the mention of Josie's name, Chase's heart stuttered. His gaze flicked back to the glass and renewed pain sheared through him. She'd left her seat and once again had her arms around the boy, comforting him with whispered reassurances that she must have known were false. Oblivious to his dark future, the boy clung to her, crying quietly, his eyes filled with equal parts hope and dread.

Chase cleared his throat of the lump that had lodged there and turned to his boss. "I'll go and break the news."

Riley merely nodded, his face grim.

Chase drew in a deep breath and then shouldered open the door to the interview room. Josie straightened upon his entry, but stayed close by Daniel's side, guarding him like a mother lion. The pain in Chase's gut twisted like a knife. He'd hate every second of what he was about to do.

He schooled his face into a carefully bland expression, refusing to let her see how much the next few minutes were going to affect him. She wouldn't react well and there was no other way he knew how to deal with it. He had a job to do. It was as simple as that.

Doing his best to keep his voice even, he addressed the boy. "Daniel, I need you to come with me."

"What's happening? Has his mother arrived?"

He met Josie's anxious gaze and swallowed another sigh. "No. I'm going to take him through his evidence again, this time for the record and then he'll be taken to the charge room."

A frown marred the smooth, golden skin of her forehead. "The charge room?"

"Yes. He's going to be charged with murder."

"You asshole."

The word hit him like a ten-pound hammer right between the eyes. He did his best to hide his pain.

Did she think he was enjoying this? That he wanted to charge the kid? How could she think such a thing? Didn't she know him at all? Was ten years really that long ago for her to have forgotten every little thing about him? Surely it wasn't.

She stared at him like he was a stranger—a distasteful one at that. Shock and anger widened her eyes and flushed her cheeks with color. She shook her head in disbelief, looking like she was beyond words. A moment later, she found them.

"How *could* you? Haven't you been *listening?* Have you heard even a single word that he said? That animal was ra—" She swallowed the word with difficulty, her gaze skating to the boy. Chase did his best to ignore her and proceeded to carry out his job.

Pulling out a pair of handcuffs, he gently restrained the boy. Ignoring his cry of anguish and the gasp of horror from Josie, he led the child out of the room.

"Handcuffs? You're handcuffing him?"

"It's standard procedure."

"You have to be fucking kidding?"

"Josie, that's enough."

The stern command came from Riley and Chase swallowed a sigh of relief. Her anger reverberated through him, weighing him down with sadness and grief. With quiet determination, he blocked out everything but his job.

As if wading through a pond of molasses, he went through the motions required. Twenty minutes later, it was done. Daniel Logan was charged with murder and remanded into custody. He'd be brought before the judge as soon as the courthouse opened.

CHAPTER 6

Kelly Logan stared at her reflection in the bathroom mirror and hated what she saw. It had been more than a week since the attack and yet it replayed in her head continually, as clearly as if it had happened the night before: The smell of unwashed body; the guttural grunts and groans; the weight of the man forcing her into the mattress. And then, the rancid breath; the sharp rasp of stubble; and worst of all, the feel of him violating her.

No, that wasn't the worst of it. The worst part was when she glanced up and saw her son, his face stark with shock and horror and disbelief. That was by far the worst. That was the memory she'd never escape.

What followed was a nightmare she didn't think she'd ever wake from: The man pounding into her; the crack of the gunshot. The noise of it smashed into her brain, even as her attacker collapsed on top of her without another sound.

Warm blood and tissue had sprayed across her face, blinding her, choking her, horrifying her. And all that time, Daniel had stared at her, his face a frozen mask of terror and incredulity. She didn't even remember calling the police, but all of a sudden, they were there and from that moment forward, everything passed in a blur.

Paramedics examined her. In muted tones, they declared her in shock, but otherwise unharmed. *Unharmed?* Had someone really said that? Compared to the animal on the bed with his brains splattered across the wall, she probably was, but she was far from feeling unharmed. She couldn't imagine ever feeling normal again.

Police officers had surrounded her, asking a barrage of questions that blurred into a kaleidoscope of murmurs and static noise. They'd spoken to her gently, with concern etched deep into their faces, but it hadn't made any difference. Her mind had refused to settle. Her thoughts skittered and skated like hot fat melting on a griddle until all she'd wanted to do was scream.

Daniel had been taken out of the bedroom by one of the officers and for that, she'd been eternally grateful. She was in no position to help him or to give him what he needed. She'd been taken by ambulance to the hospital and the nightmare had continued. More questions; more intrusive examinations. The phrase 'rape kit' became part of her vocabulary.

Afterwards, the doctor urged her to take a sedative and she was more than willing to comply—anything to stop her from remembering the nightmare that had suddenly become her life.

Because of the lateness of the hour, she'd been kept in the hospital overnight. It was the next day before she'd been well enough to see Daniel. A part of her still wished she hadn't.

She'd cried out in anguish in the visitors' room at the police station when they'd brought him from the cells. The sight of his blank expression, his dead eyes, his refusal to say a word haunted her even now.

Where was her beautiful son? The boy who laughed and joked and teased? The boy who was always telling a story, who couldn't be solemn if he tried? *What had they done to him?*

She hoped and prayed with quiet desperation that his emptiness was a temporary thing; that once he was home and in a familiar environment, he would return to something that resembled his normal self.

She never expected him to forget what happened. Heavens, *she* couldn't forget it. But she hoped the resilience of his youth would help him put it behind him in the best way he could. The fact that there were bloodstains still on the carpet didn't help, but she'd done her best to remove them—even Trevor had tried.

At the thought of her husband, she sighed anew. Fresh waves of pain and despair washed over her. She clung to the edge of the sink, increasing the pressure until her fingers hurt. She didn't know what to do about Trevor. Every time he looked at her, he grew angry.

It wasn't that he blamed her for what happened, but the mere sight of her looking so depressed and withdrawn reminded him of the attack and how he hadn't been there to prevent it. The guilt of it was eating him alive. He'd told her as much amidst sobs of anguish three nights ago.

And then there was Jason. Oh, God. Her poor little boy. He walked around the house like a ghost, lost and bewildered. It was almost as if he didn't recognize them anymore. She could hardly blame him. The family he'd known was gone; disintegrated like ashes in the wind. How could she make this better? She didn't know how to fix it, to make it better, to help him like he needed.

She'd always been the strong one, the one that had remained calm in the face of a crisis; the one they'd turned to; the one they expected to make things better, to put them back on track. Now, she didn't know what to do to help any of them. She couldn't even help herself.

She'd been on edge since her return home, feeling numb and detached and exhausted. Nothing felt real. Nothing felt safe. The feelings were foreign and frightening. She'd become a stranger watching her life through a lens that wouldn't focus and she had no idea what to do about it.

———————————

Josie checked the time on her watch and frowned. Her two o'clock appointment was late. If there was something that irritated her to no end, it was tardiness. It wasn't fair to her other patients who arrived on time and were then forced to wait.

During the past week and a half, she'd done her best to push thoughts of Daniel and Chase from her mind and had been wholly unsuccessful. She didn't need a therapist to tell her the bad mood she'd been in since she'd last seen them had everything to do with both Chase and the tragic circumstances that had once again brought them together.

The phone on the desk near her elbow shrilled, breaking the silence in her office. Whilst she was contracted to the Rural Health Authority, it was her responsibility to locate suitable premises to work from. She'd been lucky to find office space in an old weatherboard home that had been converted to suites for professionals.

A doctor, a physical therapist and a chiropractor also shared the house, each with a generously proportioned room and a shared reception area. For a small additional fee, Josie had the use of the services of Moira Barnes, the clinic's ageing but oh-so-elegant secretary.

The terms of Josie's contract with the Health Authority meant that she was obligated to see any patient they referred to her. In return, she was entitled to keep most of the fees her patients generated, less a small percentage that was remitted back to the Health Authority. In addition, she was entitled to see other patients who came to her from other sources.

The phone rang again and she picked up the receiver. "Josie Munro."

"Josie, it's Moira. I have Detective Barrington on line three."

Josie's heart lurched. Stealing a breath, she took the call. "Hi, Chase."

"Josie, I'm glad I caught you."

His familiar, deep tones triggered another flurry of nerves. He'd always had that effect on her, ever since high school when a chance meeting at an inter-school football game altered her world forever.

She'd been seventeen. He was a year older. The

charming smile, the teasing glint from his emerald-green eyes had catapulted her head over heels in love. Now she frowned at the memory and forced it from her mind. She was upset at Chase for so many reasons she might never feel kindly toward him again.

"What is it, Chase?" Her tone was distinctly unfriendly.

"It's about Daniel Logan. His matter was mentioned in court today. His lawyer has requested Daniel undergo a psychological assessment and the request has been granted. The prosecutor has contacted me. He wants you to do an assessment for the Crown. As the defendant, Daniel has a right to silence, but if the defense seeks to present a psych report, in the interests of fairness, the Crown will also tender one."

"Why me? I'm sure there are plenty of psychologists more qualified. Have you called anyone in Grafton?" she said, referring to the nearby city that was four times as big as Watervale.

"No. I want you."

Josie's heart leaped into her throat and then she silently cursed under her breath. *Did he mean...?* She couldn't fall for that. It wasn't possible he felt the same way she did. Besides, she was mad at him. She refused to yearn for things to be different.

"I-I'm not sure I'm the best person for the job. I've never—"

"Daniel's mother called me. She asked me about you. She wanted to know who you were. Daniel's barely spoken since your initial interview, but he's been asking for you. Apart from the *doli incapax* issue, the prosecutor wants your report to include an opinion on whether the boy's fit to stand trial."

"*Doli* what? I don't have a clue what that means. Like I told you, I've never done any court work before."

"I'm sorry, I didn't mean to sound pompous."

He sounded genuinely apologetic and Josie modified her tone. "So, what *does* it mean?"

"*Doli incapax* is a Latin term that means incapable of

criminal intention or malice. The law presumes a child under the age of fourteen doesn't know their actions might be wrong in a criminal sense, such as shooting a man dead. It's up to the prosecution to prove the child has the mental capacity to form this understanding. If they don't, the case will be thrown out."

Josie closed her eyes and supported her head in her hands. The memories of that awful night, the memories Daniel could never erase, crowded her mind until she could barely hear the rest of what Chase said. The bleak desperation, the fear, the uncertainty in the young boy's eyes—it broke her heart anew.

"I know you think I had a choice in laying charges against the boy, but the fact is I—"

"Okay, I'll do it," she said, cutting him off, not wanting to hear his explanation. "When do you need it?"

"The matter's been stood over for a couple of months to enable both parties time to obtain their reports. Right now, he's out on bail. I believe he's at home...with his family."

The way his voice trailed off, Josie knew he wanted to say something more, but after taking down the contact details of Daniel and his mother, she forced herself to end the call. She understood that Chase had only been doing his job, but she didn't have to like it. Besides, she was still angry at him for not bothering to explain his abrupt departure from her life. As much as she wished it were different, the hurt he'd caused just wouldn't go away.

Trevor Logan tilted the beer glass toward his mouth and emptied it. He swiped at the froth left behind on his lips and promptly ordered another. He'd been at The Bullet since the sun had gone down. It was now going on for ten. His eyes had long since blurred over and his legs just wouldn't move like they should. But no matter how drunk he got, the pain just wouldn't go away. Even the alcohol taunted him.

Every time he closed his eyes, he replayed the scene in his head. He might not have witnessed the attack, but the police gave him enough details of what had happened and the rest he'd pieced together.

It had been morning before they'd reached him. He'd been on the road for twelve hours and had pulled into a truck stop for the night. He'd turned off the two-way, set his alarm for six and then settled down to sleep. Three or four beers and some quiet music on his iPod usually did the trick.

He'd spoken to Kelly and his boys before he'd gone to sleep and had then switched his phone off.

He should have pushed harder to be home. If he'd been there, this never would have happened. His wife would be the happy, chirpy woman she'd always been and his boys would be driving him insane. Their rousing was always done with little rancor, but it happened all the same. Now, he would kill to see them rumble around. It would reassure him that his world hadn't been tilted off its axis. It would assure him they were normal.

Normal? Who was he fucking kidding? His family would never be normal again. They'd had the life torn out of them and ripped to shreds. To make things worse, he couldn't even hunt down the animal who'd done it. The prick was dead and good riddance to the filthy scum, but Trevor couldn't help but wish he'd been given the opportunity to put a bullet in the son of a bitch. He wouldn't have stopped at just one.

The bartender placed another glass in front of him and Trevor murmured his thanks. He reached for his wallet, but the barman stayed his hand.

"It's all right, mate. This one's on me."

Trevor bit his lip against an immediate surge of anger, but merely nodded his thanks. The barman's pity infuriated him. There was nowhere he could go to escape it. Everywhere he turned, people knew he was the husband of the woman who'd been raped by a monster fresh out of jail. They knew he was the father of the boy who'd murdered the prick.

It wasn't like they blamed Daniel for his actions. Most of

them were more than happy to admit they'd have done exactly the same thing. But Trevor couldn't help but notice the occasional frown sent his way, the look of calculation in the eyes of some of the men as they shook their heads and muttered that it wouldn't have happened if he'd been there.

As if he didn't know that. As if it weren't tearing him up inside, the guilt staring back at him every morning and weighing his gut down every night. He needed to be strong, for his wife, for his boys.

The problem was, he couldn't be. He couldn't even look at them without imagining the horror of what had happened and that made him furious all over again. Not at them, never at them, but he couldn't be near them, either. He didn't want to punish them, but he had to stay away. For the very sake of his sanity which he was barely clinging to, he had to stay away.

At the other end of the scarred wooden bar, Chase took a sip of his drink. The single malt whiskey slid down his throat in a ribbon of smooth, liquid fire. Try as he might, his thoughts kept circling back to Josie and he couldn't help the yearning that filled him. *If only things had turned out differently...* If only the timing hadn't been so bad.

The day after he'd met her at the football game, he'd called her and asked her out. She'd lived in Grafton, a couple of hours away, but the distance didn't deter him. He'd known from the very first instant that she would be his, forever. Besides, he'd turned eighteen and had a license. He'd even saved enough to buy a cheap car. He didn't care how much the fuel cost or how many miles he drove, he couldn't get enough of her.

Of course, they were both still in school and in reality, their meetings were mostly confined to the weekends. Even then, those were fitted in around sporting engagements, dance lessons and other things.

They made it even more difficult for themselves by choosing to keep their love a secret. Josie had five very protective older brothers and her father was a District Court judge. Not that Chase let that daunt him, but he agreed with her just the same: It would be easier if they didn't tell anyone, at least, not until after they'd finished school.

They emailed and texted and spent hours talking on the phone. Chase told his mother he was dating a girl in his class. Josie's parents thought she was spending time with her girlfriends.

It killed Chase not to take her as his date to his high school graduation, but Josie told him it was for the best. Her father was not at all keen for her to have a boyfriend. She was seventeen, but still very much his little girl. He urged her to concentrate on her studies, finish high school and perhaps after that, when she went to university, she could look at dating.

For twelve more months, they kept their relationship a secret. Chase had been accepted into the Goulburn Police Academy and spent much of his time hours and hours away. Still, his love for Josie didn't waver and he longed for the day he could tell her family and the world his true feelings. When she asked him to be her date to her high school graduation, he'd been over the moon.

She told him her family had been surprised at her choice, not having even heard of Chase Barrington. They wondered aloud how the two of them had met and were satisfied with vague references to high school. Besides, Chase was on his way to a career in policing, and law enforcement ran thick through Munro veins. By then, all of Josie's older brothers were serving police officers. Her father had given his tacit nod of approval.

Memories of that magical night swamped him and emotion burned behind his eyes. He'd never seen Josie look more beautiful. When she'd whispered shyly that she wanted him to make love to her, he thought he might combust from the heat of his desire. Until then, their relationship had remained purely platonic. He'd wanted her to be sure and wanted her first time to be special.

And it had been. It was his first time, too. They'd made love and it had been as beautiful as he'd imagined. Afterwards, he'd kissed her and held her and promised one day he'd make her his. They'd even talked about their children and had gently argued over names. They'd agreed to meet with her parents the next day and confide in them their secret. Chase had been counting the hours.

And then tragedy struck and for him, it was all over. One moment he was head over heels in love and planning a forever future with the girl of his dreams and the next he was flat on his back in a hospital bed, his whole world turned on its head.

Even now, he couldn't think about it, didn't want to think about it. Life had knocked him down and he'd dealt with it the best way he could, the *only* way he could. At least, that's how he'd felt at the time. Now, he wasn't so sure.

Seeing Josie again had stirred up so many long-buried memories and with them, excruciating guilt. But not only guilt, there was also uncertainty. *Had he made the right decision when he walked away from her all those years ago?* He couldn't help but wonder what might have happened if he'd told her the truth.

A soft, warm body pressed against him and he blinked to clear his head. A woman in her early twenties smiled at him and flicked back her glossy brown hair. She had a body meant to drive men crazy and her cherry red lips were full and open in invitation.

She put a manicured hand on his arm and leaned in, making sure he noticed her impressive breasts. It was hard not to. They were barely contained in some kind of black, lacy mesh and for an instant, his body stirred.

Once upon a time, not so very long ago, she would have caught his interest. After all, one night stands were his specialty—nothing permanent required. No commitment offered or sought. Just a few moments of reciprocated pleasure before both parties moved on in the morning.

But after seeing Josie again, knowing that she was in town, not even the pretty young starlet who looked like she'd stepped off a Hollywood movie set could tempt him. She pressed against him again and asked him to buy her a drink. Her voice was low and throaty, but he politely shook his head no. Tactfully angling his body away from hers, he finished his drink and set the glass back down on the bar.

"I'm sorry," he murmured. "I'm flattered, but I'm not the man for you. Trust me." Ignoring the flash of disappointment in her eyes, he left the bar, cursing himself and Josie Munro every step of the way.

CHAPTER 7

Josie stared at the woman and her son seated across from her. It had been two days since she'd spoken to Chase and then had made the call to Kelly Logan. It was obvious Daniel and his mother weren't faring well. Josie's greeting to him a few moments earlier had gone largely ignored and his mother's response was only slightly better.

Kelly Logan looked like she was in her late thirties. Though her shoulder-length brown hair hung lank around her face, her skin was clear and well maintained. Remnants of nail polish remained on her fingers, evidence of an earlier manicure. Once upon a time, a time before the assault, she'd been a woman who took care of herself. Swallowing a sigh, Josie tried again to establish a connection.

"Mrs Logan, thank you for coming in and for bringing Daniel to see me. I explained a little of the reason for your visit when we spoke on the phone."

"Yes, you did. Something about the prosecutor wanting a report."

"That's right. Daniel's lawyer has arranged for him to be assessed by a psychologist. It's normal procedure for the Crown to do the same. The purpose of the report is twofold. The prosecutor has asked me to assess Daniel's fitness to stand trial. He's a little concerned your son may still be too traumatized to deal with the reality of a hearing and to provide his lawyer with adequate instructions. The other purpose is to determine whether Daniel knew what he was doing was wrong."

The woman's frown was fierce. "Of course he knew it was wrong. Do you think we've raised our boys to be lawless animals?"

Josie hurried to explain. "Of course not, Mrs Logan. I'm sorry, I didn't mean to give you that impression. I'm sure Daniel's a good boy. I'm sure he knows right from wrong. What I'm talking about has to do with how the law perceives these things.

"*Doli incapax* is a term the law uses when dealing with children under the age of fourteen. A child between the ages of ten and fourteen can be charged with a criminal offence, but the burden rests on the prosecution to prove the child knew what he was doing was wrong."

Kelly Logan opened her mouth again and Josie hurried on. "Not merely in a naughty sense or something for which he might be punished, but wrong in a criminal sense. It's an important distinction. If the Crown fails to prove Daniel's *mens rea*—his mindset—in a criminal sense, the case against him will be dismissed and the charges will be dropped."

Hope flared in the woman's tortured eyes. "Really? They could drop the whole thing? H-how likely is that to happen?"

Josie swallowed a sigh and answered as honestly as she could. "I don't know. It depends upon Daniel. I interviewed him the night it happened. He recounted a set of events. Based upon this, he was charged with murder. I don't know if the interview will be admissible. That's for the court to decide. It's my job to dig a little deeper, to find out exactly what he thought at the time of the offense, how he felt, what made him act the way he did. My recommendation to the court will depend upon my findings."

Daniel's mother stared at Josie with eyes that had been through more than anyone should have to bear. Quiet tears slid down her cheeks. Josie bit her lip against the surge of emotion that tightened her chest and made breathing difficult.

"I'm so sorry, Mrs Logan," she whispered. "I don't know what else to say."

"Of course you don't. No one does. Not even me. I close my eyes, I try to sleep, but all I see is *him*. I *hear* him. I *feel* him. I—"

"Mrs Logan," Josie interrupted and stole a look in Daniel's direction. She was relieved to find him staring blankly at the wall beside him, his head turned sideways, away from them. He appeared oblivious to his mother's quiet but furious outburst.

Josie reached across her desk and placed her hand over Kelly's. "Mrs Logan, you need to seek some professional help. Please tell me you're seeing someone."

The woman closed her eyes as if to block out the pain. Her hand fisted under Josie's. "Th-the nurse at the hospital put me in touch with a counselor. D-Diane something or other. She came to see me while I was there, in the hospital, that first night."

Josie nodded. "Have you seen her since?"

Kelly shook her head. "No. I-I can't even think about it, let alone talk about it."

"I know how you feel, and believe me, it's perfectly normal, but talking about it will help you heal, it will help you release the burden of anger and guilt. These emotions are perfectly normal, but they will consume you from the inside out if you don't do anything about this."

The woman stared up at her with a hard expression. "You know how I feel? How in heavens name would you know? Have you ever been ra—?"

"No, but I've been a psychologist for a number of years. I know what I'm talking about. I know the effects of trauma and how to help people deal with them."

Anger flashed in Kelly's eyes. She snorted in disgust. "You've learned it out of books. That's what you mean to say. You don't know what it's like, how it *feels*. You don't have a clue. You don't go to bed too scared to turn out the light, wondering... Knowing it won't happen again, sure it won't happen again, but not really believing it."

Josie blinked back tears. The woman was right. She didn't know. She couldn't even imagine how it felt and she prayed she never would. Guilt surged through her at the thought.

"You're right, Mrs Logan, I don't know how it feels, but that doesn't mean that I or some other therapist of your choice can't help you."

"And how am I going to pay for it? My husband hasn't been able to return to work. He thinks if he leaves, something bad is going to happen." Her voice dropped to a ragged whisper. "He thinks this is his fault."

Josie drew in a deep breath and let it slide out over her taut lips. Trevor's reaction was understandable and was a form of survivor's guilt. It pained her to know that this family who had already suffered so much was now hurting even more.

"I'll call a friend of mine in Grafton and see what she can do. Her name's Phoebe Jamison. She's a therapist working for the base hospital. I'm sure there'll be some form of counseling you can access free of charge. Daniel, too. Phoebe will know for sure. Anything would be better than nothing." She paused before adding gently, "In fact, it would be a good idea if all of you attended counseling. Has your husband talked to anyone?"

Kelly shook her head and dropped her gaze to her lap. A moment later, her shoulders shuddered and she gasped on a sob. "He won't even talk to *me*." She shook her head back and forth. "I don't know what to do. I don't know what to do. I just...don't know what to do."

Josie's gaze shot to Daniel. He'd turned to face his mother, his blank expression replaced with one of torture.

"Please, Mom. Please, don't cry. Please." Tears ran silently down the young boy's cheeks and Josie's heart clenched in pain. Moisture formed in her eyes, but she steadfastly ignored it. She was breaking every rule by allowing herself to get involved, but she couldn't help it: She'd been involved from the moment Riley called her in the early hours of the morning to come to the aid of a desperate child. There was no way she could shut off, or turn her back on them now.

It was a long time later when Kelly and her son managed to get their tears back under control. Josie's composure had been severely tested by the sight, but she had a job to do and she couldn't let her emotions get in the way.

She offered them a box of tissues and then quietly addressed the boy who sat across from her.

"You heard me talking to your mom about the report I need to do." He nodded, his eyes red.

"This report is very important. It could mean the difference between you standing trial for shooting that man or going free." She paused and looked at him, purposefully holding his gaze. "Do you understand what I'm saying, Daniel?"

He eyed her steadily. She was filled with a surge of admiration.

"Yes, I understand."

Josie swallowed a sigh of relief. "Okay, well, I think we've been through enough today. I want you to go home and think about what I've said." Her gaze encompassed both of them. "I'll see you here again tomorrow."

Closing the door to her office behind them, Josie leaned against the wooden panel. Her shoulders slumped on a heavy sigh. A moment later, she gave herself a mental shake. She wasn't the one who had suffered unspeakable violence. She wasn't the one who needed help. She vowed to do whatever she could to assist the Logan family.

First on her list was calling Phoebe Jamison.

———————

Chase glanced up from his desk and spotted Riley as he walked through the doorway. For the past couple of days, they'd been on opposite shifts and Chase hadn't had a chance to catch up. He wanted to talk to Riley about Josie, but the opportunity hadn't presented itself. Now, it seemed fate had played into his hands.

"Ah, boss, you got a minute?"

Riley stopped and looked up. "Sure, but follow me. I'm expecting a phone call in my office."

Chase pushed away from his desk and followed Riley into

the small room, partitioned from the rest of the squad room with glass walls.

"What's going on?" Riley asked as he lowered himself into his chair.

Now that he had Riley's attention, sudden nerves tightened Chase's throat. He took his time arranging himself in the other chair that stood across from Riley's desk. Paper and files and reference books were piled high all over the floor. Even more paperwork covered the desk.

"Don't you ever get sick of all that crap?" he joked, indicating the mess.

"Yep, every single moment of every single day, but it's like this: The quicker I finish with one pile, another pile appears. It's like magic. I never even see them coming."

Chase tried out a grin. "*Mm,* and you're the boss. What hope do the rest of us have?"

Riley took the teasing in stride and returned Chase's grin. "So, what's been happening? How are things going with the Logan boy?"

"Daniel's lawyer requested he be assessed by a psychologist. The Crown has followed suit. I called Josie. She's agreed to provide us with a report."

"Good, you can rely on her to do the right thing. Let's hope we can all live with it."

"If it's the truth, then I guess we'll have to," Chase replied.

"Yeah, that's the way it usually goes. Now, is there anything else?"

"I finished up the report on that break and enter and the highway patrol officers brought in a couple of DUIs last night. They sobered up in the cells and were given court attendance notices this morning."

"Good. Just another day at the salt mines."

"Yeah."

Riley waited for him to leave. When he didn't, Chase was subjected to a slight frown. "Is there something else, Chase?"

Chase squirmed in his seat, trying to find the words. Nobody in Josie's family had an inkling of what had gone on between them. As far as anyone knew, he'd been her date for her high school graduation, a one-off event that had happened and had been forgotten just as quickly.

"How long has Josie been back in town?" he blurted before he lost his courage.

Riley's frown deepened momentarily and then he shrugged. "I don't know, a month or two. When Dad suffered that bleed on his brain right before Christmas, she started talking about moving back. I think she wanted to be closer to Dad and Mom. Nothing like having one of your parents spend a night in the ICU in a coma to put things into perspective. They're not getting any younger and Josie's always been close to them. I think she wants to spend more time with them, while they're still here. Why do you ask?"

Chase averted his gaze and cursed the heat that spread up his neck. "No reason. Just curious. I haven't seen her since we were teenagers."

Riley chuckled. "She hasn't changed much. Still as headstrong and determined as ever, but inside, she's as soft as melted ice cream." Riley chuckled again. "Don't tell her I told you that."

Chase forced himself to return the grin. "Of course not. So," he said as casually as he could manage, "is she married? Does she have any kids?"

Riley shook his head. "Nope and nope, much to Mom's despair. She was hoping both of my sisters would have found someone by now, but it hasn't happened. Of course, Josie's always talking about the swag of kids she'll have one day. She's already been over twice to babysit the twins and she refuses to take any payment. Kate and I think it's fantastic."

Chase gave a half-hearted smile while his heart beat fast with pain. *She still wanted kids.* Of course she did. It was one of the things they'd talked about. She couldn't wait to have a baby.

"Why all the interest in Josie all of a sudden?" Riley asked, his eyes narrowed in suspicion. "You're not what she needs. No offense, but you're the last person I want my little sister to date."

Chase grimaced, but didn't argue back. He'd worked hard at cultivating his playboy image and if he were honest, the title was well deserved. He could hardly tell his boss it was all a façade—that it had been the only way he could think of to get over the woman he'd loved with all his heart and then lost.

He kept his hurt carefully concealed behind another forced grin. "Of course not. I wouldn't want my little sister to date me either."

"You don't have a little sister."

"Well, if I *did*."

"Exactly, I'm glad we see eye to eye. Now, get out of here. Don't you have work to do?"

CHAPTER 8

Scott Jones grunted from exertion and forced the weights in his hand up a final time. One hundred and fifty pounds of lead on either end of the steel bar and forty repetitions had his muscles screaming for release. He savored the burning sensation a moment longer before letting his spotter lower the bar back down.

"Fuck, you nearly busted yourself, Scotty. Why do you go so hard? You're already the buffest bloke in here. Besides, you can always come back tomorrow. It's not like you're goin' anywhere." Weasel laughed at his own joke.

Scott looked up at him. Weasel was quickly becoming annoying. Okay, so everyone needed a mate, especially in a place like this and Weasel was always happy to tag along. Jail was hard on the toughest of them and Long Bay wasn't known for its comforts. But he missed his old mate, Neil. Life inside just hadn't been the same since he'd left.

The two of them had made quite a team. It was a brave bloke who dared to defy them. They even had the guards eating out of their hand. He and Neil had controlled the jail with an iron fist and didn't hesitate to remind anyone who needed it that they were the real ones in charge. He couldn't remember how many fights he'd been in or the number of times he and Neil had cracked the heads of anyone stupid enough to step out of line.

The guards thanked them for it, too. It helped keep everyone happy. The fact that a little paperwork had to be completed by the management every time Scott or Neil put someone in the infirmary was a small price to pay.

A sly but cowardly inmate by the name of Dudley sidled up close to Scott.

"Nice work there, Scotty. You'll be liftin' tractor tires next. One in each hand."

Scott glared up at him, suspicious of the snicker he was sure he could hear in the man's voice.

"What the fuck do you want, Duds? You don't belong out here."

Dudley refused to look insulted or even the least bit scared. "I've got some news for ya, Scotty. It's about ya mate, Neil. I thought ya might like to hear."

Scott stilled and then his heart took off at high speed. He swallowed and did his best to get his panic under control. He could tell from the look on Dudley's face that the news wasn't good. Unwilling to show how much it mattered, he offered a disinterested shrug.

"How the fuck would you know anything about Neil? He's on the outside now and you're still stuck in here."

A sly smile turned up the edges of Dudley's narrow, puce-colored lips. "I got me sources, don't you worry. How much is it worth to ya?"

Anger boiled at the edges of Scott's consciousness and he itched to slam his fist into Dudley's face, but he needed to know what the fucker was talking about, so he breathed through the fury and forced a smile.

"Come on, Duds. I thought we were mates. You should tell me just because you're a good bloke. I shouldn't have to pay you."

"Ha!" Dudley laughed. "As if I'd fall for that one. You of all people know how it goes. I've got somethin' you want. When you give me what I want, then I'll tell ya what I know."

Scott growled low in his throat, impatience surging through him. He ought to just smash his fist in the side of Dudley's head and be done with it, but then the fucker would spend a week in the infirmary and Scott wouldn't be any the wiser about the prick's news. If it really was something to do with Neil, Scott wanted to know.

Forcing another smile, he sighed dramatically and stepped away from the bench press. Weasel stood nearby, jiggling nervously from foot to foot.

"Get me a fucking towel, Weasel," he growled, "and hurry up about it. It's hot as hell out here." Weasel scurried away, across the other side of the exercise yard. More than a hundred other inmates, all garbed in prison green, walked or talked or smoked or did all three along the yard's perimeter.

Scott turned back to Dudley and narrowed his eyes. "All right, Duds, here it is. I'll give you three joints and a handful of pills. That's it. Now, hurry up and spit it out before I change my mind."

"Throw in a couple of packets of ciggies and I'll tell ya everythin' I know."

"Deal." They shook hands and Scott held his breath and waited to hear the news.

"A mate of mine from up the coast rang me last night after dinner. He told me Neil had taken a bullet. Apparently, it was all over the news up there a few weeks ago."

Scott swallowed his shriek of pain and schooled his features into an emotionless mask. He forced himself to ask the question. "Dead?"

"Yeah. At least, that's what they said on the news."

"Fuck. What happened? Did Vladimir find him? That son of a bitch always threatened to get him the minute he got out."

Dudley shook his head. "Nah, nothin' like that. Nothin' to do with drugs. Some kid from the fuckin' boondocks gave it to him. Neil was stickin' it to the kid's mother and the kid pulled out a fuckin' gun. Blew his fuckin' brains out."

A buzzing started in Scott's ears. The sound drowned everything out. He stared at Dudley's mouth. His lips were moving, but Scott could no longer hear the words. Pain tore through him at the thought of Neil dead. *Neil.* His mate. The big brother he'd never had.

He shook his head and slapped at his ears in an effort to

clear them of the roar of noise. Grabbing hold of Dudley by his shirt front, he pulled the other man close. With his face only inches away, he spat, "You'd better not be fucking with me, Duds."

Dudley paled, but shook his head adamantly. "I'm not fuckin' with ya, Scotty. I swear. It's the truth."

Scott closed his eyes against the weight of realization. Forcing them open again, he stared hard at the other man.

"Tell me everything."

———————

Josie's strokes were sure and even. The cool water kissed her skin. She reached the end of the pool and did a neat racing turn and started once again for the other end. She'd lost count of the number of laps she'd done, but it had to be at least forty. Her arms and legs were growing tired. It was a sure sign she was on the downhill run.

She'd always loved swimming. As a child, it had been her favorite thing to do. She'd escape into the water and her troubles would wash away like magic. She'd climb out and everything would feel clean and new.

Even now, all these years later, she still used swimming as a form of relaxation. The pool was a place to clear her head, a place to forget about the world. It was fortunate that Watervale boasted a nearly new aquatic center which included an Olympic-sized pool. An indoor heated pool was also part of the complex. It would come in handy during the winter months when the temperature dropped below zero.

Her thoughts shifted to Daniel and she made a mental note to touch base again with Phoebe. Josie hoped her friend had managed to arrange counseling options for Kelly Logan and her family. From what Kelly had said, none of them were faring well.

Not that Josie was surprised. A traumatic event such as the one they'd suffered would have long-term, far-reaching effects. She only hoped they received the help they needed.

Tucking her legs up underneath her, she made the final turn and headed for the finish line. Her arms were aching, her legs were leaden, but she loved the feeling of deep satisfaction she always felt after the conclusion of a hard swim. There was something about pushing her body to the limits that just felt right.

Her hand came into contact with the end of the pool and she came to a stop. Her breath puffed out fast and hard. She made an effort to slow it down. Too much carbon dioxide was never a good thing.

"I see you still choose the pool to do your workout."

She looked up in surprise, squinting against the morning sun. Chase loomed high above her, his face in shadow. He was dressed in tailored charcoal-gray suit pants and a crisp white business shirt that hugged the width of his shoulders and tapered down to narrow hips. Her pulse once again quickened and it had nothing to do with her recent exertion.

"W-what are you doing here?" She hated that she sounded so breathless and hoped he'd put it down to her efforts in the pool.

"I came to see you. I wanted to know how things are going with Daniel. Have you met with him yet?"

"How did you know I was here?"

Chase shrugged. "It's a small town. Plus, I dropped by your office. Doctor Wheeler imparted the information that you swim most mornings of the week." He scowled and Josie wondered what had soured his mood. It certainly wasn't like he didn't know how much she loved the pool. She'd been swimming all her life.

"How did you come to be sharing office space with him, anyway?"

His disgruntled question registered and all of a sudden she understood the origin of his frown. Chase was jealous of Rohan Wheeler.

In his late twenties, the doctor was not only good-looking, charming and funny, but according to Moira, he was also entirely available.

Josie had noticed Rohan's interest, but so far, she hadn't

done anything to encourage it. She'd relocated to Watervale to take stock of her life, to spend time with her parents and to find contentment in her career. She had no intention of rushing into a relationship with the town's most eligible bachelor, no matter how much her body urged her to break her self-imposed man drought.

At the reminder of how long it had been since she'd had sex, Josie bit back a sigh. The fact that her intimate encounters with men had been few and far between since she'd graduated from high school had everything to do with the male specimen who stood above her, his eyes hidden behind a sexy pair of aviator sunglasses.

Concealed behind her goggles, Josie suddenly realized she had the same advantage. She could look her fill like she wanted to and not be concerned he would know. The mirrored goggles were a perfect match for his sunglasses and she bit back a mischievous smile and let her gaze drink him in.

Until her return to Watervale, she'd never seen him in a business suit. His visits from the Academy had been on weekend furloughs and he'd mostly favored casual clothes. Of course, she'd seen him naked and the memory had been burned into her brain. He hadn't felt the need to cover up, like she had, and despite the dim light, there was no mistaking the honed planes of his hairless chest, the flat belly taut with muscle, the length and power in his muscular legs, covered in fine, soft hair.

Her heart beat faster at the memory of what had come after and needs long denied overwhelmed her. Despite the cool water, she burned from the inside out and only Chase could put out the fire. Knowing that the thought of her with Rohan had sparked his jealousy, her heart lurched with a sudden burst of hope.

Perhaps he cared for her more than he was willing to admit? No one got jealous over someone they didn't have feelings for. Could it be possible that he wasn't as immune to her as she thought?

The idea sent a surge of excitement running through her

and then she remembered the way he'd dumped her and some of her keen anticipation died away. She'd believed all this and more a decade ago—and where had that gotten her? Lonely and alone and broken hearted.

It wasn't like she'd forgiven him... But maybe, maybe the hurt she'd carried around for so long was easing and now that he was here, back in her life, they could talk things through and work things out and somehow, some way, make it happen.

"Are you finished in there?" Chase pulled off his sunglasses and a single dark eyebrow was raised in query. A curious smile played upon his face.

Josie's lips tugged upwards in answer and all of a sudden, she felt better than she had in a long, long time.

"Afraid I'll turn into a wrinkled, old prune?" she quipped and then followed it through with a wink.

She heaved herself from the pool and strode passed him, feeling his gaze on her every step of the way. She pulled off her goggles and tugged off her cap and then collected her towel from where she'd left it. Wrapping it around herself, she flicked her wet hair out of her eyes and squeezed out the excess water from her ponytail. At last, she stole another glance at him.

He stared at her, his eyes burning with an intensity that did funny things to her tummy.

"Who cares about old and wrinkled? You'll always be beautiful to me."

His words caressed her. Heat surged throughout her body and she flushed, feeling naked beneath his gaze. She secured the towel tighter around her, grateful she hadn't chosen a bikini. He hadn't seen her this close to naked since high school and even then, she'd had the protection of the night. When they'd made love the sky had been lit with nothing more than the faint illumination of the moon.

It had been the first time for both of them and it had only happened once. She'd never felt more beautiful than when he slipped her graduation dress off her shoulders and trailed kisses all over her skin.

He'd kissed every inch of her, loving her with his mouth. When at last he slowly entered her, she'd gasped at the wonder of it and the feel of him deep inside her. She'd breathed through the pain and had enjoyed each exquisite sensation, under the canopy of stars.

Every moment had been perfect, to savor and cherish and wonder at, over and over again—except it hadn't turned out that way. He'd taken her home amid murmured words of love and tender kisses and promises to see her again the next day.

But, he hadn't called, hadn't texted, hadn't tried to contact her at all. A week later, she found out through mutual friends he'd returned to Goulburn. She didn't hear from him again.

Chase watched the emotions come and go across Josie's beautiful face and guessed she was also reliving their past. He forced himself to remain unmoved, but it was difficult, especially when the shadows of sadness in her eyes tore him apart. She didn't know why he'd abandoned her and the guilt would stay with him all his life.

So what if she was better off without him? So what if he'd broken off their relationship for her? The problem was plain and simple and had been for more than ten years: He could no longer offer her what she wanted most. No matter how he wished things were different.

He'd love her with his dying breath, but he couldn't let her see his true feelings, ones he'd worked so hard to mask for such a long time. What was the point in telling her how he felt and possibly reigniting all that they'd had when it wouldn't make any difference? It had been hard enough to turn his back on her the first time. He'd never have the strength to do it again.

So, he cleared his throat and ignored his pain and focused on his job. To maintain the distance between them was for the best, for both of them.

"I was wondering how the Logan case is progressing and if you've started the report?"

The shadows in Josie's eyes were gradually replaced with steel. Chase bit down on a stab of regret.

"I've met with him three times already and I'm meeting with him again this afternoon. Don't worry, I'll have my report to you in plenty of time."

"What are your initial impressions? Are the charges going to stick?"

Her eyes narrowed and he cursed silently, wishing he'd used more tact. *What was it about her that made him lose his mind?* He couldn't think straight around her. He never had.

"I'd rather not say at this point in time. I'll wait until after I speak with him again. He's a young boy, terrified out of his wits. His family's falling apart. I'm going to give him all the time he needs to speak and give me what I need. Whether the charges stick or not is of no consequence to me. My job is to determine the truth of his state of mind and his capacity to know right from wrong."

Chase flushed under her anger. "I wasn't implying you'd be influenced one way or the other. If I didn't believe in your professionalism and your ability to do the job, I'd never have recommended you to the prosecutor."

Josie continued to glare at him. "Good. As long as we understand each other."

"Good," Chase nodded, hating the childish attitude that had crept into his voice.

Josie turned away from him and began to gather her things into a brightly striped canvas swimming bag. She dropped her towel on a nearby bench and tugged a short cotton dress over her swimsuit. He tried not to notice her long, tanned limbs or the way her lithe muscles flexed when she moved.

The dress was a pale blue that set off her eyes and hugged the curves of her breasts. Not that he needed to be reminded of how they looked. They'd been amply displayed in her swimsuit. He was sure she hadn't meant the modest one piece to be so alluring, but the fact was, she could have been wearing a chaff bag and he would have noticed.

Blood rushed back to his groin and his cock hardened. He cursed under his breath, hoping she wouldn't notice. He was grateful for the suit pants that went a long way to concealing his desire. It wouldn't be fair for her to get the wrong impression. He should be showing more restraint and doing everything he could to show her they were over, not having bursts of jealousy or having his body react like a teenager's whenever he saw her. And what was that stupid comment he'd made about her always being beautiful?

So what if all of it was true? He'd vowed every night since he'd met her at the station to make sure she understood they were over, in case she held any illusions to the contrary. There was no future for them. There hadn't been a decade ago and nothing had changed in the years since. He had to make sure she knew it.

An idea formed in his mind. It was so awful he could barely contemplate it and yet, it made perfect sense. It would be just the thing to convince her they were never going to be a couple again. The more he thought about it, the more he knew if he managed to pull it off, it would be the end of them.

Deep sadness and regret filled his gut and tightened his chest until he had to gasp for a breath. He had to do it. It was the only way. He prayed for the courage to see it through. Forcing a smile, he cleared his throat and hoped she didn't notice the strain.

"What are you doing later, Josie? Perhaps we could catch a drink at The Bullet?"

Her eyebrows flew up in surprise and he could understand her confusion. One minute he was hot and the next he was frozen. He had to stop this waffling, this inner weakness, while he still could. The Bullet would give him the perfect venue and opportunity.

"I-I guess so. My last patient's at five-thirty. How about I meet you around seven? That will give me enough time to go home and change. I need a shower after a day in the clinic."

His thoughts flew to her wet and naked and soapy and his jaw tensed on a groan. Scrambling around for something to distract him, he said the first thing that came into his mind. "Where are you staying?"

"I took a short term lease on the old Holloway place, out on Whiskey Creek Road."

"So you're not in town?"

"No. After living in Brisbane for the last decade, I can certainly handle the daily commute. Ten minutes feels like nothing. Besides, I like the serenity of the countryside. My nearest neighbor is more than four miles away."

"You must have a good view of the mountains up there?"

"Yes, it's spectacular from my bedroom window."

As if only just becoming aware of what she said, Josie averted her face, but not before he caught the crimson blush as it spread across her cheeks. His heart turned over, even as another rush of blood went straight to his groin.

Knowing what he planned for later, his body's reaction sent a burst of self-disgust flooding through his veins. He intended to carry out a plan that would devastate the woman he loved. He had no right wanting her.

But wants and needs were distinct and separate things and the two of them often didn't coincide. He wanted nothing more than to have Josie in his life; what he *needed* was to set her free, once and for all. Though his plan would paint him a prick of the highest order, he was doing this for her.

Kelly Logan heard her husband's heavy tread in the hall, heading in her direction and pulled the blanket up over her head. The sun was way up in the sky and yet she still hadn't been able to bring herself to climb out of bed. The energy it took to dress and prepare herself to face yet another day was beyond her. Not even for her family could she find the strength required to make the effort to look like she cared.

The phone on her nightstand peeled shrilly in the stillness and she snatched at the receiver: Anything to avoid having to make conversation with Trevor. It had been nearly a month and he still couldn't bring himself to look at her.

"Hello?"

"Is that Mrs Logan?"

"Yes," she answered, her voice low and cautious. Ever since the assault, she'd been bombarded with calls from the media. It was a sad indicator of the deterioration of her relationship with her husband that she'd rather risk speaking with a journalist than talk to the man she'd been married to nearly half of her life.

"It's Phoebe Jamison. I'm a psychologist at Grafton Base Hospital. I'm also a friend of Josie Munro's."

"Yes. I remember. She told me she'd call you."

"She did and I apologize that it's taken me awhile to get back to you. We have an enormous backlog of patients needing our services."

"It's fine," Kelly muttered, wanting nothing more than to end the call.

"Josie asked me to look into what counseling options might be available to you," the woman continued. "Unfortunately, there are no government funded face-to-face counseling services available, but she told me a little about your circumstances and I...I'd like to help your family, free of charge."

Kelly frowned and did her best to follow the counselor's conversation. Trevor entered the bedroom and stood a short distance away, staring at the floor. A cup of coffee and a plate of toast were on a tray in his hands. Her heart lurched at his thoughtfulness.

"Mrs Logan? Are you still there?"

"Y-yes," she managed. "I'm still here."

"Would you like to make an appointment?"

Kelly closed her eyes and tried to block out the pain. The

sane, logical part of her brain urged her to respond with an affirmative, but the ever-present blackness overshadowed it. She didn't want to make an appointment. She didn't want to ever have to think about that nightmare again. She couldn't think of anything worse than reliving the terror of it before a stranger—or anyone. Not even her husband.

"I'm...I'm sorry, Ms Jamison. I really am. I appreciate your call and your very kind offer, but I don't think so."

"Talking about it with someone can help, Mrs Logan." The woman's gentle reply brought tears to Kelly's eyes. She turned her face away from her husband and bit her lip against a sob.

"I-I'm sorry, I have to go." Quickly, she returned the receiver to the cradle and then buried her face against her pillow. The pain she'd tried so hard to hold at bay seeped from her eyes and sent a paroxysm of shudders through her body. She thought she was all out of tears, but fresh ones kept coming. They ran down her cheeks and dampened the pillowcase.

A rough hand swiped gently across her hair. She tensed and then forced herself to relax.

Trevor. It was only Trevor. It was the first time he'd touched her since it happened. She cried like she'd never stop.

CHAPTER 9

Josie stared at the untouched chicken and mayo roll on her desk and swallowed a sigh. She'd dashed out between patients and purchased it from the café around the corner, but hadn't gotten around to eating it. Now, as she waited for Daniel Logan, her appetite disappeared.

While she'd refused to share her thoughts with Chase, she was fairly certain in which direction they were headed. From all accounts, Daniel was a well-mannered, well-behaved preteen who had been raised with courtesy and respect. While he'd been through severe trauma, the kind she wouldn't wish on anybody, it couldn't be said that he was unable to grasp the seriousness of what was going on. In their last session, he'd even asked about the court process and how long a matter like his might take.

No, she was sure that his fitness to stand trial and his ability to comprehend what was going on was unquestionable. What she was less certain of was his ability to discern right from wrong in the criminal sense that the Crown required. Secretly, she hoped when she questioned him in this regard, he would display obvious signs that he didn't quite understand. The last thing she wanted was to see him stand trial.

He'd killed a man, but who wouldn't have done the same in similar circumstances? Most of the townspeople were appalled he'd been charged, men and women alike. Some were hailing Daniel a hero. Even others were calling for a bravery award. She hadn't heard a single whisper that the law had played it right.

It tore Josie up inside. She was among the people who wanted to laud the boy as a hero, but they were part of a society that lived and died by its rules—rules that were imperative to survival and were necessary to ensure order. Without them, there would be anarchy.

She couldn't imagine what would happen if people were free to shoot and kill as they pleased. No one had the right to be judge, jury and executioner, no matter how despicable the crime. Laws were put in place for a reason. It wasn't up to a twelve-year-old boy to decide when and if he would follow them. Her thoughts turned to the police and the difficult job they faced.

She wondered about Chase and Riley and the pressure they both must be under. Helplessness and compassion tightened her chest. She hoped the people of Watervale understood that the police were merely doing their job. She remembered her outburst when Chase informed her that charges would be laid and she felt a stab of guilt. She'd been unfair. The Chase she'd known wouldn't have made the decision lightly.

She recalled his invitation earlier that morning to get together for a drink and her heart skipped a beat. The invitation was not something she expected and just the thought of meeting him sent heat coursing through her. It was foolish to get so excited at the thought of seeing him again socially. Years ago, he'd dumped her without a word of explanation. His actions shredded her heart into so many pieces, it had taken her years to heal. He'd taken the one thing she offered him so freely and lovingly, something she could never regain, then turned around and left her without looking back.

He was just like the boys her mother had warned her about; the ones who were only after one thing. Josie used to smother a smile every time her mother said it: *'They're only after one thing'*—like her mother couldn't bring herself to say the word sex.

The fact that her mother had been right saddened her; that Chase was the one to take her innocence and leave without a word devastated her even more.

And yet, here she was, a decade later, contemplating forgiving and forgetting the past. Did she love him that much that she'd be willing to overlook his cruel and callous behavior, the way he exited her life the very day after she slept with him? *Despite everything, did she still want more of him?*

She sighed heavily, scared that the answer was yes, regardless of the reasons why she should not. Somewhere buried deep within her, she hoped he'd finally offer her an explanation; one that would blow all the heartache away; one that she could nod and smile in relief and say, 'Of course, that's why you didn't call; why you left without a word.'

She glanced at her watch: Three more hours before she was due to meet him; three more hours before, hopefully, she'd know the truth and if that truth could set her free, then maybe, just maybe, she'd feel his lips on hers again.

Excitement, apprehension and uncertainty surged through her. The tangled web of emotions sent a tingling sensation all the way down to her toes. She remembered the way he held her, like she was the most valuable thing in the world. She remembered his soft caresses, of the feel of him deep within her. It had been too long since she felt cared for and loved. She'd been so lonely. All of a sudden, the time to meet him couldn't come soon enough.

The phone at her elbow buzzed and she picked it up and answered the call.

"Josie, it's Moira. I just wanted to let you know your next appointment is here."

"Thank you, Moira. I'll be right out."

———

Josie watched Daniel from out of the corner of her eye

and made notes on the pad in front of her. She was a little surprised to discover he'd come to the clinic alone. He looked drawn and tired and defeated—and who could blame him? The past month since the attack couldn't have been easy.

What had the school yard been like? Was he teased? Did they ask him questions he didn't want to answer? Or had the attitude of his fellow students been more supportive, like the people of the town?

Knowing the townspeople were behind him may have helped restore his flagging spirits, but nothing would change what had happened that ill fated evening. No one could turn back time.

"How's your mother?" she asked quietly.

"I dunno. She's all right, I guess."

"Do you know if she's been seeing anyone, a counselor?"

He shrugged and stared at the floor. "Maybe. She spends an awful lot of time in bed. I dunno how she can stay in that room. I can't go anywhere near it."

Josie closed her eyes briefly against the sorrow his words evoked and continued making notes.

"How did you get here today, Daniel? Did your mother bring you in?"

"No, Dad did. He said Mom wasn't up to it."

"Well, thank you for coming in. I really appreciate it."

"You need to see me to write your report. Isn't that what you said? You said you'd write a report that would make them see they'd have to drop the case."

She stared at the earnestness on his face and her heart broke a little more. She had to make him understand it wasn't as simple as that.

"I do need to see you so that I can write the court report, but it's not up to me to decide. The judge will listen to arguments from the prosecutor and from your lawyer. It's then up to the judge to decide."

His eyes blazed with anger. "Then why am I here? If what you say doesn't matter, what's the point of rehashing it all? Do you think I enjoy reliving it? Remembering what I saw?"

"No, of course not," she replied calmly. "I can't imagine how hard it must be."

"You're damn right it's hard! Every time I close my eyes I can see him with my mom. I run to the shed and I get the gun, but this time I can't find any ammunition. It's not where Dad left it. I look around the shed, but it's dark and I end up turning in circles. I hear Mom screaming, shouting for me to help. I know what that man's doing to her and I just want to make him stop."

His breath came hard and fast. His eyes were wide with fear. Josie fought against the urge to take him in her arms and soothe the pain away. She had a job to do and she had to see it through.

"What was he doing to your mom, Daniel?"

"He was... He was raping her! He had his pants down around his knees. Her nightgown was all bunched up. What the hell do you think he was doing?"

"It was wrong, wasn't it, Daniel?"

"Of course it was wrong! He was hurting her. He was hurting my mom." His voice caught on a sob and once again, Josie struggled against the urge to offer him comfort.

"You decided to get the gun."

"Yes, it was the only way I could think of to make him stop."

"You knew where the gun was? You knew where your dad kept the bullets?"

"Yes! Yes! I'm with my dad all the time when he goes to the gun safe. We shoot rabbits and crows and kangaroos. Sometimes we go to the rifle range and shoot at targets."

"You knew the combination to the safe. You knew which gun to choose. Did you load it with ammunition?"

"Of course I did. I couldn't have shot him without it."

"So you went for the gun, knowing you were going to shoot him?"

"Yes, are you *stupid*? I had to make him stop. I was the man of the house. Dad told me I was responsible for Jason and my mom. The man was way too big to tackle and I had nothing to hit him with. All I could think of was getting the gun."

"When you loaded the gun and brought it back into the house, did you still intend to use it?"

"Of course I did!" he shouted. "Haven't you been *listening*? There was no other way to make him stop."

"So you went back into your mom's bedroom and the man was still there. What did you do, Daniel?"

"I lifted the rifle to my shoulder and I looked through the scope. I put the crosshairs on him."

"Where did you aim, Daniel?"

He paused and stared straight at her, his eyes hard. "I aimed for the back of his head."

"Did you know that it might kill him?"

Daniel scoffed mirthlessly. "Of course I did. I've shot rabbits. I've shot kangaroos. I know what happens when they take a bullet. They darn well don't get up."

"Is that what you wanted?"

He stood suddenly and leaned forward over her desk, his face only inches from hers. "I wanted him to stop. And he did."

Josie remained where she was and held his wild stare. Slowly, the tension left his body and he crumpled back onto the seat.

After awhile, she spoke again, her voice soft and gentle. "Is killing someone wrong, Daniel?"

He gave her a jerky nod.

"Are we allowed to go around killing people?"

"No," he responded, just as quietly.

"What should we do if someone is doing something wrong, like breaking the law?"

Daniel drew in a deep breath and let it out on a heavy sigh. He slumped forward and covered his face with his hands. His voice came out muffled when he finally replied. "We call the police."

"Why didn't you call the police, Daniel?"

"I live twenty-five miles from town!" he cried in a voice that broke her heart. "It would have been too late. Don't you understand anything?"

"Do you think it was wrong to kill that man?"

"Yes, it was wrong, but I bloody well don't regret it. He was hurting my mom and I had to make him stop." He looked up and stared at her, his expression coldly determined. "I'd do it again if I had to."

Chapter 10

Josie added another coat of red lipstick with a hand that wasn't quite steady. A quick glance at the clock on her nightstand showed her it was nearly seven o'clock. With a ten-minute drive into Watervale, if she didn't hurry up, she'd be late. With a final swipe of the brush through her long blond hair, she collected her handbag off the kitchen table and headed out the door.

Chase had given her directions to The Bullet and on the dot of seven, she pulled into the car park adjacent to the bar. She was surprised at the number of vehicles already there. It was relatively early and a week night at that and yet the parking lot was brimming with cars, mostly pick-ups and SUVs. Her father's sleek, little Mustang stood out in the crowd.

Slinging her handbag over her shoulder, she climbed out of the car and picked her way across the loose gravel that covered the lot, cursing the four-inch red heels she'd slipped on to complement her short, form-fitting dress. Its white cotton fabric gleamed almost iridescent blue in the dark which was broken by the fluorescent lighting interspersed throughout the car park.

Smoothing her hands down the sides of her dress, she flipped her loose hair off her face and tried to quell her nerves. It wasn't like she was meeting Chase for a date, for heaven's sake. She had no right being nervous. They were friends from the past. They were catching up. Nothing less, nothing more.

But, try as she might, she couldn't get the idea that it was kind of a date out of her mind. He'd asked her to meet him for a drink. They had a history, a romantic history. They'd been much, much more than friends. Her heart took flight alongside her thoughts and no amount of self-talk would bring them to a halt.

With a sigh of acceptance, she let her spirits soar and opened her heart more than a little to all the possibilities that lay ahead. A smile widened her lips until she was grinning hard. The weight of the world and of the past month in particular lifted from her shoulders. Chase was inside, waiting for her. All of a sudden, she was overwhelmed with anticipation and hope.

———————

Chase glanced surreptitiously at his watch and looked across to the doorway that led inside The Bullet. He'd been at the bar for the last half an hour, passing the time with the same girl he'd given the brush off a fortnight before. Her name was Lucy and she was a beauty therapist at one of the day spas in town. He'd learned she was twenty-three and had dropped out of school at sixteen. She'd never wanted to do anything more than paint pretty pictures on people's nails. Next on her list was to get married and have babies.

She'd shared all of this in a matter of minutes in a breathy, little-girl voice he imagined she thought he'd find sexy. He didn't. It was irritating him to the point of madness. Or maybe it was her inane chatter that was driving him crazy. He grimaced.

His foul mood had nothing to do with the annoying young thing beside him. It did however, have everything to do with what he was about to do with her. The very thought of it had him on edge.

He'd noticed the way Josie had looked her fill at the pool while she'd hidden behind her goggles. She'd all but licked her lips. Not that he minded—hell, he'd loved every minute of it—but it was further proof that the spark that had always been there would take very little to reignite.

He couldn't let it happen.

The heavy wooden door to The Bullet swung open and Chase caught a flash of spun gold. Josie stepped into the dimness and paused, waiting for her eyes to adjust. Chase's gut twisted inside and out, but he knew if he didn't act now, no matter how much his heart cried out against it, he'd be leading Josie toward huge disappointment and far away from the future she desperately wanted and deserved.

Spinning around, he grabbed hold of Lucy and drew her hard against him. He covered her mouth and swallowed her gasp and kissed her for as long as he could manage. After her initial surprise, the girl melted against him. Reaching up, she held onto his head and kept his mouth on hers long after he wanted to end it.

She pressed herself against him until every inch of her was plastered along his front. His body instinctively reacted to her nearness, even as his mind rebelled. Knowing he had to see it through and make it look convincing, he cupped her ass and lifted her until she was snug against his crotch. She growled low in her throat and he inwardly winced and prayed that it would soon be over.

Surely Josie had spotted them by now? The bar was fairly crowded, but not impossibly so. He didn't know how much longer he could put up with Lucy's tongue down his throat without gagging.

His answer came soon enough when a pitcher of iced water was dumped all over his head. He gasped and blinked and Lucy yelped. They both turned to stare at Josie.

"You asshole. *How dare you!*"

Her eyes spit fire and anger suffused her cheeks. She'd never looked more beautiful. One tear, then another slid down her face and Chase was shredded with agony. He turned away, unable to bear the sight of her pain—pain he was responsible for, yet again.

He convinced himself it was for the best and then he tried

to remember why. *She wanted children, remember?* She deserved to live her dream, just not with him. That's what had pushed him to such drastic action, to carry out such a despicable act. Even now, it was obvious how much she cared. He knew her well, and she wouldn't react with so much hurt and anger if her feelings for him had died so many years ago.

He ought to be floating on cloud nine, knowing that she still felt something for him and he would have, if her lifelong yearning for children had disappeared, even diminished. But it hadn't. So he wasn't.

Chase had seen her with Daniel. He'd noticed the special way she had with him, her natural ability to offer him comfort. She loved kids. She always had. Riley had even confirmed it.

The one thing she wanted and longed for, was the one thing he could never give her, no matter how much he wished he could. It was never going to happen. The cancer had seen to that.

———

Josie thought she knew what devastation felt like, but what she'd felt a decade ago didn't come close to the torture she was suffering right now. *How could he?* How could he have invited her for a drink and then have her find him locking lips with a woman who looked like she was on the prowl?

He'd known Josie was coming. They'd even agreed on a time. He also knew she was punctual. *It was almost as if he'd planned it...*

She shook her head in a whirlpool of uncertainty and confusion. None of it made sense. All she knew for certain was that Chase Barrington didn't deserve her tears. Not back then and definitely not now.

She shook her head again. If he hadn't wanted to renew their relationship, why hadn't he been forthcoming from the beginning and simply said so? Why invite her here tonight and rub salt in old wounds...and so callously at that?

She groaned aloud and stabbed her car key viciously into the slot. Turning it hard, she pulled the car into gear the minute the engine caught. Spinning her tires, gravel flying every which way into the night, she sped out of the parking lot. It was reckless and would probably chip the paint off someone else's car, but at that moment, she simply didn't care.

Hot tears blinded her and she angrily swiped them away. She was through crying over Detective Sergeant Chase Barrington. With grim determination, she vowed he would never hurt her again.

Thank goodness she'd almost managed to finish her report. When she was done, she'd deliver it to the prosecutor's office herself. After all, he was the one who required it, not Chase. There would be no need for her to ever spend another minute in Chase Barrington's company again.

At least, until the trial. *If* there were a trial.

All of a sudden, the stress of the past month caught up with her. Her shoulders slumped and her breath hitched in despair. Though she willed it away, a sob tightened her chest and escaped through her tightly compressed lips and then, like a dam bursting, it was quickly followed by another and another until the road in front of her was blurred from a deluge of hot tears.

No matter how much she wished it were different, there was no escaping two facts: Chase Barrington was an asshole and Daniel Logan had the capacity to stand trial.

It was clear to her that at the time of the offense, the young boy knew what he was doing was wrong. He meant to shoot the intruder and he meant for the man to die. She was convinced he'd do exactly the same thing again, given similar circumstances. Against her emotional inclinations to find a way to get him off, it was her duty to inform the court.

Chase was the officer in charge of the case. There would be no avoiding him come the trial. But that could be months away. For now, she'd keep out of his way. She'd go back to the place she'd begun to think of as home and spend some time licking her wounds. And then she'd come back stronger than ever and Chase Barrington could go to hell. She'd survived his rejection once; she knew darn well she could survive it again.

As the lights of her cottage came into view, she let her anger build. Anger was good. Anger was great. It gave her something concrete to focus on. If she spent too much time thinking about what had just happened, she'd splinter into a million pieces and she flat-out refused to allow that to happen. She'd been there once before. It wasn't pretty.

Chase finished the bottle of scotch and stared out into the quiet night from his position on the balcony of his condo. Despite the late hour and the impressive amount of alcohol he'd consumed, his brain wouldn't let him rest. No, tonight it played a tortuous game, replaying the scene with Josie over and over again. No matter how hard he fought to push the images into oblivion, he couldn't escape them.

Her anger, confusion, shock and utter devastation were so clearly imprinted on his mind that no amount of alcohol would get rid of them.

And he was the one totally and utterly responsible for her pain and broken dreams. The knowledge pierced his heart and while he would forever regret every moment of her pain at the bar, he still felt that he'd had no choice.

As soon as Josie had cleared the room, he'd disentangled himself from Lucy. She'd blinked hard. Her surprise and confusion had quickly turned to anger when he told her he was leaving. Her slap across his cheek had stung, but it was nothing less than he deserved.

He was a jerk, a cad, an utter prick. He didn't deserve anyone's sympathy or understanding. He deserved to be alone, unloved and unhappy. Tears burned behind his eyes.

In weak moments, his youthful dreams of a normal life haunted him. As Josie did... No, never again could he go there.

Once again, he cursed the cancer that had taken root in his cells a decade ago and forever changed his life. He'd gone from a nineteen-year-old man with the world at his feet to a boy who was scared and confused. The future he'd dreamed of with the girl that he loved had vaporized before his eyes. Instead, words such as malignancy, chemo and oncology ward became part of his everyday life.

He'd discovered the lumps in his testicles six months before Josie's graduation. They hadn't given him any trouble and seemed more of an anomaly than anything else. It was only during the physical drills required throughout his police training that one of them became annoying. It rubbed and chafed and was sometimes downright irritating, but it hadn't caused him pain. That was the reason he ignored them for so long.

Away in Goulburn, at the Academy and with end-of-year exam pressure looming, his visits home had become fewer and further apart. He ached every night he spent away from her, but he didn't have a choice. She was busy too, immersed in her final exams and he needed to get through his course. He wanted to build a future for both of them and for that, he was willing to make sacrifices.

When Josie asked him to be her date for her high school graduation, the lumps were suddenly the last thing on his mind. He spent every leisure hour planning every minute of their night. It more than lived up to his expectations.

The memory of the night he'd spent with her was burned inside his brain. The softness of her skin, the sweetness of her lips, the indescribable feeling of being buried deep inside her. He was with the woman he loved with every fiber of his being and words couldn't come close.

He came home late, but his mother was still awake. She noticed the change in him right away. Unable to keep it to himself a moment longer, he revealed his love for Josie. After all, now that she'd finished high school, it was only a matter of time before they declared their love to the world.

It was during the conversation with his mother that he mentioned the lumps. Being a nurse at the local hospital, she immediately became alarmed. Her reaction caused the tiniest fissure of fear to creep in and wind its way into the love that filled Chase's heart. He hadn't wanted to think about what the lumps might mean and how they could affect his future. Their future.

His mother insisted he see a specialist and she arranged it for the very next day. Although he protested, she insisted and instead of spending promised time with Josie, he waited in a hospital for a diagnosis.

In the rush to leave the house, he'd forgotten to take his phone. All the agonizing hours he spent in clinics and he hadn't even been able to let her know. He couldn't find the courage to make the call from a payphone. He didn't even tell her that he was thinking of her and praying—every minute, every second of that day.

Then finally, the doctor had called them in and he'd followed behind his mother. They'd taken seats opposite the doctor's huge desk and Chase had waited with dread to hear the news.

"I'm very sorry, Chase…"

It was all he needed to hear. All he *could* hear. The roar in his ears had drowned out the rest of the doctor's words. He'd caught snippets such as 'surgery' and 'chemo' and couldn't believe they were talking about him. He was young; he was healthy. There had to be a mistake.

He couldn't have cancer; it wasn't possible. Cancer was for old people, or people who'd spent their lives in the sun. It wasn't for young people like him. He'd barely had a cough or a cold during the entire nineteen years of his life.

But the doctor's words kept coming and the noise in Chase's ears slowly receded. His mother's grip on his hand got tighter and he forced himself to listen.

He had cancer inside both testicles. It was rare, but that's the way it was. The tumors were deep inside the tissue. They needed to remove the tumors and along with the cancer, all of one testicle and most of the other. The doctor hurried to reassure him that in time he would feel normal sexual urges again. Surviving with even part of one testicle was a little like living with one kidney. After the surgery, he could supplement Chase's hormone levels with synthetic testosterone and he said Chase could go on to have a full and productive life. There was no reason to think it couldn't happen.

It was his mother who raised the question about his fertility. The doctor assured her he could function with even just part of one testicle, but of course, there was no guarantee about healthy sperm. It was unfortunate that the chemotherapy couldn't be contained to only one part of Chase's body. The risk that the chemo might make him sterile was very real.

Then again, the doctor added, no one knew if they were fertile until they tried to make a baby. There were men with both testicles who couldn't make that happen; Chase's cancer didn't definitively make it so.

The doctor was doing his best to put a positive spin on it, but all Chase heard was the possibility of sterility and his heart shriveled and died. Josie was born to be a mother. She couldn't wait to have a family. As soon as she finished university, they intended to marry and work on making that a reality.

If Chase was now infertile, and they were together, her dream would die in the dust. He knew she loved him, but he didn't want her to hate him for being the cause of her dream's demise. He couldn't bear that thought and he couldn't bear the deceit. He'd have to tell her and let her decide: *Did she want him more than she did a baby?*

How badly he wanted to ask her, but he couldn't bring himself to do it. He couldn't face rejection for something he had no power to change. He couldn't force her to give up her dream for his happiness. Night after night, day after day, sitting in a chair with a needle in his arm, filling his body with the poison that would keep him alive, he imagined the scene before him and he still couldn't find the words.

How could he put her in such a position? How could he ask her to choose? She'd dreamed of a large family. Who was he to take that dream away? He loved her too much to force her to choose.

And so, he said nothing. Instead, he walked away. He buried his own dreams deep inside him and refused to ever think of them again. As the years went by, he hoped she'd found a man who deserved her. He hoped she had the family that she craved. Everything inside him screamed out against giving her up, but all he wanted was to see her happy.

And then she'd come back into his life and she wasn't married and she didn't have any kids and no matter how hard he tried, knowing those things had suddenly filled him with a hope so glorious he could hardly contain it. From the moment Riley told him she'd returned, he found it hard not to shout out his joy. And now he'd gone and ruined any chance of that. Again. And the worst thing of all was, this time it had been intentional.

He lifted the bottle of scotch to his lips and cursed when he found it empty. Despite his best efforts, the pain in his heart was still there. He thought he was doing what was best for her. It was obvious she still wanted kids. He still had part of one functioning testicle, but what if it wasn't enough? *What if the chemicals that had killed the cancer had also killed the very thing he wanted for her, above all else?* He hadn't found the courage to discover the answer and now it was probably all too late. After what he'd gone and done tonight, he was sure Josie Munro would hate him forever.

CHAPTER 11

Josie forced her eyes open and did her best to resist the pull of a few more moments of mind-numbing sleep. After fleeing The Bullet and arriving at her rented cottage in record time, she'd spent the night alternating between pacing the modest confines of her living room and tossing and turning in her bed. Images of Chase and the young woman were emblazoned on her mind and fresh anger bubbled to the surface.

He was a jerk of the highest order and she was a sad and lonely fool. For more than a decade, she'd held on to the secret wish that he'd come riding in on his white stallion, begging her forgiveness and proclaiming his undying love. It was obvious she'd read too many romance novels and it was way past time to stop living on dreams. She was twenty-eight years old and mature enough to face the facts, no matter how painful.

Chase was her high school sweetheart, her first love. It was natural she'd harbor feelings for him and that he would hold a special place in her heart. No one forgot their first love. If things between them hadn't ended so abruptly or if he'd even attempted to explain, she would have put it down to experience and moved on, pushing the episode firmly behind her.

But it *had* ended abruptly and he hadn't tried to explain. The reality of that gnawed at her like a slowly festering wound, always there to remind her it needed tending to.

Like a thorn wedged so deep under her skin, it took years to emerge and when it did, it exploded in a mess of ooze and puss and infection.

Well, she had no intention of letting this wound get any bigger. She didn't know what kind of game Chase Barrington was playing, but she was sure as hell through with it—and him.

The phone rang on her nightstand and she rolled over and picked it up. "Josie Munro."

There was a moment of silence on the other end and then Chase said, "Josie. It's me."

A white-hot wave of fury gushed through her veins. *How dare he call her the very next day? How dare he have the nerve?*

"Josie, please, don't hang up. I'm so sorry."

She scoffed in his ear. "Sorry? You have to be kidding? Sorry doesn't even come close."

"I don't know what else you want me to say."

"That's the thing, Chase. I don't want you to say anything to me. Nothing. Not one word. Not ever." She went to hang up the phone and heard him call out.

"Josie, please, wait up. It's about Daniel Logan."

Her hand paused mid-air and she reluctantly brought the phone back up to her ear. "What about Daniel? I'm almost finished my report. I'll deliver it to the prosecutor later today. It's ahead of schedule so you shouldn't have anything to complain ab—"

"It's not about your report." Chase's tone filled with quiet dread. Sudden fear turned Josie cold. She forced herself to ask the question.

"What is it, then?"

"It's…it's about Daniel's mother, Kelly. She—"

"She what? Tell me, for heaven's sake!"

"I just took a call from Riley. He's at the Logan farm. I'm about to head out. I'm sorry, Josie. Kelly Logan committed suicide. Her husband, Trevor, found her early this morning."

Josie gasped in horror and a hand flew to her mouth. She

thought of the sad and broken woman she'd met in her office and tried to hold back the pain.

"H-how?" she stammered, needing to know.

"She overdosed on sleeping pills. They'd been prescribed for her by the doctor who examined her after the assault."

"Does Daniel know?"

Chase sighed. "Yes. Riley told me Trevor broke the news to his boys right after he called us."

Josie shook her head against the tragedy of it all. *How much was one family meant to endure? How much could one family endure?*

"I wanted to tell you before you heard it from someone else. I know how close you've grown to Daniel."

"I-I only spoke to his mother a fortnight ago. I tried to get her some help. A psychologist friend of mine from university works in Grafton. Phoebe was going to call her... I-I can't believe it. That poor family. That poor, poor boy. I have to see him. I have to be there. He'll be blaming himself. I know he will. I—"

"I'll call Riley," Chase interrupted, his voice gentle. "I'll find out if the children are still at home. Their mother's bedroom is once again a potential crime scene. They might have been taken someplace else."

Josie drew in a deep breath laced heavily with sadness. "Thank you," she whispered. "I appreciate your call."

"Anytime," Chase whispered back. "It was the least I could do. I'll call you right back."

Daniel sat on the old floorboards at the far end of the porch with his legs tucked up to his chest and his arms tight around them. His chin was on his knees. He stared blindly across the front yard. The sun was bright and shining, oblivious to the darkness inside the house. Like a rerun of a bad movie, the yard was once again crowded with emergency vehicles. He rocked back and forth on his butt.

It was all his fault. If he'd never blown that asshole's head off, his mother might still be alive. People survived rape; he'd seen it on TV. And yet, his mother was dead. She'd taken too many pills.

His father told him it was an accident; that she hadn't meant to die. She'd simply taken too many by mistake. She'd done it in the middle of the night and probably hadn't wanted to wake him by switching on a light.

But Daniel was having none of it. He'd seen enough to know. People didn't take a handful of tablets by *mistake.* Nobody did that kind of thing. It made him mad to think his dad thought he might fall for that lame explanation. Jason, perhaps, but he was only eight. Tell Jason that kind of made-up rubbish, but don't try to sell it to *him.*

The tired floorboards creaked under measured footsteps and Daniel lifted his head. He stared at the police officer who made his way toward him. It was the same one who had attended their house a month ago; the one who had taken him to the station.

The man reached him and hunkered down on his haunches, bringing his face up close. Daniel could see the tiny flecks in his bright green eyes.

"Daniel, my name's Chase Barrington. I'm a police officer in town. You might remember me?"

Daniel nodded and lowered his gaze, not needing the reminder of how they'd come to meet.

"I've spoken to your dad. He said he told you what happened."

"He told me a bunch of lies, that's what he told me." The words spewed from his mouth in a gush of pain and anger. The officer's expression didn't change.

"Why do you say that?"

Daniel looked away and shook his head, avoiding any further conversation with the officer. He was beyond trying to explain. All he wanted was for the nightmare to be over; for his life to go back to the way it was.

"It wasn't your fault, Daniel."

The gentle tone and the kindness in the other man's eyes

undid him. Tears stung his cheeks. The officer leaned forward, as if to offer him comfort, but Daniel shuffled out of the way. He didn't want comfort; he didn't want to be touched. This *was* his fault, no matter what anyone said.

"I've spoken to Josie Munro. She's the psychologist you've been talking to. I just thought you might like to know, she's on her way over."

For the first time since he'd woken that morning and been given the news by his dad, hope flared in Daniel's chest. *Josie.* The beautiful woman with the long blond hair who listened and understood. He didn't have to pretend or be guarded when he talked to her. She made him feel safe. Now, she was coming out to see him. He'd get to stand close to her again. Or maybe they could just sit right here, out on the porch, out of sight.

He was a little in love with her already. She filled many of his dreams and in each and every one of them, she smiled and laughed and had eyes only for him. It was stupid. He was only twelve years old. *Nearly thirteen.* She was way older than that; way too old for him.

Still, the impossibility of it only made it more enticing. A look, a glance, a touch… Thinking about those things kept the fear and pain at bay that surfaced when he woke. The excitement of his dreams was what got him through the day because once dawn arrived, everything came crashing down and the awful reality of his life took hold until the end of another day.

———————

Josie picked her way across the tidy front yard that bordered the Logan house and tried to ignore the dread that weighed her down. Three police vehicles and an ambulance were parked haphazardly nearby. The back doors of the ambulance were open and she noticed the gurney was missing. *It must be inside.* The thought only added to the heaviness that engulfed her. She couldn't imagine how members of the Logan family were feeling.

She'd just stepped out of the shower when Chase had called her back. He told her that Daniel and Jason were still at the farmhouse with their father; apparently they had nowhere else to go. The family had been in the area for only a matter of months. They hadn't made friends with many in the community and they had no relatives living close by. Josie's heart broke at the thought of them suffering alone, without the comfort of extended family and friends and she resolved to do whatever she could to help.

She walked up the front steps and strode across the porch. She pulled open the front screen door. It squeaked loudly in protest, making her wince. The air around her was still and quiet. She couldn't even hear the murmur of voices. Knowing she couldn't turn around now, she swallowed a sigh and forced herself across the threshold. A moment later, she entered the house.

The morning sun filtered through clean but tattered curtains that covered a wide window in the front room. A large, faux leather brown sofa, paired with matching armchairs, filled most of the modest space. A low coffee table was stacked with magazines and a flat-screen television hung on the wall.

The next room led into the kitchen where a pile of dirty dishes filled the sink. Stale bread, an opened cereal box and half a dozen empty beer cans littered the counter. After the tidiness of the front room, Josie could only surmise Kelly Logan hadn't ventured into the kitchen too often since her assault.

Continuing down the hall, she saw a bedroom that contained a set of bunk beds. A motorcycle print hung on one wall. Underneath it, a row of medals on ribbons that looked like they were for running events hung from a handful of nails. Josie stepped closer and turned one of the medals over; the weight of it was heavy in her hand. Her heart skipped a beat at the words inscribed on the back: *Daniel Logan; Watervale Public School; twelve-years boy cross country champion.*

A noise behind her snagged her attention and she looked up. Daniel stood in the doorway. He stared at her and at the medal still in her hand. His eyes were huge and shadowed in his pale face. His blond hair was mussed and untidy, like he'd only just climbed out of bed. He still wore his pajamas. Her heart filled with sympathy.

"Daniel, I-I just heard about your mother. I-I'm so sorry."

He stared and blinked and stared again and then she saw him swallow. Tears glinted in his eyes. With a sudden need to console him, she closed the distance between them and pulled him into her arms. She didn't care if it crossed professional boundaries; he was a child who was in desperate need of comfort. He'd endured more horror than anyone should and she wasn't going to stand by and let him deal with his pain alone.

His arms came around her waist and his body shuddered against her. Sobs poured out of his mouth in a torrent of tortured gasps. She held his head against her breasts and blinked back tears of her own.

His obvious pain tore right through her and she groaned at its force. Then, thrusting it aside, she concentrated hard on the boy in her arms and murmured wordless noises of comfort. Her hand brushed through his soft, messy hair over and over again.

"*Shh*, honey. It's going to be all right. *Shh*. I'm here. I promise everything's going to be all right." The words tasted acrid on her lips, but at that moment she meant every word. Her brain might have tried to argue differently, but she refused to listen to reason.

She'd all but completed her report that declared Daniel fit to stand trial. She'd also offered the opinion that he had sufficient capacity to know that his actions were wrong. If her report was accepted by the court, he was going to be tried for murder and she would be instrumental in allowing it to happen.

How could she go through with it? The very boy at the center of it was distraught and desolate in her arms. The rules of society dictated that he be brought before a court of law to answer for his actions. He'd shot a man dead; a criminal, a man who was raping the boy's mother. The laws of the society they lived in demanded there be consequences for not conforming to its rules.

But who would it serve if he was sent away to spend months, even years in juvenile detention? It wouldn't serve his mother and it sure as hell wouldn't make a difference to the way Daniel felt about his guilt. He had been convinced his actions were necessary. He did what he had to do to protect his mother; to bring an end to her pain. If he was put in similar circumstances, he'd do the same thing all over again.

Locking him up wouldn't change his outlook; it wouldn't make him see the error of his ways. He had to live with his actions every single minute of the rest of his life and that was punishment enough—worse than being imprisoned, as far as Josie was concerned. All she wanted was to take him home and comfort him and promise to make everything better. She wanted to treat him like the young, lost boy he was.

But that choice wasn't hers to make. Society stated otherwise. Soon, the contents of her report would be argued from both sides of the bar table. She didn't know what would be contained in the psych report obtained by Daniel's lawyer, but she hoped it carried some convincing arguments that the boy be left alone. He was now without a mother. He'd suffered way too much. *Surely the judge would see that?* She could only hope that this tragic mess would be sorted out and that Daniel, through some miracle, would be given another chance at life.

———————

The funeral home was dim and quiet and gave Trevor Logan the shivers, but he forced himself inside the room where he'd been told his wife lay in repose. A moment later, he spied her, or at least the polished wood of her coffin and he moved toward her in a trance, until finally he reached her side.

He'd been told there had been an autopsy, but she still looked just the same. With a trembling hand, he brushed the hair off her beautiful face. Her skin was cold and waxy, but she looked so calm and peaceful—she looked like she was sleeping. The shadows under her eyes were gone and so was the pain of the last month. He was glad she was no longer hurting. He wished he could say the same.

The truth was, he was struggling desperately and he didn't know what to do. The guilt was slowly eating him from the inside out and every day the blackness grew until it was almost like he no longer existed, and all that was left was a shell: a shell filled with anger and helplessness and more than an ocean of blame—all of it directed at him.

It had taken him nearly a week after the attack to even bring himself to look at his wife. He'd tried so hard, but he couldn't do it, even when he knew his avoidance was tearing her apart. Each time he went to gaze at her, all he saw was the animal who'd violated her.

It was ludicrous because he hadn't even set eyes on the perpetrator. The body had been long removed when the police made contact with him and he'd finally made it home, but it didn't stop him from imagining the scene over and over again and every time he did, the anger and fear and utter helplessness returned tenfold to overwhelm him. If he'd walked in and saw what was happening he would have done exactly what his son did. There was guilt there too, that he hadn't been there for his family.

Then there were his boys and the toll it had taken on them: Daniel most of all. Another wave of guilt pounded into him from all sides. *He* was the one who'd taught Daniel about guns, about hunting, about safety, and it was he who'd told his eldest son he was the man of the house while his father was away. All Daniel had done was follow his father's orders. He'd protected his mother and brother, like his father had asked him to. The guilt of the consequences for his son nearly overwhelmed him.

Daniel, his beautiful boy, was shattered. He moved through the house like a ghost. The worst of it was, Trevor had nothing left to give him. It was all Trevor's fault that his son had reacted the way he had to defend his family, yet now it was all Trevor could do to keep himself upright and to keep up the appearance that he was still functioning halfway normal.

He scoffed in the silence. He was so far from normal, the mere thought of it was a joke. Still, he did his best to alleviate the concern he saw in the eyes of well-meaning neighbors who dropped by and he tried hard to make it appear that he was coping.

He should have been home when that son of a bitch came calling. It was as plain and simple as that. If Trevor had been home with his family, the nightmare would never have happened. The drug-crazed fuck might have still chosen their house, but he wouldn't have found a woman and children alone and undefended. Trevor would have been the one to take the gun to the fucker and he would have gladly faced the consequences.

It shouldn't have fallen to his twelve-year-old boy to take on such a responsibility. The whole nightmare was wrong on so many levels. Even still, with his wife lying there in a coffin, he couldn't help the surge of pride for his son, a boy who'd managed to do to the scum what he'd imagined doing himself.

Trevor couldn't believe the police had charged his son. *How fucked up was that?* Daniel had done what any man would have done and now he was the one in trouble.

It was a fucked up world they lived in. Of that, he had no doubt. And now his beloved Kelly was dead. Gone, just like that. Life for him and his boys would never be the same again.

A surge of emotion overwhelmed him and hot tears sprang to his eyes. *How in fuck's name was he going to live without her? What the hell was he meant to do?* He leaned over the open coffin and buried his head against her chest. The smell of the embalming fluid burned his nostrils. She was stiff and cold, even through her clothes. She felt like a stranger.

"How could you *leave* me? How could you leave our *boys?*" he sobbed, with all the pain and desolation in his heart.

The stranger remained coldly silent.

He sobbed like he'd never stop.

———

Scott Jones stared at the calendar on the wall and marked off another day. Three more weeks and counting before he was out of this shit hole. Three more weeks before he could take the first step toward seeing his plan come to fruition and seek revenge for his mate.

The prison siren wailed in the distance, indicating it was time to eat. Scott gathered the newspaper clippings he had spread across his bunk. After hearing about Neil's murder, he'd scouted around for anything he could find. A few ciggies here, a pill or two there and he'd managed to gather quite a collection. He'd even gone on the Internet while he was down in the prison library and had Googled Neil's name and the location: *Watervale.*

Within moments, he found what he was looking for and had printed out the map. It would take him about six hours to drive there, longer if he had to take the bus. Still, it would be worth every minute of the wait—of that he had no doubt.

CHAPTER 12

The day of Kelly Logan's funeral was dreary, wet and gray. It was the kind of day that made you want to linger inside the warmth and comfort of your home, away from the cold and misery outside. But there would be no warmth or comfort today, inside or out, and there was no escaping the feeling of despondency that plagued Chase.

The bleak weather only served as a harsh reminder that soon Kelly Logan would be laid to rest. Her misery was finally over and his own misery came to mind. He accepted that any chance he had of being with Josie, the woman he loved, was as good as buried, too.

It had been three days since he'd spoken to her and it was agony to know that despite her living so close, she couldn't be further away. For a decade, he'd struggled to forget about her—like a long raging war, the memories advanced and retreated back and forth in the depths of his mind. At those times, even sleep became his enemy and offered him no repose.

While his heart had clung to the hope that things might be different someday, his mind cruelly reminded him that all hope had been extinguished at The Bullet not so long ago.

That she would be at the funeral, he had no doubt. He'd seen her with Daniel at the farmhouse. The boy had clung to her with a poignant desperation that tore at Chase's heart. It pained him equally to see the despair and sadness etched onto Josie's face as she'd held the young boy tight.

Neither of them had noticed him, so absorbed in each other they'd been. It only reinforced for him how much she needed to be a mother. It would give her purpose, fulfil her in a way nothing else could. He'd always known that was the way of it, just as he'd known the chance he could give that to her was likely to be zero.

With a sigh, he pushed the depressing thoughts from his mind and shrugged into his coat. Bracing himself against the blast of cold air, he opened the front door of his condo and hurried through the rain to his car.

Josie drew her jacket around her and bent her head against the wind. Watervale was only a couple of hours inland from the coast, but it was nestled at the base of a mountain range. The town was no stranger to ice and snow. Fall had come and gone and it would be only a matter of time before the quiet of winter would set upon them and the hot, sunny days and pleasant nights would be nothing more than a memory.

With her shoulder, she pushed open the heavy wooden doors that led into the church and took a few moments to get orientated. Rows of wooden pews lined both sides of the generously proportioned church. A crucifix hung from high above the altar. The altar itself was marble inlaid with gold and gleamed in the dull light. The stained glass windows weren't shown to their advantage because of the overcast day outside, but she could imagine how spectacular they would be in the bright sunshine.

Earlier, waking to the sound of rain, Josie had let out a quiet groan of despair. As if attending the funeral of a loved one wasn't difficult enough, now the Logan family was going to have to do it on a cold and dismal day. The weather seemed to set the tone of the morning and she'd been on edge ever since, reluctantly admitting that her turmoil not only had to do with Daniel and how he'd cope, but with Chase as well.

Chase would be at the funeral, no doubt, along with many people from the town, including her brother, Riley. The Logans may not have been in Watervale long, but word had quickly gotten around. It would be a very rare person indeed who hadn't heard about what had happened. First the sexual assault and murder and now, the devastating suicide. There wouldn't be many in the tight-knit community whose hearts remained untouched.

To her surprise, the church was only half full and she didn't have to search long to find an empty seat. She chose one close to the front, but far enough away that she wouldn't be mistaken for family. She wanted to be there for Daniel and to show him her support, but she was also conscious of not wanting to intrude. Daniel sat with his father and brother and from the familiar features of one of the women in the front row, a maternal aunt.

Josie's gaze alighted on the coffin where it stood in the center of the aisle. It was a dark cherry wood casket, its top laden with a bouquet of sweet-smelling lilies. White in color, they contrasted starkly with the darkness of the coffin, but somehow they seemed appropriate and their heavy perfume filled the air.

She breathed in deeply and began to ease the air out between her lips. When she turned her head slightly, she caught sight of Chase and what was left of her breath came out in a rush.

He looked as handsome as ever, tall and broad shouldered in his dark, tailored suit. His curly brown hair was damp from the shower, or maybe it was from the rain? Either way, it only added to his good looks. He was a man who demanded attention, whether he sought it out or not.

She thought of the woman draped all over him in the bar and her jaw tensed. Chase had appeared more than happy with the situation and the woman sure as hell hadn't forced him to hold her that close.

Despite Josie's best efforts, shards of jealousy once again pierced her heart and tears burned behind her eyes. She wished she could put this all behind her. She wished she didn't care. But the truth was, she still loved him and would always love him. She'd cursed herself because the truth was, it was Chase Barrington, or no one else. She'd proved it over and over again. The crystallization of this reality was like being damned to hell.

Not that she'd been promiscuous, but she'd done her best in college to forget him. It had only been after several short and futile relationships that she'd finally faced the truth: She'd never feel for other men what she felt for her high school love. Despite the way he'd left her and the agony of pain he'd caused, her heart still yearned for him and there was not a single thing she could do about it.

She watched while Chase took a seat not far from her on the other side of the church. Her sigh of relief was tempered with disappointment. She hadn't expected him to sit beside her, but it would have been nice if he'd at least acknowledged her presence.

She caught a glimpse of another dark suit from the corner of her eye. The next moment, Riley squeezed in beside her, folding his long limbs into the tight confines of the pew.

"How are you, sis?" he whispered, his dark eyes full of concern.

A surge of emotion tightened her throat and she blinked back a rush of tears. Trust Riley to break through her defenses, he'd always had the knack for doing that. Despite being five years older, they shared a very close bond. He was dark as the night and she was as fair as the day, but somehow their characters meshed and they saw into each other's souls.

If there was anyone she could have confided in all those sad years ago, it was Riley. Her love for Chase was so big that she wondered how she'd contained it and kept it from her family. She'd wanted to sing it from the rooftops, to tell everyone who might want to hear, but she'd kept the knowledge a secret and now she was glad she had.

When it all went wrong, there were many times she wished she'd had a sturdy shoulder to cry on, but by then,

Riley had left home and she'd felt too ashamed to call him because she'd kept the truth hidden for so long.

Knowing that she'd misjudged the one man who she'd loved beyond all others made it even harder to seek comfort in her older brother's arms. In a way, she was glad no one else knew. She'd crawled into a deep hole, undisturbed, and mourned the loss of her love in private—and there had been so much mourning to do.

She'd mourned the loss of her future; she'd mourned the loss of her past. She'd mourned the loss of her innocence... She'd never trust her heart to another again. She worked hard over the years not to grow bitter and she was sure she'd succeeded on that front. She wasn't bitter. Angry, hurt, confused...yes. But she still believed in love. She only had to look at her parents and her married siblings for confirmation of that.

Her parents were still going strong after forty years. All five of her brothers were married. She didn't have to spend much time with any of them to feel the depth of love between them and their chosen mates. While the knowledge they were happy filled her with joy, she couldn't deny during the dark and lonely depths of the night, she yearned to feel the same.

Aware that Riley stared at her with a look of growing concern, she stammered out a few whispered words of reassurance and hoped he put her reticence down to the solemnity of the occasion. As if sensing her fragility, he put an arm around her shoulders and drew her in close against his side. She breathed in his warm, familiar smell and leaned into him, grateful to have him near.

Gradually, the church filled and the service started with a hymn. The beautiful words of *Amazing Grace* brought a burst of fresh tears to her eyes. Riley shot her another look of concern tinged with understanding and pressed a soft kiss against her hair. She squeezed his hand and did her best to concentrate on the minister when he began to speak.

The woman Josie guessed to be the older sister of Kelly Logan was halfway through the eulogy when Trevor gave out a cry of pain. Reaching out to the coffin, he threw his arm over it, his hand tangling up in the flowers. He hugged the coffin close and tears streamed down his cheeks. Josie bit her lip, devastated by what she witnessed.

Her gaze shot to Daniel and her heart broke right in two. The desolation on the young boy's face was enough to unravel her. She stirred, ready to go to him, only realizing at the last minute what she was doing.

Riley's arm restrained her gently and she slowly relaxed back against him. It wasn't her place to offer Daniel comfort. He had a family who could give him that. She was nothing more than the psychologist who had assessed him at the request of the prosecution and it wouldn't be long before everyone would know the contents of her report. She was the woman who was about to ruin what was left of the tattered shreds of his life. He didn't even know it yet.

Chapter 13

Chase typed in the necessary information and finished his report. A fight had broken out earlier that morning between two men over the sale of fifteen pigs and it had taken him most of the day to get to the bottom of it. He loved his job in rural policing, but every now and then he found himself wondering what it would be like to be a detective in the city. Sydney or Melbourne, it didn't really matter which one. Maybe, even Brisbane. He frowned at the thought. *No, not Brisbane.* He couldn't imagine living there without thinking of Josie.

He hadn't seen her since the funeral, more than a fortnight ago, and even then, it had only been from a distance. She'd appeared clearly shaken in the church, fraught with sadness and sorrow. Overcome with emotion, she'd sought comfort in Riley's arms. Chase had quietly bemoaned the injustice of it—it should have been him offering her solace that day, *his* strong arms keeping her safe, just like he promised her.

But there was no turning back and no rewriting their history. He could only assume she was still angry over the stunt he'd pulled at The Bullet. The very thought of that evening weighed heavy in his heart but, short of telling her the whole sordid truth, there was nothing he could do to explain his actions.

And now, there was her report.

John Wall, a mountain of a man and a veteran prosecutor,

who was in charge of the Logan hearing had recently delivered it to him. The matter was scheduled to be heard in a few days and when John had given Chase a copy of Josie's findings, the contents stayed with him long after he'd read them. Although he'd guessed much of what her report would say, he knew better than anyone else how difficult it must have been for her to arrive at her conclusion.

He wished he was brave enough to phone her; to dial her number and ask her how she was, but more than anything, he wished he had the courage to ask her why she wasn't married with a handful of children, like she'd always wanted.

"How's the Logan matter going? Do you have a copy of the psych report from the defense, yet?"

Riley's question cut abruptly into Chase's thoughts and he focused on his boss who stood a few feet away.

"Not yet. They have until the end of the day to serve it on us. I'm guessing it will say the exact opposite of what's contained in Josie's."

"No surprises there. What date is the competency hearing?"

"It's slated for first thing Tuesday morning. We have four days to prepare and that's counting the weekend."

A smile tugged at the corners of Riley's mouth. "Sounds like John's going to be busy."

"Lucky for us he's the best in the business. I'm sure he'll be ready and raring to go."

Riley nodded and turned away. He was halfway across the squad room when he stopped and turned back to face Chase.

"Oh, I nearly forgot. Kate asked me to invite you to a barbeque this Saturday night. She said it's been ages since we had you over. In fact, I think the last time we got together was the night of the tragedy at the Logan place."

Chase grimaced. "Yeah, we sure can do without a repeat of that."

"You can say that again. I've invited Josie, too. She's been in town more than three months and I've barely seen her outside of work."

Chase dropped his gaze and did his best to keep his expression from showing the sudden discomfort he felt. Despite his efforts, Riley moved closer and frowned.

"Are you okay with it, Chase? I mean, I know you took her to her high school graduation, but that was it, wasn't it? You don't have a thing for her, do you?"

"A thing? Of course not." Chase hoped the heat he could feel rising from his chest and creeping up his neck went undetected. Riley turned away again and Chase swallowed a sigh of relief. It was short lived. A moment later, Riley spun on his heel again and faced Chase.

"What about Josie? She hasn't been carrying some kind of flame for you, has she?"

"No, no I wouldn't think so. We... We barely knew each other back then." Chase almost choked on the lie.

"Good. I wouldn't want to make things awkward, for either of you."

"Nope. No awkwardness here. You're more than welcome to invite her over. She's your sister, after all."

"Yes, she is and it's been great to have her back. Mom and Dad are beyond thrilled. For too long, I've been their only child to live within a hundred mile or so radius."

Chase thought wistfully of the parents he'd lost five years ago. They'd been killed instantly in an automobile accident. He was grateful they hadn't suffered, but being an only child now meant he found himself alone, disconnected, and with no family to speak of. Every now and then he wondered what it might be like to have a sibling or two—or six, like Riley.

"It must be nice to know they care," he murmured.

"Yeah, it is. As much as they drive me nuts sometimes, I wouldn't trade them for all the money in the world."

Daniel stared at the cobwebs on the ceiling high above his bed and wondered about what it would be like to be a spider. Not a big hairy one that everyone wanted to swipe with the broom or drown with insect spray, but a harmless, useful one like a huntsman—one that could live its life spinning its intricate web in the dark corner of a room, far from everything and everybody, coming and going as it pleased without being noticed. It sounded so far removed from the reality of his life since the murder he could scarcely imagine it or remember what life had been like before the arrival of Neil Whitcomb.

Neil Whitcomb. Daniel had finally discovered the man's name. His lawyer had given him a copy of the police report when they'd met earlier in the day. His competency hearing was a handful of days away. His lawyer wanted him to be prepared.

Reading through the police account, Daniel felt detached, removed from the events that unfolded on the pages—like he was reading about someone else.

Neil Whitcomb. It sounded like such a normal, ordinary name. It sounded like the name of a man who had never done any wrong; the kind of name belonging to a man Daniel could be introduced to at the farm store and think nothing of it; the kind of name that could have belonged to his neighbor.

There was nothing to indicate that a man with the name of Neil Whitcomb would break into Daniel's home and rape his mother and drive Daniel to murder. There was no disguising or denying what it was and no way to minimize the event. In the blink of an eye, it had happened—just like he'd told Josie and according to his barrister, she'd said as much in her report.

Everything she'd written was true, and he couldn't blame her for her honesty. He'd always known his actions were wrong and that he'd probably go to jail, but he didn't care. He still didn't care. He was scared to death of the thought of being locked up, but if he came across the same situation again, he'd act exactly the same way.

If there was one thing he *was* sorry for, it was the way it had affected his family. His beloved mother, the woman he'd tried to spare from pain, was dead. His father might as well be, too. When he was there, he moved around the house like a ghost, his face devoid of emotion, blank and expressionless. He'd returned to work out of necessity and even though he no longer did the long hauls from Melbourne to Brisbane, more and more often, he'd come home late, well past the hour of bedtime.

Before the shooting, Daniel had never been scared; he'd been proud of the responsibility his father had entrusted to him, but now, he'd lie in the dark, grateful for the presence of his little brother and pray for his father's return. He was beyond relieved that his dad no longer stayed away overnight. Every creak, every sigh, every whisper of the wind would stir the fear that lay dormant within him during the day, but would reveal its ugly head during the night. He wanted to sleep with the gun behind the door of his bedroom, but his father expressly forbid it.

The sound of Jason turning over in the bed sent Daniel's heart leaping in fear. With a soft curse, he forced himself to relax. What he wouldn't give to turn back the clock, to return to a time when his worst nightmare was whether he was going to wake up with a zit.

The ever-present fear and nervousness he'd been living with for more than a couple of months was eroding his mind. He'd barely slept since it had happened and the deprivation was taking its toll. He'd done his best to put on a cheery façade for his brother and his teachers, but inside, he was falling apart.

Like the broom that destroyed the spider's web with a single, vicious swipe, his life had taken too many hits in too short a time and had fragmented into a million pieces. He'd never be able to put them together again, no matter how hard he tried. But the thought of not trying terrified him. *If he didn't try, what then?*

There was no one he could turn to. Not to his father, not to Jason, not even to his friends. He hadn't been in Watervale long enough to have made friendships strong enough to withstand the kind of pressure he'd put one under. The only other person who came to mind was Josie and her report to the judge put him one step closer to jail.

He had no one.

He was all alone.

Just like the spider.

Chapter 14

The delicious smell of smoky barbeque wafted toward Josie's nose and her stomach grumbled. Having woken late after another restless night, she'd skipped breakfast in favor of a swim and had then headed to her office to finish up paperwork on patients she'd seen late on Friday afternoon. She'd worked through lunch and by the time she arrived back home, given that she was shortly heading over to her brother's place for dinner, there hardly seemed any point in eating.

Riley had called her earlier in the week and had invited her over for a barbeque. Despite her sleepless night, she looked forward to sharing a few pleasant hours with him and his family. No doubt the adorable identical twins, Daisy and Rosie, would clutch at her legs and plaster her with sticky hugs and kisses like they usually did. She'd learned months ago not to arrive at the Munro household wearing white pants. At least the girls would distract her, even for a little while, from the turmoil and chaos in her head.

Riley's two-storey, modern rendered brick house sat on a large corner block in a very nice part of town. The manicured lawns and neat garden beds overflowed with colourful blooms, evidence of Kate's green thumb. A couple of small tricycles along with an array of balls and plastic toys littered the concrete path that led to the front door.

Josie skirted around the side of the building, assuming everyone would be at the back. From the tantalizing smell of the barbeque, she figured it was almost time to eat. She rounded the corner and came up short, almost stumbling over her feet.

Chase stood with his back to her, less than ten yards away. As she watched, he threw back his head and laughed at something Riley said. Her brother spied her and waved to her with the barbeque tongs and then said something else to Chase. Unaware of her presence, Chase's laughter rumbled out once again.

Josie forced air into her suddenly depleted lungs and tried her best to gain control over her traitorous heart. She hated that he still had an effect on her, but there was nothing she could do about it.

If she'd known Chase was invited, she would have found an excuse to decline. Anything to avoid having to spend time with him, exchanging nothing more than superficial pleasantries that only served to mask her hurt. She hadn't forgotten how he'd flaunted the bar floozy right before her eyes and no matter how often she analyzed it, she'd drawn the only obvious conclusion: He'd wanted to send her a clear message that night—it was over and had been over for more than a decade. He'd moved on and she should too and the sooner she surrendered to that fact, the better.

And now he was in her brother's backyard, looking super comfortable, a bottle of beer in his hand and a lazy smile on his face. She looked around a little frantically for signs of other guests and found none.

Surely it wasn't just the four of them? Oh God, she'd be forced to sit next to him. Her panic ratcheted up another notch. All she could think of was escape.

"Aunty Josie! Aunty Josie! You're here!"

Before she could turn on her heel and sneak away like a thief in the night, two chubby little bodies dressed in matching denim dresses and cute white sandals with bright pink bows launched themselves at her legs. With her chances of escaping undetected fast evaporating, she bent low and scooped up both of the toddlers in her arms. She swung them around amidst squeals of laughter and delight.

They took turns kissing her on the cheek and on her lips and on any other part of her they could reach. She kissed each of them on the top of their snowy blond heads, setting them down gently with a protectiveness that came to her naturally when she was around any of her nieces and nephews, or any other children for that matter.

"How are my favorite little princesses?" she asked, smiling at their adorable faces.

"Good," they chorused. "I'm Rapunzel," Daisy announced, flicking her longish hair. "And I'm Cinderella," Rosie added. "I have a wicked stepmother."

Josie looked suitably horrified. "A wicked stepmother? You poor, poor girl."

"Yes, and she makes me live in a dungeon and sweep up all the dirt."

"She *does*? How mean is that? Lucky you have a fairy godmother," Josie smiled.

"She's going to bring me a beautiful, magical dress. The prince will take one look at me and fall in love and ask me to be his wife."

Josie stifled a laugh. "Wow, that's...that's pretty special. You're lucky to have such a wonderful fairy godmother."

Daisy pulled at Josie's sleeve. "*I* want a fairy godmother."

"No, silly," her sister replied. "Rapunzel doesn't have a fairy godmother. She stays locked up in her castle forever."

A dark frown creased Daisy's small face and she stamped her foot. "I don't want to be locked up in a castle forever!"

Stepping between them, Josie hastily intervened before the girls came to blows. "Daisy, Rosie, it's okay. Daisy, you don't have to be locked up in a castle forever. That's what the prince is for, remember? He rides up on his strong white steed and rescues you."

She was met with identical frowns. "What's a steed, Aunty Josie?" Daisy asked.

Rosie rolled her eyes. "It's a car, silly. How else is he going to rescue you and take you away from the castle?"

Josie stifled another grin and squatted on her haunches

until she was at eye level with the twins. "Actually, it's a horse. They didn't have cars back in those days."

"No cars?" Rosie asked, her frown deepening. "How did they go to the shops?"

"Well, I guess they walked or—"

"They rode their horses!" Daisy finished, grinning triumphantly.

"Yes, that's it, Daisy," Josie smiled, drawing both of them in close for a hug. "You girls are far too clever. Whatever will your teacher do when you get to school?"

Rosie shook her head. "We're not going to school. We're staying home, with Mommy and Daddy. We're staying home forever."

Josie swallowed a sigh and hugged them both again tightly. Far be it for her to disillusion them. There were some things an Aunt didn't have to do. Breathing in the scent of their sweet-smelling hair, she looked over their heads and straight into Chase's tormented gaze.

Chase stared at Josie from across the yard and his heart tightened with emotion. With her blond head pressed close against her nieces, she could have passed for their mother. The smiles on the faces of the little girls, with their arms stretching tightly around her, told him they adored and loved her.

He'd always known she'd make a fantastic mom. She was naturally maternal, kind and gentle, patient and loving—all the things a mother should be. It wasn't right for her to be denied that gift and it wasn't right that he yearned for her to be his when he couldn't guarantee her one of the things she longed for most.

He guessed there was always adoption, but it wouldn't be the same. He couldn't imagine what it was like to carry a child, but he was certain it was an experience that couldn't be replicated.

He'd been surprised to discover that she wasn't married, that she hadn't started a family of her own. The reasons for this weren't clear to him and that was something he desperately wished he knew. Could it be that the longing she'd expressed when she was a teenager had dissipated over time? If that proved true, would fate be willing to give them a second chance? *Could he be that lucky?*

She stood and with a twin on either hip, closed the distance between them. The image of Lucy plastered all over him at The Bullet suddenly flashed into his mind, along with the pain and hurt that night on Josie's face. Pangs of guilt ripped through him. He could only imagine the names she'd called him. He wondered if she'd even speak to him now.

Unable to help himself, his gaze roved over her and took in every minute detail. She wore a fitted, cornflower-blue shirt that matched the color of her eyes. The soft fabric clung to her breasts and gently caressed her curves. A pair of denim jeans and highly polished dress boots completed the ensemble. Summer was long since over, but her skin still evidenced the vestiges of a tan.

Her cheeks were pink and her mouth was softly parted, as if she was also finding it a little difficult to breathe. As he watched, her tongue peeked out and swiped across her lips.

Blood rushed from his head and centered in his groin and it was all he could do not to groan. Instead, he clenched his jaw, turned slightly away and prayed no one would notice his predicament.

"Josie. It's good to see you, sis. Glad you could make it." Riley enveloped her and his girls in a hug and then tickled one of the twins under the chin. She giggled and the other one begged him to do it to her. He took both girls from his sister and to their matching squeals of delight, threw them up in the air.

Chase was glad for the distraction. It was difficult enough to greet Josie without her brother looking on. He cleared his throat and tried to appear casual and unaffected.

"It's great to see you again, Josie. How have you been?" He cursed silently at the inanity of his conversation, but there was nothing else to be done. Her expression grew cool.

"Fine, thanks Chase. Busy. You know how it is."

He nodded and cast around for something more clever to say, but came up with nothing. He was relieved when Kate stepped out onto the back porch to greet Josie and offered to get her a drink.

"Thanks, Kate. I'll come in and get it," she replied, looking almost as relieved as he was to put some distance between them. She hurried toward the back steps that led up onto the porch and Chase exhaled on a surreptitious sigh.

"What was that all about?" Riley asked shrewdly, his gaze narrowed on Chase.

Chase shrugged and took another swig of beer in an effort to delay his response. "What are you talking about?"

"You and Josie. You both looked like you'd bit into a moldy donut. What gives?"

Not willing to get into it, and especially not with her brother, Chase shook his head. "Nothing, mate. It's nothing. I don't know what you're talking about."

Riley stared at him a moment longer and then, to Chase's relief, dropped it.

"All right, whatever you say. Who's ready for a little barbeque?"

———

Josie held her glass out to Kate while she poured her a glass of iced tea and then took a grateful sip.

"*Mm*, that's lovely." She sighed and set the glass back on the counter. In keeping with the casual occasion, she'd pulled her hair back into a relaxed knot at the back of her neck. A strand had come loose and she tucked it back behind her ear.

"So, what have you been up to?" Kate asked and went back to slicing tomatoes for the salad.

"The usual. There always seems to be some poor child who needs my help." She gave a small deprecating grin. "I used to think Watervale was a quiet little town." She took another sip from her glass and sighed softly. "You probably know I've been working with Daniel Logan?"

"Yes, Riley told me. The whole situation's just awful. And to have his mother..." Kate shook her head sadly. "That poor family, what they must be going through. I feel sorry for you, too. I bet you didn't have anything like this in mind when you decided to move back. It's a far cry from what you're used to."

Josie closed her eyes briefly and nodded. "You're right. It's the last thing I expected, but in a way it's been a good thing. After spending years in Brisbane doing what I was doing, I'd begun to feel very disillusioned about my career choice. I wanted to help kids; I wanted to make a difference. I wanted to feel like I was needed."

She grimaced. "Little did I know how much I'd be needed and how difficult it would be. I-I've submitted my report on Daniel to the prosecutor. Unless the defense comes up with sufficient arguments in rebuttal, that poor young boy will go on trial for murder." Her shoulders slumped. "The competency hearing starts next week. I wanted so much to help him, but I'm afraid I've made things worse."

"You've done your job. Josie. You've told the truth. There's nothing to be ashamed of in that."

Kate's soft words of comfort eased a little of Josie's anguish, but she still couldn't shake the guilt that had assailed her since her decision. Daniel had trusted her, he'd opened up to her and on some levels, she'd betrayed him.

She wanted to take the contents of her report back, she wanted to change her mind, but she couldn't. She'd told the truth and there was no going back, no matter how much it hurt. Tears burned behind her eyes and she bit her lip on a sob. Kate set down the knife she was using. She wiped her hands on a cloth and came around to Josie's side.

"Oh, honey, I didn't mean to make you cry. It's not your

fault. You know that. If it hadn't been you, the prosecutor would have requested someone else. They would have drawn the same conclusion. The outcome would be the same."

Josie nodded, knowing Kate was right, but the hurt caused by her decision didn't ease. She'd heard the rumblings in the town from angry locals who didn't think a boy who'd shot and killed a rapist should be punished: Okay, a man was dead, but he was the scum of the earth and didn't deserve to live. It was just the way it was. Daniel Logan should be hailed a hero, not dragged off to jail in shame.

Josie could understand the feelings of the locals. On some level, she felt that way, too. But that didn't fit the kind of world they lived in. Not wanting to think about it any longer, she changed the subject.

"So, what's with Rosie not wanting to go to school?"

Kate eyed her skeptically and Josie wondered if her sister-in-law would insist on her verbal confirmation that whatever decision the court arrived at wasn't her fault, but to her relief, Kate answered her question.

"The girls saw the movie, *Matilda*. What more can I say?"

Josie smiled in understanding. "Ah, *Miss Trunchbull*. She even gave me nightmares, and I only read the book!"

Kate laughed. "Me, too. Roald Dahl has a lot to answer for. It's not a movie I would have chosen to let the girls watch, but they were having a playdate over at a friend's house. Unfortunately, one of the older siblings had the movie on and apparently the girls were glued to the screen. The first I knew about it was when they started complaining they were never going to school."

Josie chuckled and took another sip from her glass. Kate went back to putting the final touches to the salad.

"So, apart from being saddled with the report on Daniel Logan, what else have you been up to? How is it, being back in the country? Are you missing the city lights?"

"Not at all," Josie answered and realized it was the truth. "I've always been a country girl at heart and it wasn't until I moved home that I discovered how much I love living in the bush."

She shrugged. "The city has its attractions, don't get me wrong, but it can't compare to what's out here. I guess some people would find the silence dull, but I find it refreshing. It's nice to be able to commute to work in less time than I take to put on my makeup and here I don't have to battle peak-hour traffic—an added bonus. The only thing I really miss is the shopping."

"So there wasn't a special someone who's pining for you back there?"

Josie smiled and shook her head. "No. No one special."

A companionable silence fell between them and Josie took another sip of her tea. Kate threw a handful of sugar peas into the salad and then said, almost offhandedly, "Chase is a nice guy."

Josie choked on a mouthful of tea and scrambled around for a tissue to swipe at the mess on the counter. At least it gave her an excuse not to respond.

"He's also pretty cute, don't you think?" Kate blinked, her blue eyes wide and innocent.

Josie averted her gaze and silently cursed the blush that crept across her cheeks. "Um...yeah, I guess so. I hadn't really noticed."

"Riley would have been lost without him last Christmas when Duncan fell ill. Chase stepped up without hesitation and took over Riley's duties. It meant your brother was able to devote time to your parents without worrying about work. He was very grateful for Chase's help. We both were."

Josie nodded, not knowing what else to do. She was aware Chase had taken over Riley's responsibilities while their father had been gravely ill and she appreciated Chase's efforts then and now, but it didn't mean she was about to confess to feelings she thought she'd buried long ago. No one knew about her history with Chase and that's the way it was going to stay, particularly given his stunt last month at The Bullet.

"He's not married, you know," Kate said casually. "In fact,

he's considered one of the town's most eligible bachelors. Riley's convinced Chase is a love 'em and leave 'em type of guy, but I think he's selling him short. There's more to Chase than meets the eye and there are plenty of women who would love to snare him for their own."

Josie shook her head, unable to listen to any more. "Please, Kate. You're beginning to sound like my mom. Okay, I'm twenty-eight, and heavens above, I'm still single, but that doesn't mean I'm looking to settle down. I'm not interested, plain and simple. Besides, he seemed to be well and truly occupied when I ran into him one night at The Bullet."

The moment the words were out of her mouth, Josie wished them back. What the hell did she care who Chase Barrington dallied with? It was none of her business. Just because he'd invited her for a drink and she stupidly thought it meant more... She made a noise of frustration deep in her throat, grateful when Kate misinterpreted her vexation.

"I'm sorry, Josie," she said hurriedly, her face flooding with remorse. "You're right. I shouldn't have assumed you were in the market. Please, I promise never to mention Chase or single men in general again. Forgive me?"

Josie managed a nod and even forced a smile. "Of course, Kate. Don't worry about it. It's natural to assume I might be looking to find a mate. I'm getting older and as my mother often tells me, my biological clock is ticking. You'd think between all of my brothers and their horde of children, she'd be satisfied—but apparently not."

"She just wants to see you happy and having a man around who loves you and wants to keep you safe means she doesn't have to worry about you—well, not as much. I'm sure moms never stop worrying, but knowing there's someone else looking out for you must help to ease some of their concern."

"I guess. One day, I hope I'll find out for myself. I'm not against love or marriage and I'd love to have kids, but I don't want to do it with just anyone. I'm prepared to wait for Mr Right, not Mr Right Now."

"I'm glad you feel that way. It's a long time when you're married to the wrong one."

"Yes, as I've often explained to Mom, I'd rather be married to no one than merely someone."

Kate came back around the end of the counter and gave Josie another quick hug. "You're absolutely right, Josie Munro and I'm proud of you for having the courage to take such a stand. Plenty don't, and they end up regretting it. There's a reason the divorce rate's so high."

"Does Chase have any kids?" The words left her mouth before she could stop them. She bit her lip and immediately wished she hadn't blurted out the question that had been on her mind for some time.

Kate frowned a little, as if trying to reconcile the question with Josie's adamant disinterest.

"No. At least, not that I know of. I've never heard Riley mention that Chase has children and I'm sure I would have heard about them by now. He's a regular visitor over here. He and Riley get on so well and Chase loves the twins— almost as much as they love him. I'm not sure why he hasn't settled down. He'd make a great father."

"Excuse me, ladies, are you both finished gossiping in there? The meat's done and I'm starving." Riley's gentle chiding drifted in from the back porch and Josie swallowed a sigh of relief that was quickly replaced by an upsurge in nerves that danced in her stomach. Now she'd be forced to be near Chase again. During the course of her life, she'd never had caused to wonder at her acting abilities, but she was grimly certain that circumstance was about to change.

"Let's eat," Kate said and collected the salad bowl and a range of condiments set out on a wooden tray.

Josie forced a strained smile. "After you."

Trevor Logan caressed the smooth wood that made up the stock of the double-barrel shotgun that was propped between his legs. It was as smooth and soft as the skin on his wife's cheek and had been handled just as lovingly. He'd spent the whole weekend thinking about it and now the time had come. The gun had been in his family for more than half a century. It had been his father's and had been given to Trevor on his twelfth birthday, a whisker younger than his oldest son was now.

Daniel. Pain sheared through Trevor and left him gasping. He thought of his wife, his beloved Kelly, now dead and buried in the ground. His life had come to a grinding halt from the moment Neil Whitcomb entered his house and touched her. Everything he'd worked so hard for and everything he believed in was gone—his whole world taken from him by a twist of fate and one senseless act of violence.

His life was over. He had nothing to live for; nothing but pain to offer his sons. It was time he brought it to an end.

That had been his intention, after all, when he'd unlocked the gun safe. He'd barely been able to recall the new combination, having used the old one for so long. After the incident with Daniel, the local area commander had pulled him to one side and suggested quietly that he change it.

Then he recalled he'd written it down. After looking through the array of tools and other things on his workbench, he finally found the scrap of paper. Punching in the combination, he'd taken down the gun and then retrieved the ammunition box. With shaking hands, he'd loaded it, putting a cartridge in both chambers. He wanted to be certain, after all.

The boys were at school. He'd put them on the bus. Nobody would be home for hours. Long enough for him to get the job done. Long enough for it to be over.

He ran his hand up and down the length of the stock once again and gazed down at the twin chambers that stared back at him. Their black emptiness promised oblivion, a chance to escape the pain.

His chest tightened with emotion and a sob rose up in his throat. He choked in an effort to hold it back, but it proved too much for him. With tears streaming down his face, he put the gun in his mouth. The acrid, metallic taste of the barrel bit into his tongue, but he paid it no heed. He needed to get this over with before he lost his nerve. It was for the best.

He was good for nothing anymore, least of all his boys. He'd failed them just as surely as he'd failed their mother. Most days, he could barely drag himself to work, even to keep food on the table. There wasn't a second that went by where he didn't wish he could run away from the nightmare his life had become and hide somewhere deep in a crevice of darkness. His wife had managed it, surely he could too. And then they'd be together again.

His finger hovered over the trigger. He pulled the barrel out of his mouth and drew in a deep, unsteady breath, casting around for the courage he required to face the final moment. His gaze snagged on photos of his sons where they stood on the mantelpiece. The pictures had been taken earlier in the year, at school. They both smiled at the camera.

Pain tore through him and he gasped from the impact of it. He hadn't seen his boys smile since the night of the attack; the night their lives had been destroyed forever. And then Kelly, his sweet, beautiful Kelly had abandoned them...

Why hadn't she told him how bad it was? Why hadn't she held on? They could have gotten through it. Surely, together they could have put it behind them?

But she hadn't given them a chance. She'd given up, given in...and now they were left alone, to battle on without her.

He choked on another sob and swiped at the tears on his face. The gun was heavy in his hand, as heavy as the grief in his gut. He bent forward and once again closed his lips over the barrel. Once again, his finger hovered over the trigger. The stares of his sons from the mantelpiece felt accusatory—which was just plain stupid. They were photos, for Christ's sake. His boys had no idea how he felt, how close he was to escaping the pain.

He wondered fleetingly how they would cope without him and where the two of them would live. Kelly had an older sister somewhere; she'd shown up for the funeral, but he hadn't seen or heard from her since. His folks had died long ago and with no brothers or sisters, his family stopped right here. He guessed the police would track his sister-in-law down when the time came.

The thought sent another shaft of pain surging through him, but he angrily pushed it aside. He bit down hard on the barrel until his teeth hurt. *God dammit, why couldn't he pull the trigger?* All he had to do was exert a little more pressure and it would be over. He could be with Kelly once again. They'd be happy, like they used to be, before the nightmare began, before his boys...

His boys. They'd have no one. Some aunt they didn't know who lived in some dumb-ass town he'd never heard of. That's what would happen to his boys. As if they hadn't already endured enough pain...

His chest tightened on a surge of emotion. He couldn't do it. He couldn't do it to his sons. He couldn't abandon them like their mother had abandoned them. He loved them way too much.

His jaw clenched, but a sob escaped, quickly followed by another. The gun slipped out of his hand and landed with a thud on the floor. Bent over, he held his head in his hands and cried like he didn't know how to stop.

"I'm sorry, Kelly. I'm so sorry," he gasped. "Forgive me, darling. I can't do it. I want to, but I can't. I can't do it. I can't do it."

He shook his head back and forth with increasing vehemence and began to claw at his hair. The sobs came harder and faster and tore him up inside. He needed help and he needed it now. For his boys' sake, he had to make the call.

Stumbling out of the chair, he made his way to the phone and fumbled for the receiver. With hands that trembled violently, he dialed the police.

Chapter 15

Josie pulled out the file for her next patient and glanced at her watch. It was a little after three. She bit down on a sigh. The child was late. The phone on her desk rang and she picked up the receiver.

"Josie, I'm sorry, it's Moira. I've just had a call from Sandra Duckworth. Her daughter's been sick in bed all day. She rang to cancel their appointment."

Josie bit her lip in annoyance, but kept her tone light. "That's fine, Moira. I wish she'd let me know a little earlier—like before her appointment started, but thank you anyway."

"No trouble, honey. Some people are so inconsiderate. Can I get you a— Hang on, the phone's ringing again. I'll be right back."

Josie hung up the phone and collected the file off her desk and returned it to her filing cabinet. One good thing about having her last appointment for the day cancel was that she could go home early for a change. She might even pour a glass of wine and enjoy the breathtaking view of the mountains from her back porch. It was one of the reasons she'd been drawn to the place. And then, she could run a bath...

With her mood picking up, she pulled on her jacket and smiled in anticipation.

The phone on her desk rang again and she shook her head slightly and gave a wry smile. It was probably Moira apologizing for cutting their conversation short. She picked up the phone.

"Coffee, cream and one sugar, thanks Moira," she chuckled.

"Oh, I'm sorry, Josie. I-I have Belinda Murphy from the Department of Family and Community Services on line three. She wants to speak to you about the Logan children."

Josie frowned. She'd only met Daniel. She wasn't sure what she could say to the woman about his younger brother. With a shrug, she answered. "Okay, thanks," and she switched lines. "Josie Munro, can I help you?"

"Doctor Munro, it's Belinda Murphy. Thank you for taking my call."

"No problem. I understand you're calling from Family Services about the Logan boys."

"Yes, I am. I hope you don't mind, but I was given your name by an officer at the police station. I believe he said he was your brother. Riley, isn't it?"

"Yes, Riley's one of my brothers. Is anything the matter?"

"Your brother received a call from Trevor Logan a short time ago. I understand he called the police in a distraught state of mind and told them he was thinking of committing suicide."

Josie gasped in shock. "Oh, my goodness."

"From what I understand, he's in pretty bad shape. He begged the police for help. They've contacted me because the children are due out from school shortly and no one's at home. The police and ambulance have attended the Logan farm and Trevor's been taken to the hospital. I believe he's undergoing psychiatric assessment as we speak."

Josie shook her head slowly, still struggling to take it all in. "I'm so sorry to hear that, Ms Murphy, but I'm not sure what you want me to do."

"Your brother told me you've been meeting with Daniel and he's comfortable with you. He knows you and he trusts you, or so I've been led to believe. Unfortunately, the Logans have no relatives living close by and our regular foster parents are already overloaded. I'd go down to the school and collect them myself, only right now, I'm in Grafton. It will be late when I return. My colleague has been off all week with the flu. There's no one else to call. I was hoping... That is, I was wondering if you'd be able to collect the boys from the school and perhaps keep them with you for a little while. Just a few hours, if you wouldn't mind? Or perhaps overnight? I'm not sure what time I'll be back..."

Josie's head spun with the sudden deluge of information. Realizing the woman was waiting for a response, she shuffled through the flood of thoughts surging through her head and stammered out a reply.

"Um...I...I...um..."

"It will only be for tonight, I promise and maybe tomorrow morning. If you could just get them to school... Please, I wouldn't be asking unless I was desperate. They're only children. They can't stay out on the farm on their own."

"No, of course not," Josie hurried to agree. "It's okay, I'll work something out. Daniel has his competency hearing tomorrow. Don't worry, leave it with me."

Belinda let out a sigh of relief. "Oh, thank goodness! You're a lifesaver. I'll call you again tomorrow."

"Sure. Um... Which schools do they attend?"

"Oh, I'm sorry, I didn't even give you that information. "Daniel's at Watervale High on Oxley Road and Jason's at Watervale East Primary School on Stubbins Avenue. I'm sure you'll find them."

"Do they know about their dad?"

"I've called both schools. The principals were going to speak to the boys in the company of the school counselor. I assume they will have been told what's going on by the time you get there."

Josie closed her eyes briefly, glad that at least that much had been dealt with. "Okay, I guess I'll head over there now. They'll probably be getting out soon."

"Yes. Daniel gets out at three-fifteen. Jason at three-thirty." After promising once again to call her the next day and offering another round of sincere thanks, Belinda ended the call.

Josie replaced the receiver. Another glance at her watch told she didn't have a lot of time if she was to get to the high school before the bell. Collecting her handbag from where she'd put it and inwardly giving up on her plan to spend the afternoon relaxing in solitude, she opened the door to her office, filled in the receptionist and left.

From his position at his desk, Chase watched his boss pick up his coffee mug and head out of his office toward the tea room. His face looked drained, his mouth tight. After the past few hours spent at the Logan farm, Chase understood why.

"How did it go with Trevor?" he asked quietly.

Riley's shoulders slumped on a heavy sigh. "You were there. It was bloody tough." He ran a frustrated hand through his hair. "For Christ's sake, how much of this shit is one family supposed to take? Right now, I could do with a stiff drink, but I guess I'll have to settle for a hit of caffeine."

"Let's hope Trevor gets the help that he needs."

"Yeah, he's been voluntarily admitted to the psych ward for assessment and observation." Riley bit his lip and shook his head, as if chasing away the memories of the way they'd found Daniel's father after his desperate call.

"He's a broken man, Chase. He's endured more than any man should have to bear. I don't know if anyone will be able to fix him."

Chase nodded grimly. "His family's been torn apart through the worst circumstances imaginable. I can understand why he might be feeling a little less enamored with his life."

"Yeah, there but for the grace of God... I honestly don't know what I'd do if something like that happened to me. Just the thought of someone assaulting Kate... Christ, I don't even want to think about it."

"I can't help thinking about Daniel. He's not even thirteen! How the hell is he going to deal with something like this? Grown men would struggle with it. And now, he knows his father considered blowing his brains out. Please tell me it wasn't with the same gun?"

"No, we still have that one in the evidence room."

Chase breathed out on a sigh of relief. "Perhaps we should confiscate whatever other firearms he still has? If I remember right, he had at least three or four rifles in that safe. No sense in tempting him unnecessarily."

"Yeah, that's a good idea. I'll speak to him about it straight away."

"What's going to happen to the kids while he's in there? The other boy is even younger than Daniel."

"Jason. Yeah, he's eight. I called Family and Community Services. Unfortunately, they're out of options at the moment. Their foster families are at capacity and the two women who man the Watervale office are unavailable. I gave them Josie's number."

Chase sat up in surprise and straightened in his chair. "You mean, they're going to see if she can take the boys in?"

"Yes, at least for tonight. They can't stay at home alone and she's had a fair bit to do with Daniel, at least. Given the circumstances, she seemed like the best person to call."

"Yeah, I guess and of course, they can't return home without a parent in tow." He paused and did his best to slow his pulse rate that had taken off at the mention of Josie's name. "Is-is Josie agreeable?"

"Yes. She called me a short time ago. She's on her way now to collect them."

A pang of emotion tightened Chase's chest. Josie would get her chance to be a mother, if only for a little while. He wished the thought didn't hurt so much and then immediately felt guilty. She was doing what any good, decent person would do. She was offering help to two young boys who were greatly in need of it. He couldn't help but admire her for her courage. There would be plenty who'd turn away, unwilling to get involved.

"She always wanted kids." Chase didn't realize he'd said the words aloud until he noticed Riley's sharp look.

"I thought you only took her to her graduation? I didn't realize you knew her that well."

Chase blinked and quickly hunted around for a reasonable explanation. "Yes, um…that's right. We did a lot of…talking…between dances." Heat stole up his neck and he kept his gaze fixed firmly on the floor.

When his boss didn't respond, he risked a glance upwards and then wished he hadn't. Riley's eyes were narrowed in suspicion.

"Are you sure you didn't know her before that? I noticed the two of you seemed quite familiar with each other at the barbeque. More than what I'd expect from people who'd spent only a matter of hours together a decade ago."

"Well, we'd been liaising over the Daniel Logan matter. It wasn't like I hadn't spoken to her since she arrived in town."

The suspicion in Riley's eyes barely lessened. His lips pursed. "It's funny, you know. Kate told me last night that Josie asked about you. She wanted to know if you had any kids."

Chase's heart stuttered in surprise and he felt a momentary sense of elation. *She had asked about him.* Just as quickly, his heart plummeted, quieted and almost stopped. The fact that she still cared was exactly the reason he'd stuck his tongue down Lucy's throat at The Bullet. He wasn't what Josie needed. He had to accept it and move on. Riley's voice intruded on his dark thoughts.

"Do you know why I think it's funny? *You* asked me much the same thing a couple of months ago." Riley closed the distance between them until he was mere feet away. "What's going on with you two?"

Chase yearned to tell Riley the truth, but ten years ago, he'd made Josie a promise and even though he'd broken it when he'd told his mom, this was different. There was no longer any expectation of a happily ever after. It wasn't his place to breach Josie's trust with her brother. Besides, hadn't he already convinced himself to let her go?

"Of course not. Like I said, we're just friends, that's all. Until that night at the station, we hadn't seen each other since her high school graduation. We've spent a little time catching up, reminiscing—you know how it is—and of course, we've been communicating over the Logan case. The competency hearing's on tomorrow."

Riley's stern expression relaxed marginally. "Just so you know, if you break her heart, you'll have me and four other brothers to answer to, you got it? She doesn't need to get caught up with a bloke like you. We both know you're not into commitment. Josie deserves more than that and I'm going to make darn sure she gets it. Are we clear?"

Chase held Riley's gaze and did his best to swallow his anger. There was no point antagonizing his boss over it. He and Josie were never going to work, no matter how much he wished things were different.

"Yes, sir. We're clear," he said, his voice steady and strong.

"Good," Riley replied dismissively. "Now, I need coffee."

Josie walked into the Watervale High School office and tried to quell the bundle of nerves that somersaulted inside her. Having completed her senior schooling in Grafton, she'd never stepped foot inside the grounds of Watervale High and although she'd been an exemplary student, being summoned to the principal's office was always cause for disquiet, even a decade after she'd finished high school. Coupled with the reason for her visit, it was no wonder she was on edge.

She'd missed the bell by five minutes and most of the students had vanished. The school looked deserted. She approached a woman who appeared to be in her late fifties, sitting behind a desk in the reception area. The woman looked at Josie curiously, but didn't seem surprised by her arrival.

"Hi, I'm Doctor Josie Munro. I believe your principal has spoken to Belinda Murphy?"

The woman stood and moved closer. "You're here about Daniel Logan, is that right?"

"Yes."

The woman smiled kindly. "I'll let Mr Ledingham know you're here. Daniel's in with him."

Josie nodded her thanks and turned away, folding her arms across her chest. She heard the receptionist murmur into the phone and a few moments later, a door at the end of the corridor swung open and a tall man with an enormous belly strode toward her, his expression grave.

"Doctor Munro, I'm Stewart Ledingham, the principal of Watervale High. Thank you for coming."

Despite his awkward appearance, his tone was respectful. Some of Josie's nerves receded and she acknowledged his greeting with another nod.

"Daniel's in my office. Come on through."

Josie hesitated. "Does he know about...? What... What have you told him?"

"On the advice of our school counselor, I've kept it as vague as possible. He doesn't know about the attempted suicide, if that's what we're calling it, but he knows his father's been hospitalized and is receiving treatment for depression."

"Is he aware I'm here to collect him?"

"Yes, I told him you were going to take him and his brother to your place for the night. He seems okay about it."

A little more of the tension that gripped Josie's stomach since her arrival at the school dissipated. She breathed out slowly and sent a silent prayer heavenwards that things would work out.

"I'd like to see him now, if you don't mind. I have to be at the primary school shortly."

"Yes, of course. And, look, if you don't think he's up to school tomorrow, please feel free to keep him home." He shrugged and looked away. "We do our best, but we can't shield him from everything. I'm sure there are students who have approached him about what happened. After all he's been through, I'm not sure he's able to focus on anything school related and to tell you the truth, that's the least of the boy's worries at the moment."

"His hearing starts tomorrow. Don't worry, he won't be at school."

The man in front of her blushed profusely and Josie just shook her head. He should have made it his business to know when Daniel would next go before the court. It was as simple as that.

With a blustering attempt to cover his tracks, the principal turned away and headed back the way he'd come. She drew in a deep breath, squared her shoulders and followed him.

Josie glanced over at Daniel who sat in the front seat of her car. He held himself stiffly and his head was turned away from her. Apart from a murmured hello when she'd greeted him in the principal's office, he hadn't spoken a word.

She was a little taken aback when she saw him. He seemed to have lost weight—pounds he couldn't afford to lose—and his eyes were ringed with dark circles. His expression was hallow, haunted, void of any emotion. A pang of sympathy went through her and she wished she could take away his pain. His mother was dead; he'd been charged with murder and now, his father was in hospital suffering from demons of his own. No wonder the boy was upset.

"Do you live in town?"

The quiet question came from the child in the back seat and Josie eased her breath out on a surreptitious sigh, thankful that the silence in the car had been broken. At least Jason was talking to her. In fact, although he looked drawn and pale, he appeared to be holding up better than his brother. That was understandable. Jason wasn't the one who'd witnessed his mother's rape or was looking at being put on trial for murder.

Knowing the boy waited for her answer, she cleared her throat and replied, "No, I don't live in town, but I'm not too far out."

"So, you live on a farm then," Jason said.

"Yes, kind of, but not a farm like yours. I only live on a few acres. I'm renting a cottage from the Holloways, out on Whiskey Creek Road. Do you know where that is?"

Jason shook his head. "Nope. We haven't been here long. We're only renting, too."

"Where did you come from?" Josie asked, wanting to keep the conversation going.

"Melbourne. It was closer to Dad's work there. We moved here because Mom wanted to get out into the country. She hated living in the city."

"I know what you mean," Josie replied. "I used to live in Brisbane and while it's nowhere near as big or busy as Melbourne, it has its fair share of drawbacks. I'm more than happy I made the move back to the bush."

Jason sat forward a little in his seat. "So, are you from Watervale?"

"No, I was born in Grafton and my parents still live there. It's nice to be close to home again."

"Yeah, as much as Mom hated Melbourne, I miss being near my friends. At least there were people who we knew down there."

"What about other family members? Do you have any aunts or uncles? You won't have to stay with me forever. In fact, I'm not sure if your principal told you, but it's probably only for the night. Mrs Murphy who works with the Department of Family and Community Services will speak to your dad tomorrow. If he's not well enough to come home, I'm sure she'll call one of your relatives."

"We don't have any relatives," Daniel stated bluntly. "None that we're close to, anyway. Mom has a sister way out west, but the first time we met her was at Mom's funeral."

Josie was glad Daniel had entered into the conversation, but his stark words sent quiet slivers of pain through her heart.

"What's wrong with Dad, anyway? No one will tell me," Jason said softly.

Daniel tensed beside her. Josie wondered what to say. She wanted to be honest with them, but she also didn't want to cause them any more pain. Besides, once their father had received some proper counseling and perhaps some medication, there was no reason why he couldn't return home and be there for his sons.

"Your dad's still struggling a little with the things that happened to your family a couple of months ago," she said gently. "It's perfectly natural and perfectly understandable. Losing a family member can make you sad for a long, long time."

"Yeah, I'm still sad about losing Mom," Jason replied, his voice little more than a whisper. "I wish she was still here."

"Dad wishes he was dead. Just like I do." Anger laced every one of Daniel's harsh words. Utter devastation ravaged his face. Josie tried hard to contain her shock and sadness and to keep her attention on the road.

Easing off the accelerator pedal, she took the turn into her driveway, grateful that they were nearly home. She couldn't properly deal with this situation while behind the wheel. She brought the car to a halt outside the fenced yard that surrounded the cottage and then turned to Daniel.

"Would you like to come inside?"

He turned to look at her with a tortured gaze and vehemently shook his head. Her heart sank, but she knew better than to push him. He'd come in when he was ready. Instead, she turned to Jason and asked, "Could you help me bring the things in from the car?"

They'd stopped at a local department store and had purchased a few necessary items: pajamas, toothbrushes and a change of clothes. Josie had chosen not to return to their farmhouse and hoped what she'd purchased would be enough to see them through until Belinda could make alternative arrangements.

To her relief, Jason nodded and climbed out of the car.

Josie followed suit. Together, they carried the sacks of clothes and other items into the cottage. Daniel ignored them, steadfastly staring out the window. Josie's heart broke anew at the anguish on his face, but knew the best thing to do was to leave him alone.

He'd been through so many traumatic experiences in such a short time and hadn't received near enough professional help to deal with all of it. She'd done her best from the beginning, but she'd been brought in not as a counselor, but as a servant of the court. Her role in his life had not been to offer him help, but to decide whether he was capable of answering for his actions. As far as she knew, he hadn't seen anyone for *him*; he hadn't been given any strategies to help him heal.

Well, for now the legal system could be damned. She'd done what was asked of her and submitted her report. No one could accuse her of bias if she offered him her support now. There was no way she could stand by and watch his pain and desolation ravage him like a disease and simply ignore it.

All her life, she'd wanted to help children. She'd studied child psychology with that single goal in mind. She'd grown up in a safe and secure, happy household, but wasn't immune to the fact that plenty of children didn't. One of her best friends in the fourth grade went through a terrible time when her parents divorced. Josie could still remember how Annie Faraday would cry herself sick in the bathroom each lunch time, recalling events that had happened at home. Josie's heart would break, right alongside her friend's. She'd done all she could to make Annie feel better.

It had given birth to a fierce determination to learn how to offer help; to somehow, in some small way, develop skills to help other children get through painful situations such as these. And she'd done it. She'd graduated with a PhD in child psychology.

Doctor Josie Munro, Child Psychologist. Her parents had been so proud. Josie had been eager to get out into the real world and make a difference.

And then she'd taken the job in private practice and had begun to lose her way. In a way, she was grateful for the ruptured brain aneurysm her father suffered last Christmas. The shocking reminder of the fragility of life had woken her up with a jolt. She'd returned to Brisbane immediately after the festive season and had handed in her resignation. It had been fate and a whole lot of luck that a private health service in Watervale was looking for a child psychologist to open up a practice.

And here she was, with a boy so damaged, she didn't know if she could help him and another boy who needed her almost as much. Jason might not have suffered through the same trauma Daniel had, but he'd suffered just the same. No one could experience the death of their mother, let alone by suicide and not bear some deep and penetrating scars. Josie was just glad he was still able to talk about it, even a little. It wasn't a lot, but it was something. She could tell Daniel hadn't come that far.

Swallowing a sigh, Josie pulled the last of the sacks from the trunk, these ones containing the makings of dinner, and halted alongside Daniel's window. Setting the grocery sacks on the ground beside the car, she squatted down until they were at eye level. He immediately averted his gaze.

"Hey, Daniel. It's okay. I'm not going to pressure you to come inside. You stay out here for as long as you need to, all right? I'm going inside to make up a bed. There's one for you and your brother. Then, I'm going to prepare dinner. I have cookies and milk in the kitchen if you'd like an afternoon snack. You just come in when you feel up to it, okay?"

He gave her a jerky nod, but remained silent. Even so, Josie was relieved. Any communication was better than none. She stood and collected the sacks at her feet and began to walk away.

"Josie?"

The quiet cry brought her to a halt. Slowly, she turned around to face him. "Yes?"

"Thanks."

Tears burned her eyes and she hurriedly blinked them away. He needed her strong, secure, impenetrable. She drew in a shaky breath and answered him. "That's okay. Like I said, you come in when you're ready."

———————

Chase turned into the driveway that led to the old Holloway place and was relieved when he saw the lights on in the cottage. After Riley revealed Josie had asked about him, he couldn't get the idea out of his mind that he'd screwed up good and proper.

Could he have been wrong to hide the truth from her, to not give her the opportunity to make up her own mind? At the time, he'd kept it a secret so that she didn't feel obligated to stay. It felt like the right thing to do, even though it tore him apart.

But he was desperately unhappy and she was still on her own. *She'd asked about him.* He was sure she still cared. Had his actions to push her away done nothing more than cause even more heartache for both of them? The thought saddened him.

All afternoon, he'd wrestled with the idea of going out to visit her and had eventually given in. Whether it was a good idea or not, he no longer cared. He wanted to see her. He *needed* to see her. It was as simple and complex as that.

She probably wouldn't be happy to have him arrive on her doorstep. They'd mostly avoided one another at the barbeque, but he had a ready excuse if she wondered why he was showing up at her home. He only hoped she'd buy it.

He pulled up in his unmarked police car next to her fully restored forest green Boss 351 Mustang. The car was unoccupied. A garage stood a little distance from the house, its door open. Curious as to why she hadn't parked such a classic car under cover, he strode across the dirt track to the garage and stopped just inside the doorway.

Inside the garage was dimly lit, but he could make out

the silhouette of a TT600 Triumph Motorcycle with enough horsepower to make him catch his breath. He shook his head and whistled, impressed. *Was it hers?*

The knowledge that he didn't know for sure saddened him. They'd missed so much of each other's lives over the years since they'd parted—years they could never get back.

"What the hell are you doing? Why are you here?"

Chase spun on his heel and faced Josie. He'd been so caught up in his thoughts, he hadn't even heard her approach.

"H-hi. Riley told me about the Logan boys. That...that you've taken them in for the night. I just came by to see if you needed anything. I can't imagine you're set up for a couple of kids."

Her gaze narrowed dangerously and he cursed under his breath. *Why did he always say the stupidest things when he was around her?* It was like he couldn't help himself.

"Why do you always say such stupid things?" she demanded, her eyes spitting fire in the dimness.

So, they were still in sync in one way. He wanted to smile, but forced his lips still. Aggravating her further would be far from wise. Instead, he went for conciliatory.

"I'm sorry, Josie. That came out wrong. What I meant was that, seeing as you don't have any kids, I figured there might be something you needed. I came out to offer my help."

"How do you know I don't have any kids?" Her tone was far from friendly.

"*Do you?*"

She folded her arms defensively across her chest. Chase tried not to notice how the action pressed her breasts upward into the open V of her blouse.

"As a matter of fact, I don't," she answered. "Not that it's any business of yours."

"You're right, except that I happen to know you were asking about *my* status as a parent, so I guess that makes us even, right?"

Even in the twilight, Chase could make out the dark blush

that stained her cheeks. He'd bet a month's pay on the fact that she'd like to be cursing her brother out something fierce right about now. He struggled to keep the grin off his face.

"What do you want, Chase?" Her tone was slightly less aggressive.

"Like I said, I just wanted to check that you were okay and that you didn't need help with anything. It's Daniel's hearing tomorrow. That's got to be rough on you all."

She stared at him a little longer, suspicion still lurking in her eyes. A long moment later, her shoulders slumped on a sigh. She threw her head back, her expression one of challenge.

"Okay, Mr Good-doer, if you want to help, then help." With that, she headed back to the house.

CHAPTER 16

Josie left Chase standing in the dark and did her best to get her heart rate back under control. As if she didn't have enough to deal with tonight without him showing up. They'd barely exchanged a handful of words at Riley's barbeque and she hadn't seen him since. While she wasn't surprised he knew she was looking after the Logan boys, she never imagined he'd turn up on her doorstep, offering to help.

From the look of his rumpled shirt and disheveled hair, he'd had a hard day at the office. The last thing he probably felt like was offering her his assistance, and yet he'd come. As much as she wanted to prevent it, she couldn't help the warm spurt of pleasure and gratitude that had filled her when she realized why he had come.

When she'd found him poking his head into her garage, she'd been mad. He had no right to know anything about her or the woman she'd become. He'd dumped her right after graduation. The fact that she'd discovered the thrill of riding fast motorcycles was of no concern to him and was absolutely none of his business. Just like she'd told him when he'd offered his quip about her kids—or lack of them.

She had to concede he'd scored a point when he told her he knew about her conversation with Kate and she gritted her teeth and cursed Riley to hell. She was certain her brother had been Chase's source of information. She should have just kept her mouth shut, pretended a total lack of interest in Kate's obvious attempts at matchmaking and *darn*—she'd nearly managed it. If only she hadn't asked about whether or not he had kids.

Swallowing a sigh, she opened the door that led onto the front porch. It was too late, now. What was done was done. She had two real kids to deal with and if she were honest, she was grateful for Chase's help. She may have been trained in child psychology, but the reality of seeing to the needs of the boys was a little overwhelming, even if it was just for the night.

"Watch the step," she muttered, knowing he probably wouldn't see the loose floorboard in the dark. He murmured his thanks and she held the screen door open for him.

"If you could help set up the beds, I'd really appreciate it," she said and then walked into the house. Chase followed behind her.

"Sure. Where are they?"

"Down the hall, second room on the left. The owner left a little furniture in the place. Unfortunately, the spare beds need to be assembled. Riley helped put mine together when I first arrived, but I wasn't expecting visitors quite so soon."

"It'll be quicker if we do it together. You can hold onto one end and I'll hold the other."

Josie inclined her head and nodded. "All right. Just let me see to the boys and check on dinner. I'll be with you in a minute."

She found both boys seated on the couch in the living room, watching something on the television. Daniel's expression was sad but stoic. At least he appeared more in the present than he had in the car. Jason gave a slight chuckle at something on the TV and Josie's heart tightened. At least one of them had the ability to laugh, to be a little carefree. She only hoped that Daniel would make it back to that state of mind again and that his spirit hadn't been damaged forever.

After letting the boys know about Chase's arrival, she checked the contents of the oven and then returned to the spare room where Chase was assembling the spare beds. She stole a few moments watching him from the doorway.

He worked with focused determination, his hands as confident with tools as they'd been when he'd touched her body. She chastised herself for letting her thoughts wander to places they shouldn't go. Straightening her shoulders, she entered the room.

"Something smells good," he said with a smile.

She shrugged, a little embarrassed. "It's just fish and chips and I've thrown together a salad. I wasn't sure what the boys liked and I wanted to keep it simple."

"Fish and chips sounds good to me." As if only just realizing what he'd said, Chase blushed profusely.

"Um...I'm sorry, Josie. I didn't mean to invite myself to dinner. I just meant... Most kids like fish and chips."

Memories of the two of them lying on the beach during that last summer, with a box of fish and chips between them, flooded through her. It had been one of their favorite things to do. Chase would drive over to Grafton from Watervale early on a Saturday morning. She'd tell her parents she was going to the mall with her friends and would then meet him at the bus stop. They'd spend the day together, swimming, surfing and sharing their dreams and eating fish and chips.

She looked at him and could tell he was remembering that time as well. An awkward silence fell between them before Chase eventually broke it.

"If you give me a hand, I'll have these beds put together in no time and I can get out of your hair. I'll leave you to your dinner."

Knowing she was probably going to regret it, but wanting him to stay, Josie blurted, "No, don't rush off. Stay for dinner." She indicated the half-assembled bed in his hands. "It's the least I can do."

Chase stared at her, his expression way too solemn. "Are you sure?"

"Of course. There's plenty to go around. I'll set an extra place at the table."

Josie noticed her voice had risen, but there was nothing

she could do about it. Without another word, she turned and left the room and took refuge in the kitchen. Forcing a few deep breaths into her lungs, she opened a drawer and pulled out another setting for the table.

Chase tightened the last bolt on the second single bed and stood, stretching out the muscles that had cramped while he'd been assembling the furniture. Josie hadn't made another appearance and he'd finished the job to the sound of her banging around in the kitchen. It was such an everyday, mundane sound, it shouldn't have affected him like it did, but he couldn't help it. Knowing she was just down the hall making dinner warmed him all the way through.

It should have been *their* home, *their* kids, *their* bed he'd been assembling. She should have been his wife. That's the way they'd planned it, before life intervened; before cancer raised its ugly head and everything went to shit.

Years later, the injustice of it still angered him, even when he'd learned to let it go. He was alive and back in good health. It was more than some people were granted. A lot more.

Shaking off his ingratitude, he picked up the mattresses where they were stacked against the wall and put one on each bed. At least the Logan boys would be comfortable tonight. He assumed Josie had enough bed linen.

Collecting the Allen key he'd used to assemble the beds, he left the room and made his way into the kitchen. The smell wafting from the oven made his stomach grumble and he was reminded how long it had been since he'd eaten his store-bought chicken salad sandwich at lunch time.

Josie caught sight of him standing in the doorway and smiled. His heart somersaulted. He glanced behind him in an effort to distract himself and noticed Daniel and Jason on the couch in the living room.

"Um, I was wondering if you have any bed linen? Sheets

and that kind of thing? I'll make up the beds, if you like."

"Oh, you're finished. I'm sorry, I meant to come back and help."

Chase brushed away her apology. "It's fine. All done now. All except the sheets."

"Yes, the sheets. Right. I have some in the linen closet, left over from when I was at college. The closet's in the hall, just before you get to the spare bedroom. I'm just about to serve up dinner. I'll get the boys to help you."

She wiped her hands on a cloth and Chase stepped aside to let her pass. Her perfume drifted toward him and he did his best not to think about how sweet and familiar it smelled, even after all the years. He heard her speaking to the children in the next room and a moment later they appeared.

"Daniel, do you remember Detective Barrington?" The boy glanced at him and then quickly looked away.

"Yes," he murmured. "You're the one who charged me."

Josie tactfully ignored Daniel's comment and turned to his brother. "Jason, this is Detective Barrington. I'm not sure if the two of you have met."

Jason stuck out his hand and Chase shook it.

"Were you at the house with my mom, Detective Barrington?" the younger boy asked.

Chase nodded, his expression somber. "Yes, mate. I was. You probably saw me there. And please, call me Chase. I'm here as a friend."

Josie flashed him a grateful smile. "Chase came out to see if we needed any help. He's put your beds together in the spare room. If you'd like to help him make them up, I'll serve dinner."

She turned and went back into the kitchen and Chase walked down the hall. He found the linen closet and pulled out two sets of single bed sheets and a couple of pillow cases and handed them to the boys. Spare pillows were stacked high on a shelf, along with extra blankets and he reached up above his head and snagged two of each.

A small calico cushion bounced out and hit him on the

head. He leaned down and picked it up and realized what it was. His heart pounded. It was the cushion Josie used to bring with her to the beach. They'd lain together, side by side, with their heads sharing the small, soft mound. One day, she'd produced a permanent marker and had drawn two love hearts intertwined. She'd added their names and more love hearts around the side.

Chase turned the cushion over and found what he was looking for. The words *Chase loves Josie* were exactly where he'd written them. The moment in time when he'd put them there was forever emblazoned on his mind. She'd turned to him and kissed him softly on the mouth. "I love you too," she'd whispered.

His heart had swelled with so much happiness, he thought it would explode right out of his chest. He couldn't wait for the day when she'd finished high school and he could tell the world that she was his.

And she'd kept it. After all these years and countless moves, she'd kept the cushion close at hand. God, what he wouldn't give to ask her why.

"I don't think we need that one," Jason said, pointing to the cushion in Chase's hand.

Chase stared at the boy for a moment and then blinked. "You're right," he said and returned the cushion to where he'd found it. Forcing a smile, he turned back to the boys and gave both of them a wink.

"Okay, I can't say I'm the best bed maker in the world, but let's see if we can pull this off."

Chase stared at Josie from where he sat opposite her at the kitchen table and tried not to think about how beautiful she looked with the soft glow of the lamplight behind her turning her hair to spun gold. Dinner was over and the dishes were done. The boys had been tucked into bed. He could tell she'd wanted to say something more to Daniel, but the boy had muttered a soft goodnight and had turned to face the wall, probably worried about the hearing the next day. Chase had felt her sadness at the boy's withdrawal, but was sure she understood it.

Even now, more than an hour later, the sadness lingered in her eyes. He knew how she felt. The boy had suffered unimaginable horror and it wasn't over yet. Wanting to help him but not knowing how was beyond frustrating for Chase. He couldn't imagine how much more difficult it was for Josie. She'd been trained to help and yet it was clear to him that the boy kept pushing her away.

"Don't keep beating yourself up, Josie," he said quietly. "You're doing the best that you can. He's very lucky to have you on his side."

He could tell from the tightening of her jaw and the flash of denial in her eyes that she disagreed.

"How can you say that?" she demanded, pitching her voice low in deference to the sleeping children. *"I'm* the one who has recommended to the prosecutor that the court proceed with the matter."

"It isn't just you, Josie. Okay, you've provided the Crown with your opinion and I assume you still stand by it, but it's the judge who will make the decision. He'll read both reports—don't forget, the defense will tender one too—and both sides will get to argue. Don't think for a moment that it all comes down to you. Not wanting to belabor the point, but your report's only a small part of the whole."

She made a sound of frustration. "I can't help but think Daniel won't see it that way."

Chase stared at her, but there was nothing he could say. What she said was true and he could only hope the boy was mature enough to understand Josie's role in the proceedings. He made a mental note to have a talk to him.

Josie sighed. She picked up her glass of red wine and drank from it. She'd brought out the bottle not long after the boys had gone to bed and wanting to prolong their time together, Chase had been only too happy to share it. A sense of comfortable intimacy had fallen between them and a little while later he found the courage to mention the motorcycle.

"I saw the Triumph in your garage. Is it yours?"

"Yes. I've had it for quite awhile."

"I'd have never guessed you were into motorbikes."

She contemplated him over the rim of her wine glass, her expression tinged with sadness.

"It's been a long time since you knew me. I was a kid in most respects back then. I guess over the years, I grew up." A tiny smile tugged at the corner of her lips. "That, and my brother Declan bought a 1199 Panigale Ducati. Boy, has that thing got some legs."

Chase smiled back at her. "I take it you have firsthand experience?"

"Of course. Declan bought it while I was still in college. On my summer breaks, I'd go down and visit him. He lives in Canberra where the summer temperatures are sublime compared to the heat and humidity of Brisbane. Declan would escape the pressures of his job by climbing on board his motorbike and tearing up the freeway. He bought me a helmet and let me ride pillion."

"So this fascination with speed and fast bikes is your brother's fault?" Chase teased, enjoying the way she'd opened up to him.

"I'm not sure one could say it was his fault, but I'd never been on a motorbike before he let me on his." She grinned. "I'm pretty certain he's regretted it ever since. He's the first one to lecture me about getting overconfident and how powerful bikes can bring you unstuck. I've been lucky. So far, I've only had a few minor busters."

Chase suppressed a shudder at the image of Josie lying in pieces on the road, yet he tried to make light of the danger. He wasn't her husband or even her brother. It wasn't his place to express concern.

"One way to go out with a bang, I guess."

She took another drink from her glass and looked at him curiously over the rim, a single eyebrow quirked upward.

"I never picked you for a man who took life so lightly. I

was sure you'd remonstrate with me about the dangers of being a speed fiend, like the hectoring I get from my brothers. You've surprised me."

He waved her words away and picked up his glass. "I didn't say your hobby doesn't fill me with dread, but I'd be one helluva hypocrite lecturing you on the perils of riding fast motorcycles when I have one of my own."

Her eyes widened in surprise and pleasure. *"Really?"*

He grinned. "Yes, really."

"What kind of bike do you have?"

"What kind of bike do you *think* I have?"

She rolled her eyes at him, but her grin was captivating.

"Now, this is fraught with danger," she smiled. "If I say something like a Yamaha Virago 250 which everyone knows is a proper idiot's bike and you have one, you'll be wounded for life. If I guess an imported, custom built Harley-Davidson V-Rod and you're forced to confess it's way out of your price bracket, you'll be even more embarrassed. See? It's a lose-lose situation. Why don't you just tell me?"

"I'm appalled that you think my ego so fragile that it couldn't cope with your brutal honesty," he said with mock outrage and then narrowed his eyes. "That's if it is honesty you're purporting to employ. Let me tell you, I have my suspicions in that regard."

Her giggle spilled over and poured into his heart, warming it all the way through, like it used to. It was the first time in more than a decade that he'd heard her laugh. Even at the barbeque, she'd remained quiet and aloof. He didn't realize how much he'd missed hearing it until that moment.

They used to laugh together all the time. Her sense of humor and her ability not to take herself seriously were two of the things he'd loved most about her.

Loved? As in the past tense? Who was he kidding? He was still in love with her. Not his cancer or the decade that stood between them could change that fact.

When he didn't respond, the humor in her eyes slowly dimmed. "What's the matter, Chase? What did I say?"

The uncertainty on her face pierced his heart. The urge to

tell her everything, to tell her the truth of what happened all those years ago, burned through him. His heart pounded. He opened his mouth and then closed it, his indecisiveness getting the best of him.

What good would it do to tell her now? Nothing had changed. He still couldn't give her the thing she wanted most. He still couldn't guarantee her a baby.

"Why aren't you married, Chase? Why don't you have a family? I thought you wanted kids as much as I did."

The softly voiced question came from nowhere and hit him hard in the chest. He sucked in a breath and stared at her, wanting so much to tell her. Instead he said, "We don't always get what we wish for."

She stared back at him and he could almost see the barrage of questions on her lips. In an effort to distract her, he asked, "What about you, Josie? Why don't you have kids?"

She held his gaze a moment longer and then lowered it. "I guess I haven't found anyone I want to have kids with," she mumbled and then filled her mouth with more wine.

He mulled over her explanation and tried to ignore the hope that leaped in his chest. At the same time, his shoulders slumped. *She still wanted kids.* It was just that she hadn't found the right man to father them.

"What happened to us, Chase?"

The whispered words tortured him, along with the tormented expression on her face. Once again, he wanted to tell her and once again he backed away. He'd made the decision years ago to never tell her the truth.

Despite his earlier hope, when he thought they might have a chance, he realized that all the reasons he'd kept it from her in the first place hadn't changed. He still couldn't bear the thought of her pity, or worse, that she might stay with him out of obligation. Eventually, she'd come to resent him and any love she had for him would die.

Was he too proud to tell her? Was that what this was really about? The thought sent a surge of anger rushing through him and he forcefully pushed it away. No, this had nothing to do with pride. Would he be stupid enough to let pride get in the way of being with the woman he loved? All of a sudden, he didn't want to think about the answer.

"Someone did a good job of restoring the little Mustang," he said instead and watched her earnest expression slowly fade away, replaced by disappointment. His gut felt hollow with cowardice.

She went to take a sip from her wine glass and then realized it was empty. He watched while she set the glass back down, picked up the bottle and refilled it, then in silence, she drank once again. One swallow, two. She'd have the whole bottle drunk soon. He couldn't help the surge of guilt that rushed through him. It was his fault she felt the need to overindulge.

Another mouthful later and she finally cleared her throat. He braced himself against what was to come, but she only looked at him with sad resignation and said, "The car belongs to my dad. He's been restoring it for years. He finished it just before he suffered a ruptured brain aneurysm last Christmas."

Chase nodded, remembering. Riley had been a mess. He'd called Chase in a panic and had asked him to look after the command. Chase had been happy to help and had urged Riley to be with his family. For a little while, nobody knew if the former District Court judge would pull through. Fortunately, he had.

"He's a lucky man," Chase murmured.

"Yes. We're lucky too, for having him in our lives. He's done a lot of great things in his time. I hope I can look back some day and be as proud of the things I achieve."

She said it so wistfully, emotion burned at the back of Chase's eyes. *Were there things she wanted to achieve and yet hadn't? Could marriage and motherhood be among them?*

"I borrowed the Mustang off him not long after I arrived in Watervale. I never needed a car in Brisbane. I lived a few minutes' walk from the bus station. The times when I had to go further afield, I took the Triumph. That reminds me..." she said with a slight smile, as if recalling their earlier discussion. "You still haven't told me what kind of bike you have."

Relieved to have the conversation moved in another direction, Chase replied with a grin. "I have a Honda Fireblade, if you must know and it goes like the clappers."

An answering smile played around her lips and she nodded in approval. "A Fireblade? Nice. Yes, I can see you on one of those." She held his gaze and for the life of him, he couldn't look away.

Her praise warmed him much more than it had a right to and he tamped down on the feelings that surged deep inside him. Until he found the courage to tell her the truth, he had no right feeling anything at all for the beautiful, warm, gentle, gorgeous woman that was Josie Munro. All he had to do was get that message through to his brain...and to other parts of his anatomy.

He hadn't been with a woman since Josie's arrival in town and his cock now throbbed with heat, but the almost visceral need to be inside her had nothing to do with his self-enforced abstinence and everything to do with the woman seated across from him.

For years after they'd parted, he'd done his best to erase her memory. He'd had his fair share of women—probably more than his fair share, if he were honest. Riley's jibe about Chase's past was well and truly deserved. He had a reputation in Watervale for being a ladies' man and he'd worked hard to maintain it. A man who liked to play the field didn't receive too much pressure to settle down. Women who were looking for commitment knew better than to date the likes of him. That suited him just fine.

He'd known, since first meeting Josie that no one else could ever come close to making him feel the way she did. Each little moment spent together added up to something extraordinary. It was like they'd met in another life; their hearts and souls already entwined even before setting eyes on each other at a football game. They were young and in love, with their lives, full and glorious, ahead of them. They promised themselves to each other, forever and ever, amen.

Knowing how it had all ended still filled him with pain and the memory of the way he'd walked away from her without a word of explanation seemed cowardly and flooded him with shame. All at once, his desire deflated. He glanced at his watch and saw that it was late.

He pushed away from the table, averting his eyes.

"I'd better go. We both have a big day ahead of us and it will be here before we know it."

From the corner of his eye, he saw her shoulders slump and her face once again filled with disappointment, but she cleared her throat and answered him in a voice that was almost normal.

"Of course. I'll see you out."

He followed her into the entryway. She reached for the screen door and held it open.

"Thanks for putting the beds together. It was a real help. I-I appreciate it."

Chase nodded, hating to leave her like this and for a brief moment he wanted to kiss her, he wanted to see if she'd remember the taste of his lips on her mouth, but he quickly pushed the thought aside, knowing it was for the best.

"No problem. Thanks for dinner. It was great."

A wry smile tilted the corners of her mouth. "It was fish and chips, Chase."

"Right. Fish and chips. Best I've ever tasted."

She shook her head slowly back and forth and her smile turned into a grin that touched every corner of his heart. She was the same beautiful, sweet Josie he'd known and loved forever.

"I'll see you in court," he murmured and left her standing on the porch. He'd never felt more lonely.

Daniel listened to the quiet murmur of voices drifting into him from Josie's kitchen. He ought to be frightened of them. After all, they were both giving evidence for the prosecution. His lawyer had explained the process and although Daniel hadn't really wanted to know, he'd listened just the same. The prosecution would call their witnesses who would do their best to convince the judge that Daniel had done wrong. Then Daniel would get a turn.

But the truth was, both Josie and Chase had shown him nothing but kindness and he couldn't help but be grateful for that. Okay, so tomorrow she was going to tell the judge that he'd meant to kill the man who'd raped his mother and that was fine with him.

He *had* meant it. Neil Whitcomb had hurt his mother. The man deserved to die. It was as simple as that.

He turned over on his side to face his little brother. His pajamas, whilst a little large and smelling totally unfamiliar, were soft and comfortable, like the sheets on his bed. It was the first time in more than a month that'd he'd slept in clothes and linens that were fresh and clean.

It wasn't his dad's fault. Daniel was old enough to fill the washing machine. It's just that it had always been his mom who'd taken care of that kind of stuff. Clean clothes, hot meals, packed lunches. Before all this, he'd never given it any real thought. That kind of thing just happened. Now he wished he'd told his mom more often how much he appreciated everything she did.

Tears burned behind his eyes and he bit his lip to prevent a sob, not wanting to upset his brother who slept in the bed beside his. Despite his best efforts, moisture leaked out of his eyes and slid slowly down his cheeks.

He sighed and swiped at the tears and then put a hand against his stomach. His belly was full and he slept in a comfortable bed. He only wished he could somehow fill the emptiness in his heart and find something that could take away the sure knowledge that everything was his fault.

His little brother stirred in his sleep and then turned on his side to face him. Daniel saw the glint of Jason's eyes in the faint light that drifted in through the window. "Are you awake?" he whispered.

"Yes," his brother answered and then followed it up with a yawn. A moment later, he added softly, "I like it here."

Fresh tears flooded Daniel's eyes and he bit down hard on a sob. "I miss Mom," he gasped and then turned away to face the wall.

Chapter 17

Josie leaned back against the counter in the staff tea room and took a long, slow sip of her morning coffee, savoring the rich aromatic taste. She closed her eyes to enjoy one last moment of the morning's solitude. She was due in court at ten and although she'd cleared her schedule, after leaving Daniel at the courthouse with his lawyer and dropping Jason off at school, she'd stopped by her office in order to once again go over her evidence. The prosecutor expected her report would be tendered to the court without objection, but then the cross examination would begin.

Blake Harton Junior was a man whose reputation preceded him. Coming from a long line of lawyers and a couple of Supreme Court judges, Harton had cut his teeth defending small-time crooks and drug dealers in the Local Court. Eventually, he'd graduated to the District Court where his clients ranged from murderers, hard core criminals engaged in drug importation and distribution and worse. He was a tough defense lawyer who had a reputation for carving up a witness like a moist Thanksgiving turkey. While Josie was relieved to discover someone had secured excellent legal defense for Daniel, she was dreading the cross examination by his lawyer.

With coffee in hand, she read the first page of her report again and sighed.

"It's a bit early in the morning to be looking so glum, isn't it? Surely things aren't as bad as that?"

Doctor Rohan Wheeler's teasing smile displayed his perfect white teeth. His brown eyes sparkled with humor. Josie couldn't help but smile back at him.

"Sorry, I'm just going over my report on Daniel Logan. His competency hearing begins today in the District Court. I'm squaring off with Blake Harton, Jr. He's been engaged on behalf of Daniel."

The doctor let out a whistle. "I'm impressed. Someone must have plenty of money. A barrister of Harton's quality doesn't come cheap."

"Yes. I'm not sure who's footing the bill, but I'm pleased Daniel's getting competent counsel. Besides, if the matter proceeds to trial, it will be heard in the Supreme Court."

"So, what's happening today?"

"I've been told by the prosecutor that I'll be on the stand right after the investigating officers. My report's instrumental to the prosecution's argument that Daniel's competent to stand trial."

Rohan compressed his lips and nodded. "Good luck with it. With Harton on the attack, you're going to need it."

Josie grimaced and then took another sip of coffee. "Yes, I'm afraid you're probably right."

"How about we meet at The Bullet later? You'll probably need a stiff drink or two by the time you get through on the stand."

Josie nodded and smiled. "I'd hazard a guess that you'll be right again, Doctor Wheeler." Her thoughts landed fleetingly on Chase and the last time she'd been to The Bullet. She determinably pushed them away. "Sounds like a plan. Court finishes at four. What time can you get away?"

Chase stepped down from the witness box after undergoing a rigorous cross examination from Blake Harton

Jr, of the evidence tendered in Chase's statement. Relieved that it was over, he shot a glance in Daniel's direction to gauge how the boy was faring. He sat in the dock and was flanked by two corrections officers. To Chase's relief, he looked solemn, but composed.

Chase took a seat near the prosecutor. Senior Sergeant John Wall was a veteran in the courtroom. Large in life and in stature, he'd been with the prosecutor's office in Watervale for as long as Chase could remember. The man won more than he lost and he always played fair. Chase held John in high regard and was pleased to have him on his side.

The judge asked the prosecutor to call his next witness and when Josie's name sounded throughout the courtroom, Chase turned to look toward the door from where the witnesses entered.

She was dressed in a smart, navy pin-stripe suit. The fitted jacket emphasized her curves and the skirt skimmed the top of her knees. Shapely calves were encased in navy stockings. She wore a pair of three-inch heels that only added to her above-average height.

Her hair shone like burnished gold and had been pulled back and secured in a bun at the nape of her neck. After all these years, he still remembered what it felt like to free it from the constraints of her ponytail. Soft and silk-like, it would flow over his fingers, enveloping him in the sweet scent of her shampoo. His hands fisted at the memory, almost as if the silky strands were once again within his reach.

Josie took her place in the witness stand and it was then that he noticed her pallor. There were dark circles beneath her eyes and her lips were taut with nerves. His heart went out to her. She wasn't a cop. Unlike him, she wasn't used to giving evidence. In fact, it was quite possible this was the first time she'd ever taken the stand. He compressed his lips and sympathized with the tension that held her body in its grip.

John went through the motions and Josie's report was tendered without objection, but it was far from over. Harton came to his feet and Chase watched Josie draw in a deep breath and let it out with a slight shudder. He understood her fear. Harton's reputation for shredding the prosecution witnesses was legendary and despite what Chase had told her, Josie's report was the only thing standing between Harton's client being committed for trial and a defense application to the judge that there was no case to answer.

Knowing that the next few minutes she'd endure on the witness stand would be brutal, Chase braced himself for the onslaught. He stared at her until he caught her eye and did his best to convey his support. He offered her a smile of encouragement and was gratified when she responded with a tiny smile of her own. It was enough to leave him feeling lighter than he had since he'd left her the night before.

Harton went in hard and fast, as Chase expected him to. Josie held her own against him and Chase couldn't help but feel proud. Her responses to Harton's questions were answered with cool and calm deliberation. Despite Harton's best attempts, he couldn't shake Josie from her professional opinion and belief that Daniel Logan had capacity to stand trial.

It wasn't as if Chase wanted to see Daniel go to jail. In fact, he'd personally seen to it that Daniel was afforded the best representation in the region, but as a police officer, he needed to see that the laws would be fairly applied, no matter the age of the defendant or the circumstances. Those factors were applicable when considering a sentence, not for determining guilt. It was an important distinction and one he wholeheartedly supported.

It didn't mean he was happy about it. There would be no winners here today. Whether or not Daniel was committed for trial, no one would leave the courtroom happy. The whole tragic situation was downright depressing and sad, but there was nothing left to do but to leave it in the hands of the justice system and hope that things turned out all right.

Daniel listened to his barrister pepper the woman on the stand with pointed questions. He should have been pleased she was getting a grilling. After all, without her evidence, the prosecution had no proof he'd known what he did was wrong.

His barrister had already told him the interview he'd given to Josie that night in the police station would be inadmissible. He was twelve. Despite Josie's presence, the interview should never have been conducted without a parent, guardian or lawyer present. He wondered if she knew that.

She'd been nothing but kind to him, despite her role in the matter and it saddened him to hear the tension in her voice as she answered the raft of questions fired at her from his lawyer.

Daniel understood the man was merely doing his job and he was beyond grateful for the lawyer's presence. He'd lost count of the number of people who'd told him how lucky he was to have secured the services of a barrister with the standing of Blake Harton Jr.

He had to admit, the man looked as impressive as he sounded. Way tall and broad shouldered, he stood strong and commanding at the bar table. He was bright eyed and clean shaven and his black gown was large and intimidating. He wore a cream-colored wig that should have looked weird but seemed to add to his air of authority.

But no matter how many times Harton tried to rattle the woman on the stand, she remained calm and unruffled and her answers didn't vary. In her opinion, the defendant (that was him) knew that what he was doing was wrong. He knew more than in merely a naughty sense that his actions were against the law. He'd taken courses on gun safety and had passed. Proper use of a firearm was part of that course. He appreciated that those who broke the law would be punished. He thought that this was only fair. He agreed that he'd shot Neil Whitcomb dead and he expressed no remorse for his actions.

By the end of it, even Harton seemed to give up. With a soft sigh and a grimace, the lawyer advised the court he had no further questions of Josie and quietly regained his seat.

Daniel stared at her. A brief spurt of anger flared to life and just as quickly died. It wasn't her fault. She was only telling the truth. *He* was the reason they were all there. Everything came back to him: If he hadn't woken and found the man, if he hadn't gotten the gun. If he hadn't blown the man's head off and then admitted he was glad he did. That he'd do it again to save his mom.

It was all his fault, every last second of it. His family had been torn apart. His mother was dead. His father wanted to join her. He hadn't been told in so many words, but it didn't take a genius to work it out. He'd heard a whisper around the school yard that his dad had been found with a shotgun; that he was going to blow his head off. Now his dad was in a loony ward, too sick to even see them.

Daniel ought to do everyone a favor and just turn the gun on himself. That's how it went in the movies. The gunman always took it in the head. If it wasn't the cops who got him, he made sure he did the job himself.

Josie stood and made her way out of the witness box and he watched her measured descent. She glanced in his direction, but he looked away. He couldn't give her the reassurance she no doubt sought from him. He had nothing to give anyone—not even himself.

His chest tightened with emotion and sudden tears burned behind his eyes. She cared about him and his brother. He knew she did. He wished he was whole enough to return the sentiment.

A sob caught in the back of his throat. It had been so long since he felt he mattered to anyone. He missed his mom. God, how he missed her. It was like a heavy ache deep within him, penetrating to the depths of his soul and it wouldn't go away. As if he'd just woken from a dream, he finally understood the permanency of it all—he'd never see her again.

CHAPTER 18

Josie pushed back a strand of hair that had escaped her sensible bun and ordered a drink from the barman. The day had been long and trying and she was glad it was almost over. At least her time in the witness box had come to an end. She thought she'd done rather well under the circumstances even if the formidable Blake Harton Junior had left her feeling rattled. She hoped she'd managed to maintain an air of professional confidence on the stand, despite the fact she'd been shaking like the windows in a hurricane beneath her calm exterior.

She'd wanted to go to Daniel straight afterward and reassure him her evidence hadn't been a personal attack, but he'd turned away from her and his slight had eaten away at her courage.

Chase had been in the courtroom. She'd been aware of him all day and had been more than relieved when the judge finally called an end to the proceedings. The questions she'd put to Chase the night before had been ignored. It was almost as if he didn't *have* an explanation for his actions so long ago. Or if he did, he didn't deem it worth sharing them a decade later.

The thought made her angry and sad all at the same time and she was more determined than ever to forget all about Chase Barrington. Accepting an invitation from a young, good-looking doctor was just the thing she needed to put her past where it belonged.

The heavy wooden door to The Bullet opened and Josie looked up and spied Rohan. He was dressed as she'd seen him earlier that morning, in a stylish suit and tie, but within moments of coming to a halt by her side near the bar, he disposed of the tie and loosened the top buttons of his shirt.

"Ah, that feels better," he grinned and tucked the tie into the pocket of his jacket. "What a day! I swear every young mother in Watervale had an infant sick with the flu. I should have gone home for a shower. I'm probably covered in germs."

Josie smiled and let her gaze wander over his physique. His broad shoulders tapered into narrow hips and his stomach appeared washboard flat beneath his shirt. His brown eyes sparkled with good humor and contrasted nicely with the dark blond of his hair. All in all, Doctor Wheeler was a very tidy package. She cursed silently under her breath when her body refused to react to his presence the way she wanted it to.

Damn Chase Barrington. He was the reason she'd remained boyfriendless these past ten years. Despite her best efforts and a string of offers, she hadn't found anyone she connected with like she had with Chase. And boy, had she tried. Even her younger sister Chanel had teased her about it when they shared an apartment together in Brisbane. It became a running joke between them about who Josie might date next. Most of them didn't last long. It only took her a date, two at the most, to know it was never going to work. Just another thing she could blame on Chase.

So, now she smiled and tried her hardest to find some kind of personal connection with the handsome doctor. He was smart and funny and about her age and there was nothing stopping her from encouraging his interest. And he was definitely interested.

From the moment they'd met, he'd sent out an interested vibe and until now, she'd done her best to ignore it. Her heart was still hopelessly tangled up with Chase and her head was no better. It wasn't fair to involve herself with someone else while she still yearned to be with another, but last night it had become more than clear it was time she got over Chase Barrington and moved on with her life. The fairy tale ending she'd dreamed of was never going to happen.

"You look fine to me," she answered and flashed him another smile. "What are you drinking?"

"You're buying, are you?"

Josie shrugged and gave him a wink. "Think of it as my way of saying thank you for helping me forget such a trying day."

"How did it go?"

Josie's smile faded. "Okay, I guess. My evidence withstood the barrage from the defense. I think I came across as believable. Their psychologist takes the stand tomorrow. If the judge sides with me, Daniel will be committed to the Supreme Court to stand trial for murder."

Rohan's lips compressed and he nodded in understanding. The sympathy in his eyes nearly undid her. He stepped closer and squeezed her arm in a show of comfort. "It couldn't have been easy for you."

The gentle understanding in his voice, coupled with the comforting pressure from his fingers filled her with emotion. Tears burned behind her eyes. As if sensing her precarious emotional state, he closed the distance between them and pulled her into his arms. She rested her head against his well-muscled chest and breathed out on a heavy sigh.

Chase pushed open the door to The Bullet and headed straight for the bar. After a day in court giving evidence and watching Josie do the same, he needed a drink. Halfway across the room he spied her and came to a sudden halt.

She was pressed up against the doctor—Rohan something-or-other—who shared her office space. Some of her hair had come loose and hung in soft waves down her back. Her face was turned away and buried against

Rohan's shirt. Chase watched as she shuddered and saw Rohan tighten his hold.

Surprise followed by disbelief and anger surged through him. It was an emotion that was totally uncalled for. He had no claim on her. He'd made it clear last night that he had no intention of taking up where they'd left off. She was a free agent, free to see whoever she pleased. That she'd taken refuge in the arms of the doctor was none of Chase's business.

So why was he feeling so jealous? And jealousy, it was. He was man enough to own up to the fact that the sight of her in another man's arms was enough to drive him crazy. He wanted her and loved her, but he had to let her go. It was for the best. *Wasn't it?* Right now, he didn't know.

He walked toward them with his face on fire—from want, from need, from despair. He was almost upon them when he spun on his heel and headed in the opposite direction. He needed to get as far away from them as he could get.

He glanced over his shoulder and was relieved to see they hadn't noticed him. He pulled up a seat at the far end of the bar. With several other patrons between them, he hoped she wouldn't see him. The bartender appeared and Chase quickly ordered a beer. A moment later, the drink arrived and he gulped greedily from the glass. Making short work of it, he promptly ordered another.

"Hi, there handsome. Would you care to buy a lady a drink?"

Chase lifted his head and stared at the stranger who'd spoken. It was only a little past five on a Tuesday afternoon, but already the woman was done up for a night on the town. Her reddish dark hair was piled high on her head and her full lips were bright with red lipstick. The rest of her makeup had also been applied with a heavy hand.

She wasn't unattractive and her smile was downright nice, but the last thing Chase needed was the company of another woman. He blinked and tried to come up with a suitable way to decline the bold invitation in her eyes. Taking his silence for encouragement, she reached out and ran her hand along the inside of his thigh. His muscles bunched involuntarily. He moved her hand away and her face fell.

"I-I'm sorry," he stammered. "I-I've had a rough day and I'm far from good company. You might want to spend your time and energies elsewhere."

Her mouth tightened and her eyes narrowed, but she slid off the stool without another word and moved further down the bar away from him. His gaze once again snagged on Josie, who had separated herself from the doctor. She stood close enough that it was obvious they were together, but at least he no longer had his arms around her.

While Chase watched, Josie took a call on her phone. She turned away from Rohan toward Chase and his heart leaped into his throat. Spinning on the barstool, he turned his back on her and prayed she hadn't spotted him. He wasn't ready to deal with her face to face with the knowledge that she was in the bar with another man.

His irrational emotions weren't fair to either of them, but they were out of his control. Right now, all he wanted to do was drown his sorrows in another glass or two and do his best to forget all about Josie Munro.

Josie checked the Caller ID on her phone and then glanced back at Rohan. "I'm really sorry, but I have to take this." Turning away from him, she answered the call.

"Hi, Belinda. How are things?"

"Josie, I'm glad I caught you. I've been having difficulty placing the Logan boys. I contacted a relative this morning, but she still hasn't arrived in town. I-I'd take them home with me, but I really don't have any room. I live in a one-bedroom apartment. I'm not sure how it would work."

Before Belinda had even finished, Josie was nodding. "It's okay, Belinda. I'm happy to have them for another night. In fact, as long as you need me. I'm happy to help out."

Belinda's relief was palpable, even over the phone.

"Josie, are you sure? That would be fantastic. You don't know how much it would help me out."

"Of course I'm sure. I'm more than happy to help. I have a spare room with twin beds, so having them stay longer won't be a problem."

"Oh, thank you, Josie. You're a life saver. Giving the Logan boys a little stability right now will do them both good. I don't know what I'd do without you."

"Belinda, please. Stop thanking me. It's fine. Like I said, I'm happy to be of assistance." Josie glanced at Rohan who was trying hard not to listen. "Where are they now?"

"They're with me. I collected Jason from school earlier and picked up Daniel outside the courtroom. He's on bail until court resumes tomorrow morning."

"Okay. Give me your address and I'll come around and get them. I'm still in town."

After taking down the details on the back of a beer coaster, Josie ended the call and shot an apologetic look in Rohan's direction.

"I'm really sorry…"

He shrugged. "It's fine. You have to go. I understand."

Relief surged through her. Rohan Wheeler was a good man. She determined then and there to try harder to force her brain to see him as more than merely a friend.

"Thanks for meeting me here and for…everything," she said and meant it.

"No problem. Thanks for the drink. Perhaps we could do it again sometime."

Josie smiled and nodded. "I'd like that."

––––––––––

The night had quietly settled in and The Bullet was more than crowded when Chase lifted his head again and stared down the length of the bar. With a frown and a savage curse, he realized Josie and her companion were gone. He hadn't noticed them leaving. He hoped it wasn't hand in hand. The image sent another surge of helpless anger flooding through him and he signaled for another drink.

"Hey, Chase. Mind if I join you?"

Chase turned his head to greet the newcomer and his eyes widened at the sight of his boss.

"Riley, yeah, of course," he mumbled, indicating the empty barstool beside him. "Take a seat."

"How was your day in court? I take it things didn't go well?"

Chase narrowed his eyes at his boss. "Why do you say that?"

"Well, you look like you've just buried your best friend. I'm making a radical assumption that if things had gone well, you'd be a helluva lot cheerier than this."

Chase pressed his lips together and nodded in agreement with Riley's summary of events.

"You've hit the nail on the head, boss, only, it has nothing to do with the court case."

"I see. It's like that." Riley pulled a stool up beside him and ordered himself a beer.

"I'll have one too, thanks, boss."

A single dark eyebrow rose in silent query.

"Really? I think you might be best to sit this one out. You're due back in court tomorrow, aren't you?"

Chase nodded morosely and contemplated the scarred wood of the bar in silence. Then he shook his head. "She's something all right."

Riley frowned. "Who?"

"Your sister. She's got me running around in circles. I don't know which way is up. I love her too much to hurt her, but somehow, I just can't walk away."

"Whoa, hold up there, Chase. What the hell are you talking about? How could you be in love with Josie? You haven't seen each other for a decade."

Chase shook his head again. "I've loved her since the moment I first set eyes on her, in the bleachers at Grafton High School. I was playing football for Watervale. She was supposed to be cheerleading, only she fell over in practice a few days earlier and broke her leg."

"Hey, I remember that! I couldn't believe anyone could break a leg during cheerleading practice. I gave her such a hard time over it," Riley grinned.

"That was the first day I met her," Chase whispered. "It was supposed to be the first day of the rest of our lives."

Riley frowned. "Wait a minute. Josie broke her leg in the eleventh grade. I remember because I wasn't long out of the Academy and I was stationed north of Lismore. She had to have surgery. They put in a few screws and a couple of plates. I remember visiting her in the hospital."

Chase stared at Riley. "Yeah, that's right."

"But I thought you didn't meet her until just before she graduated? Isn't that what you said?"

"I don't know what I said, but I'm telling you now, I met her at the bleachers that day and she was wearing a big white cast."

Riley narrowed his gaze. "What else haven't I been told?"

Becoming aware he might have said too much, Chase shrugged. He'd kept their secret for a lifetime. Then suddenly, he was through with it. It was time to tell the truth.

"Josie and I dated for nearly a year before her graduation. We were in love. We were going to get married. Only...only...we didn't. Something happened and we didn't."

Riley's gaze widened in disbelief and then showed the slightest hint of anger. Chase did his best not to squirm. His head was thick and sluggish and he suddenly wished he hadn't had so many beers.

He wasn't usually a heavy drinker—three or four on a Saturday night was usually more than enough—but these weren't usual circumstances. It wasn't every day the love of your life showed up in your town, stirring up old memories. Who could blame him if he'd imbibed a little more than was desirable? He blinked a couple of times until the multiple images of his boss morphed into just one. The solemn expression on Riley's face hadn't lessened.

"What are you trying to tell me, Chase?"

Chase let the tension of the past couple of months ease out of him on a long and heavy sigh. His shoulders slumped and his head lowered until his chin almost touched his chest. The beer he'd had was playing havoc with his powers of concentration and all he could think of was his beautiful Josie and how he'd stupidly pushed her away.

All of a sudden, he yearned for someone to talk to; someone to offer him a little advice. Apart from his mom, he'd never told anyone about Josie—not when they were back in high school and not now, but in this moment the urge to talk to her brother was overwhelming.

Riley was his boss and his friend. He was also married to the love of his life. He knew what it felt like to be so connected to a woman you almost felt like the two of you were one. Riley could help him. Riley would tell him what to do.

"I once loved a woman to distraction," he slurred, pitching his voice low. Riley bent his head closer to hear.

"She was my moon, my stars, my night, my day: She was my everything. We had it all planned out, the way our lives would go. She was heading off to college; I was already in the Academy. We were going to visit on weekends and days off and when I was finished, we were going to get married. We talked about where we'd live and what kind of house we'd have. We talked about our kids and what we'd name them. Our lives stretched out ahead of us and they were going to be perfect." He drew in a ragged breath and reached for the beer glass that wasn't there.

"What happened?" Riley asked quietly, his gaze intent on Chase.

Chase let out a soft sigh. "The Big C happened. I was diagnosed with cancer."

Once again, Riley's eyes widened in shock, but Chase was grateful when he didn't offer any meaningless platitudes. It had happened a long time ago. It was obvious he'd survived.

"I had tumors in both testes. They operated and removed

the cancer and that was followed by rounds of chemotherapy and radiation. 'Just to make sure,' they said. I dropped out of sight for the best part of a year. Fortunately, not many people noticed. I'd left for the Police Academy a year earlier. Most people thought I was still there. They thought I was still living in Goulburn. Nobody knew I'd moved back home. Mom drove me to treatments in Grafton. I stayed pretty much close to home.

"Physically, I looked like shit. My hair was gone and I'd lost a lot of weight. Most days I didn't feel too good, either. The last thing I wanted to do was socialize. And then, I was given the really good news. The chemo had killed the cancer, but it had likely left me sterile."

"Did Josie know?"

The question was murmured so softly, Chase thought for a moment that he might have imagined it. Then he looked into Riley's face and saw his somber expression and the warmth and understanding in his eyes.

A band of emotion squeezed Chase's chest like a vice and he blinked hard to keep the tears at bay. He'd done all his crying a long time ago. He refused to give in to them now.

Dragging a breath deep into his lungs, he blew it out hard between his lips. Gathering his courage, he looked back at his boss and slowly shook his head.

"No."

Riley nodded once in acceptance and then lifted his glass to his lips. Chase watched while he drank until there was nothing left. With a sigh, he set the empty glass on the bar and wiped his mouth with the back of his hand. At last, he turned back to Chase.

"You need to tell her."

Closing his eyes in resignation, Chase drew in another deep breath. "Yeah, I do."

CHAPTER 19

Josie walked down the hall toward the room where the Logan boys were sleeping, fatigue dogging her every step. The night before, she'd tossed and turned over the evidence she was due to give, as well as her concerns for the boys in the adjoining room. Toss in the random image of Chase and the way they'd parted and she'd begun the day already feeling weary. Now, more than twelve hours and a tough day in court later, she was depleted, every ounce of her energy gone.

A movement from the bed where Daniel lay caught her eye and she stepped through the open doorway. The glimmer of moonlight illuminated the shadows just enough so that she could make out his shape in the bed. A closer inspection revealed he was awake and watching her.

He'd hardly spoken a word to her since she'd collected him from Belinda's office. They needed to talk, no matter how much she wished she could avoid it. Staying silent about what was happening wasn't healthy for either one of them. She swallowed a sigh and went over to his bed and perched on the very edge of it.

"How are you doing?" she murmured and then winced at the lameness of her question. She thought *she'd* had a tough day. She couldn't even begin to imagine what it had been like for him. The memory of how he'd looked after she'd finished giving her evidence—his expression of sadness and hurt and resignation—would stay with her forever, no matter how many times she told herself she'd only been doing her job. Nothing eased the heartache that weighed her down when she thought about Daniel and what lay in his future.

No matter which way she looked at it, he was in serious trouble. If the court determined he had the capacity to stand trial and answer for his crime and he was found guilty, he'd be facing a custodial sentence. Even if he pleaded to the lesser charge of manslaughter, the likelihood of him facing jail time was incredibly high. She knew it and no doubt he had some idea, too.

Her shoulders slumped with the weight of her thoughts, but she forced a smile. She wasn't sure how frank his lawyer had been with him and how much Daniel knew about the precariousness of his position, but she wasn't going to lower his spirits any more than was necessary. Not tonight, anyway.

She glanced at him again and tears burned behind her eyes. From the look on his face, his thoughts were as troubled as hers.

"Don't beat yourself up about today, Josie. It's cool. You were only doing your job."

His quiet words tore her apart with their simple honesty and heartfelt show of support. They demonstrated an insight and maturity far beyond his years and it threw her a little off balance. Emotion surged through her and she bit down on her lip. She blinked hard to hold back the tears that now pressed behind her eyelids. Daniel needed her to be strong and courageous. She wished she had even half his bravery.

"Th-thank you," she stammered, not knowing what else to say. Her evidence could make the difference between whether he went to trial and faced a probable custodial sentence or walked away a free young man. Not that he'd walk away free in the true sense—unaffected and ready to pick up his life where he'd left off. His life would never be the same again, with or without a court-imposed punishment.

"I'm sorry that your aunt wasn't here to collect you today."

He shrugged, as if it was of little consequence. "It's okay. I don't mind being here with you. Jason really likes it here."

Together, they turned to look at the sleeping form in the bed across the room. Josie was gratified to see the younger boy's chest rise and fall in a deep and steady rhythm. At least one of them was able to sleep.

"How is the counseling going? Belinda mentioned she's been taking you both to see Phoebe in Grafton."

"Yeah, I think it's helping Jason. He seems to be adjusting much quicker than I am to Mom's death and I think he's sure Dad's gonna come home soon and then everything will be better."

"How about you?" she whispered, risking a glance in his direction.

His jaw set hard and his lips thinned. His gaze dropped to the bedclothes. Suddenly, he seemed fascinated with the pattern on the bedspread.

"It's okay, Daniel. It's okay not to be doing too good. No one would expect you to be joyful or even a little bit happy. You've been through incredible trauma. First your mom and now your dad. He's—"

"He tried to kill himself, didn't he?" The harsh question blazed from his mouth in a torrent of pain and anger.

Josie shook her head, for once, at a loss for words. She scrambled for something to say. "No, of course not. Whatever gave you that idea?"

Daniel made a rude noise under his breath. He turned on his side and faced the wall and dragged the bedspread with him.

"I heard it from the kids at school. I thought *you* of all people would tell me the truth." The bedclothes around his face muffled his voice, but still the accusation stung—even more so because she'd been hedging.

Josie closed her eyes against the pain. "I-I'm sorry, Daniel. You're right. The truth is the least of what you deserve." She drew in a deep breath and blew it out on a heavy sigh, too tired to keep up the façade of normality. Nothing in Daniel's short life would be normal for a very long time to come...if ever.

"I-I don't know exactly what happened, but I understand your dad was feeling very low. He-he thought about ending his life, but he didn't attempt it. He remembered you and Jason and how much you needed him and how much he loved you and…and he didn't do it. He didn't even try to do it. He asked for help. He was brave enough to call the police and ask for help. You should be proud of him for that. It couldn't have been easy."

Her words were met with silence and then Daniel's slight body shuddered on a sob. Josie reached for him, her heart breaking at the sound of his desolation. Lying down beside him, she pulled him gently in against her side and murmured soothing noises against his hair. He'd been so brave and tough in the courtroom, trying hard to be a man. But it was all a front. Inside, he was a scared, young boy: a twelve-year-old who'd been thrust into the adult world way too early and much against his nature.

Josie would bet everything she owned, including her prized motorcycle, that when Daniel Logan reached for that gun the only thought in his mind was to help his mother. Okay, he knew by firing the gun, he'd kill a man and he understood it was wrong, but she refused to believe he could he have imagined the path his actions would take and the utter devastation that they would wrought on him and his family.

She'd done her duty to the court; she'd provided the prosecutor with a report and she still stood by its contents, but it didn't mean she had to like it or that she couldn't feel the pain and devastation that radiated in waves from the boy in her arms.

She bit her lip against another surge of emotion and tightened her hold on him. His sobs had quietened to the occasional shudder and she waited in silence for him to calm.

"It's all my fault," he whispered in a tiny, broken voice.

Josie's response was swift and sure. "No! No, Daniel. It's not. Please, listen to me. It's easy for you to feel that way, even natural, but it's not true. You had no control over the man who attacked your mom. You had no power over the way your mom and dad reacted. We all deal with things in our own way. We make our own choices. Sometimes we make good ones, sometimes we don't, but our decisions are only ever that—*ours.*"

She reached over and put her hand on his shoulder and gently turned him to face her. "Don't let anyone ever tell you different, Daniel. We're all responsible for ourselves: every thought, every word, every deed. It's just the way it is and it's the way it has to be." She paused and drew in a breath. "Do you understand what I'm saying?"

He stared at her, his eyes huge in his pale, angular face. "Yes. It's why if the judge sends me to trial, I'll plead guilty. My lawyer doesn't want me to. He wants to fight the charge. He wants to argue that I'm just a kid and I shouldn't be held responsible. He says the only thing I'm guilty of is loving my mom too much and taking my responsibility to her way too seriously."

He slowly shook his head. "I'm grateful that he wants to defend me, but there won't be a trial. I have to stand up and take responsibility for my actions. It's why you said what you did in your report. You had no choice. You told the truth. And so will I."

Tears slid down his cheeks, but he didn't look away. "I'm scared to death about going to jail. I've heard awful stories about places like that, but I did the wrong thing and I'm prepared to accept my punishment. It's the way it has to be."

The tears that Josie had tried so hard to hold at bay escaped and filled her eyes. He'd been protecting the mother he loved from harm; he'd been acting upon a normal and natural instinct that had been around since the beginning of time. For that very selfless act he was being punished and she couldn't believe how wrong it all felt.

With a harsh sob, she pulled him into her arms and gulped through the tears that choked her. It wasn't fair. It wasn't just. Like Daniel had said, it was simply the way it was.

Jason murmured in his sleep and Josie made a

monumental effort to regain control. With a shuddering breath, she eased her hold until her arms were loose against Daniel's body. Once again, he stared up at her with eyes that had seen too much.

"It's going to be okay, Josie," he whispered. "You'll see."

She bit her lip hard to stop from crying out and managed a jerky nod. She looked across at Jason and then back to his brother. Love swelled in her heart and the power of it took her breath away. These boys, almost strangers, had crept inside her heart and filled her with such longing it was almost painful in its intensity.

In that pure moment of truth between her and the boy beside her, a clarity dawned on her—loving Chase had been easy, losing him was beyond any pain she could describe, but if she ever hoped to have a chance at love again and have a family of her own, she needed to find out his reasons for leaving and finally have an answer to the question that had dogged her for so many years.

Over time, the pain of his abrupt departure had eased, but it had never gone away. Now, more than anything, she needed answers. She needed to find closure. Then, she could put it all behind her and look to the future. She could open her heart to finding love again; to making new dreams of a life filled with the kind of love only children could bring.

―――――――――

Scott Jones stared at the calendar on the wall of his jail cell. *Another day down. Four more to go.* He flexed his fingers until they cracked and bit down hard on a wild surge of anticipation. No good getting ahead of himself. He had to take things easy; plan his course of action until there was nothing left to chance.

He moved over to the small shelf affixed to the wall where he kept his meager possessions and pulled out his collection of newspaper clippings. At the thought of Neil's death, a wave of pain flooded through him and he closed his eyes hard against the anguish. Neil had been the only one who'd cared for him in this stinking shithole. Neil had been his brother, his father, his everything. And now he was dead. As dead as the cockroach Scott had squished with his boot as it skittered across the floor of his cell, headed toward his stash of candy.

No more cockroach.

No more Neil.

Anger replaced his pain and he latched onto the emotion like a drowning man who'd just been thrown a life preserver. Anger was good. Anger kept him strong. Anger kept him focused. It was what he needed.

He flicked open the clipping that lay on the top of the pile. A color photo of a woman graced the page. Doctor Josie Munro, Child Psychologist appointed by the court to determine whether the boy who'd murdered Neil was fit to stand trial.

Disgust flooded through him and his lip curled up in a sneer. They had to be fucking kidding. A pre-schooler would know that shooting a man the way the kid had shot Neil would kill him. A psychological assessment was fucking bullshit.

Scott stared down at the article again. It had been written the day the psychologist had attended court to give evidence. Due to the age of the defendant, the court proceedings were closed, so Scott had no way of knowing which way her evidence fell.

Whose camp was she in? Did she support the idea the kid was guilty? That he knew exactly what he was doing when he pulled the fucking trigger and sent a bullet straight into the back of Neil's head? A feral smile tugged at the corners of his lips. For her sake, she'd better. Soon, very soon, he'd know the truth.

The judge finally called an end to the proceedings and

Chase didn't bother to hide his relief. After another day sitting around in the courtroom, he'd just about had enough. The persistent headache behind his eyes hadn't helped matters, either. He should have known better than to get drunk when he had to spend the next day listening to the evidence of the defense expert who'd been brought in to counteract Josie's report.

Doctor Leonard Heather had spent more than a dozen sessions with the defendant and had deduced the child, Daniel Logan, had no idea what would happen when he pulled the trigger of the gun. Heather had completely ignored the fact Daniel was almost as familiar with firearms as Chase was, especially when it came to .22 rifles. The kid had his own license and gun. He and his father were regulars at the firing range. No one who knew them would believe Daniel had randomly picked up the gun and fired it without a clue about the consequences.

Still, John Wall was forced to cross examine Heather on every aspect of his report. By the end of the day, it appeared to Chase that the prosecutor had made progress, but it had come at a price. Both of them were exhausted.

"Christ, I'm glad that's over," John muttered, shaking his head.

Chase knew exactly how he felt. Wall might have been an excellent prosecutor, but he'd had a tough day counteracting the questioning applied by Harton's skillful tongue.

With no effort at all, Chase's mind focused on Josie, like it always had when he needed comfort and reassurance. They hadn't been together for ten years, and yet he'd never shaken the habit. Not that it had done him any good over the last decade, but even though she'd been absent from his life, thinking of her in times of trouble had always eased his mind.

It was no different now.

He thought back to his conversation with Riley at The Bullet the night before and his determination to tell her the truth. Nerves stirred deep inside him. He wasn't normally one to walk away from taking a risk. He had enough self-confidence and the right balance of bravery and healthy fear to make a good police officer, but when it came to Josie, all of his courage failed him and telling her the truth was fraught with danger.

What if she turned her back on him, closing down the tiniest sliver of hope he'd clung to all these years? It would kill him, that's what would happen. His heart would shrivel and die.

But what if she didn't scorn him? What if she came to accept his infertility and a life that might or might not include children? He'd have wasted ten years...

Was he willing to take the risk? Was he willing *not* to? Was it better to wonder and live in hope forever, or discover the truth, one way or another?

"What are you up to this afternoon? Fancy a beer?"

Chase stared at John and realized he'd spoken. "Um...yeah... Why not?"

"Great. I'll see you at The Bullet. Give me time to get back to the station and unload my gear and I'll be there. Order me a Bud and make sure its icy cold." The prosecutor shot him a grin and turned to pack away his files and statements and notepads into a battered old briefcase.

Memories of Chase's evening at The Bullet the night before came back to him and he suddenly shook his head. He couldn't risk running into Josie. What if she was with the doctor again? Or some other man?

A discovery like that would be the end of him. He was sure of it. Better to go over to her place and get things out in the open, once and for all. The not knowing was tearing him up inside. It was time he manned up and laid everything on the table. It was the only way they could move forward together, or on different paths.

"Ah, John, I might take a raincheck on the drink, if you don't mind. I know it's been a shit of a day, but think I'll head on home. I have a few things to take care of before I finish for the day."

John raised an inquisitive eyebrow, but gave Chase a

friendly smile. "Of course, mate. Do what you have to do. Some other time."

"Thanks. I appreciate everything you did here today. It couldn't have been easy."

"You have that right. Harton had my balls on a platter and was ready to carve them into little pieces there for a while. I managed to claw back some ground this afternoon, but it was a tough gig."

Chase nodded solemnly. "You did well. You did great. Now, it's up to the judge."

"Yep, you've got that right. I'm glad I'm not the one making that decision."

Chase nodded again, his lips compressed. "I'll catch up with you later. Call me as soon as you hear."

"You'll be the first to know."

Chase shook his hand and headed out of the courtroom. There was nothing more to be done but wait.

Josie's phone rang where it sat on the kitchen counter and she dashed across the room to answer it. She'd been waiting half the afternoon for the arrival of a plumber. She could only hope this was him. She picked up the phone and glanced at the screen and her pulse missed a few beats for an entirely different reason: *Chase.*

She hadn't seen him since yesterday when she'd finished giving evidence. And that was after her decision the night before to demand the truth. A sudden surge of nerves flooded through her belly.

The phone continued to chime and with a muttered curse, she took a deep breath and slowly blew it out. Doing her best not to sound flustered, she answered the call.

"Chase, how are you?"

"I-I'm fine. I just got out of court. I thought you might like an update."

"Of course. How did it go?"

"Yeah, another tough day, but it's over. The judge has adjourned for three days so he can deliberate over his decision."

"I heard from Belinda Murphy earlier," Josie said. "She told me a relative of the Logan boys has arrived in town. An aunt from some place this side of Bourke. The boys are going to stay with her for the next little while, at least until their father is well enough to come home."

"Good. That's good. I'm glad they have family to support them."

"Right, like I'm chopped liver... Thanks very much," Josie retorted, stung.

"Josie, I'm sorry, I didn't mean it like that. I just meant...you know. You're not...family."

Her anger wasn't appeased. "It's been a long time since I've known you, Chase. We've been apart many more years than we were together. I thought I knew you a little. Once. Now, I don't know you at all."

"Josie, please. Don't say things like that." His tone was tinged with desperation. It gave her pause.

"It's the truth, Chase. As sad as that may be, it's the truth."

"Please, Josie. Where are you? We need to talk."

The butterflies in her chest multiplied until she could barely breathe. *Was she brave enough to see this through, to finally know the truth?* Did she really have a choice?

"Please, Jose. Please, give me a chance to explain."

The tender use of the childhood nickname he'd given her all those years ago weakened her resolve and she found herself nodding.

"Okay," she whispered hoarsely. She cleared her throat and repeated it. "Okay."

"Are you sure?"

"Yes, Chase. I'm sure. It's well past time we did this."

"Are you at the office?"

"No, I'm at home. I have an issue with a toilet. I'm waiting for the plumber."

"Fine. I'll come over. I'll see you in ten minutes."

Chapter 20

With no time to change out of her work clothes, Josie ran a brush quickly through her hair and secured it behind her head in a simple ponytail. Chase had said he'd be there in ten minutes. She didn't have enough time for something more elaborate. Besides, he'd always loved her hair in the simplest of hairstyles—at least, he used to a decade ago. Now, she didn't know what he liked.

When Belinda had called her and told her the boys' aunt had arrived in town, Josie had been devastated. She couldn't believe how quickly they'd begun to matter; how quickly they'd become part of her life. She enjoyed taking care of them, of feeding them and seeing to their needs. She wanted more of it and she damned her soul to hell for wishing even for an instant that the aunt would change her mind about taking them on.

But right now, with Chase heading over to "talk," she was glad the boys weren't there. It was time to clear things up between her and Chase once and for all. It was time to put the fairy tale behind her.

The rumble of a powerful engine drew her attention and she peered out of the bathroom window. It overlooked the side yard and part of the main road. Chase sat astride a shiny, black motorcycle looking for all the world like he belonged there. Josie's heart jumped into her throat and nerves tangled deep in her belly. Heat suddenly centered in her core.

God, he looked hot. Like a bad boy out of a Hollywood movie.

He wore a black leather biker jacket and jeans that clung to his long lean legs. He brought the bike to a stop outside the gate that led into her yard and pulled off his helmet. Climbing easily off the bike, he turned to face her house. Like they had been the morning he'd come across her at the pool, his eyes were hidden behind mirrored aviator sunglasses.

Aware that he'd be on her front porch in a matter of seconds, Josie quickly splashed cool water against her heated cheeks and then patted them dry. With a last glance at her hair, she caught sight of her reflection in the mirror and shook her head in dismay.

Her eyes were wild and bright, like she was in the throes of a fever; her lips were parted and her breath came fast. Try as she might, she couldn't slow the pace of her heart and her pulse beat a rapid rhythm through her veins.

The sound of Chase's boots on the weathered porch sent a surge of anticipation rushing through her, along with more than a little dread. He'd come to offer her an explanation that was ten years in the making. She only hoped she'd survive the impact of his revelations with her trademark of calm and cool control.

She grimaced at the thought. This was Chase she was talking about. The man she'd loved with all her heart. The man who, even now, could turn her into a mass of quivering nerves and excitement just anticipating his presence. She'd be lucky if she didn't disgrace herself with a totally inappropriate emotional outburst. The probability of that was high. Way high.

But there was nothing to be done about it now. Chase's firm knock on the screen door sounded loud and clear throughout the house. Smoothing down her pale pink tailored blouse and fitted, knee-length cerise-colored skirt, she hurried from the bathroom. Her high heels made a clicking noise on the polished wooden floorboards that led down the hall and into the entryway. With a last quick breath, she opened the front door.

From the tilt of his head, she guessed Chase's gaze drifted over her, from the top of her bobbing ponytail, across her blouse and lower still. He paused noticeably at the open V neck of her fitted shirt and her heart skipped a beat. With his eyes still concealed behind the sunglasses, she had no idea of his thoughts.

"How could you have spent a day in the office and still look so gorgeous?" he murmured.

Josie swallowed the lump of nerves that had lodged in the back of her throat and tried to get her mouth to work. Stepping away, she sucked in another breath. "Um...thanks. I-I... You look good, too."

Chase shrugged and looked down at his clothes. "I've been stuck all day in court in a suit and tie, listening to evidence. I needed to get some air." He shrugged. "I dropped by my place to change and then decided to kick over the Fireblade." He looked away and Josie had the sense that he was suddenly shy. "I thought you might like to see her."

She smiled with genuine pleasure. "Of course! I heard you coming from half a mile away. She sure sounds like she has the goods. I bet she goes like the wind."

"Yep, you've got that right." He paused and then looked back at Josie. "Would you like to go for a run?"

Excitement coursed through her and she grinned a mile wide. "You bet." She looked down at her clothes and smiled wryly. "Just give me a minute to change." Before she could think through the wisdom of her decision, she turned and hurried back inside. "Come in," she tossed over her shoulder and then headed down the hall.

Once in her bedroom, she kicked off her heels and then unzipped her skirt. She shucked it off her hips and it fell in a pile on the floor. The blouse quickly followed.

A moment later, she pulled a T-shirt over her head and then slipped into her jeans. They were snug, but stretchy and she was confident she'd be able to put her leg over the bike without too much difficulty.

The power in Chase's Fireblade reminded her of her

brother Declan's Ducati and she was filled with another surge of excitement. The knowledge that she'd be pressed up close and personal against Chase's back while she rode pillion made her insides quiver with anticipation.

The thought of his nearness shouldn't have her so stirred up, particularly because they had yet to have "the talk." She had no idea if she would like what he had to say. It was why she needed to do this now because after he'd given her his reasons for abandoning her, she might never speak to him again. The very idea was beyond depressing.

Shaking the negative thoughts away, she resolved to focus on the positive. Right now, she had a hunk on her doorstep with a smile so sexy it curled her toes and he was waiting for her to climb on the back of his bike and go for a ride. Right here, right now, life couldn't get any better and she was going to seize the moment for what it was. Pulling on some socks and boots, she left the room.

Chase held the door open for her and she stepped out onto the porch. "I'll just grab my helmet from the garage," she said and sashayed down the stairs.

Chase stared after her, his mouth dry with excitement. His gaze followed the gentle sway of her hips, encased in her skintight jeans. The soft denim cupped her ass like a lover's hand and his fingers itched to do the same.

She'd always been hot to look at, but at eighteen, she hadn't fulfilled the promise in her youthful body. A decade later, and it was all he could do not to drool. She'd filled out in all the right places—from her generous cleavage, clearly outlined through the soft fabric of her T-shirt, to the gentle flare of her hips that swept down to a pair of long, shapely legs.

The only thing that hadn't changed was her beautiful, wheat-colored hair. She'd worn it long, even back then and the casual ponytail was as familiar to him as her smile. Not that he'd seen a lot of her smile lately. He determined to change that: starting right now.

He'd called her with the intention of explaining everything from start to finish—just like Riley had suggested—and he would... But...not right now. Not when her eyes were alight with excitement and she all but danced with anticipation. So what if it was all about his motorbike? He'd take whatever time he could get.

He didn't know how she'd react to his story, especially after the way he'd treated her since he found out she was in town. All this could be too little too late. Still, he'd enjoy the next few moments and make them last as long as he could. If things went badly, the memories of her on the back of his Fireblade might have to last a lifetime.

Within minutes, she returned, tugging a helmet on her head. Together, they walked to the Fireblade and Chase swung his leg over the bike. Holding it steady, he couldn't help but gasp when she climbed on behind him and wrapped her arms around his waist. The feel of her pressed up against him was heaven and he cursed beneath his breath.

What kind of hell had he just made for himself? He'd tossed his jacket aside earlier and now felt every inch of her soft breasts against his back. His skin burned beneath his T-shirt and his cock hardened with need. How the hell was he going to stop himself from dragging her into his arms later and burying himself inside her? He didn't know.

In an effort to distract himself, he pulled on his helmet and blew out his breath on a heavy sigh. If she felt his tension, she didn't say anything and a moment later, he pressed the starter button and the Fireblade's engine roared to life.

One hundred and fifty-three horsepower and more than seventy-eight pounds of torque throbbed between his thighs and the familiar bolt of adrenalin surged through him. Josie's arms tightened around him and all of a sudden he didn't care about anything but the two of them.

He intended to treasure this moment in time that might never come again. The girl he loved more than anyone else was pressed tightly against him, astride his motorbike. Life didn't get any better.

When they turned onto the main road that led into Watervale, Chase opened up the throttle and enjoyed the rush of wind against his face. He turned slightly and caught Josie's wide smile and contentment swelled in his heart. She loved it, just like she'd told him. He couldn't believe his luck. The woman of his dreams loved his hobby, probably as much as he did.

They rode along the highway without saying a word, heading further away from the town. So caught up was he in the wonder of the moment, that Chase didn't notice the light had faded until Josie tugged on his arm. They'd best turn around for home.

Switching on his headlight, he pulled onto the shoulder of the road and slowed. Coming to a halt, he put his foot on the ground to maintain their balance and then tugged off his helmet.

"So, what do you think?" he asked and smiled at Josie. She pulled her helmet off and shook out her hair. The ponytail had loosened and strands of golden silk hung in all sorts of crazy directions.

Her grin was wide and infectious. "It was great. I loved every minute of it. I thought my Triumph was fast. It's got nothing on this." She nodded toward the Fireblade and he smiled back at her, pleased and proud.

Their eyes locked and suddenly the world faded around them. The noise from the nearby highway disappeared. The encroaching evening was forgotten and all of a sudden, he couldn't breathe. His cock throbbed with desire, his heart beat double time. His mouth was as dry as sandpaper and he couldn't think of a single thing to say.

Josie seemed to be similarly affected. She opened her mouth and then closed it and then opened it once again. In the dimness, her eyes were huge and dark and...full of need. He moved closer and cupped her chin in his hand and slowly lowered his head. His lips touched hers with the lightest of pressure, but it was enough.

Familiar memories engulfed him. She tasted exactly the same. Her lips were soft and full and giving, just as he remembered. He'd never get enough. With a groan, he pulled her hard against him and kissed her like a man starved and tried to satiate his need.

"Chase," she breathed and his heart swelled with emotion at the sound of his name on her lips.

"Josie, Josie, Josie. Hell, I want you so much. It's been so long. God, I've missed you. You can't imagine how much."

Her arms crept up around his neck and she joined him kiss for kiss. Little sighs and moans of need escaped through her mouth. His cock throbbed painfully against the denim of his jeans. He'd have to slow things down or he'd take her right there, against the seat of his bike.

Their first time after a decade deserved so much more, no matter how much the idea of seeing her bent over the Fireblade's seat appealed to him. He wanted their second time to be so much more than that. He dreamed of lying her down across satin sheets and loving every inch of her with his tongue. He dreamed of her legs around him, holding fast to the frantic pump of his hips. She'd rise and meet each one of his hard thrusts and beg him for more.

As if also sensing the side of the highway was probably not the best place for an intimate reunion, Josie pulled slowly back and slid her arms away from his neck. Her breath still came fast, but she put some space between them and offered him a nervous smile.

"Phew, that was... I'm not sure if I can describe it."

He smiled back at her and nodded, knowing exactly what she meant. Relieved that she wasn't going to deny the chemistry between them, even after all these years, he pulled her back into his arms for one last hard hug and pressed a lingering kiss against the softness of her hair.

"We better get back," he murmured against the silky strands. He felt her nod.

"Yes. We better."

———————

Josie poured each of them a glass of Prosecco and carried both drinks out to the front porch. Chase was sitting on the loveseat that stood at the far end. He'd set it to swinging gently and appeared to be engrossed in the view of the yard. Only the last vestige of sunset was visible on the horizon.

Josie offered him a glass and he murmured his thanks. "It's beautiful out here."

She looked up and absorbed the red and purple and deep golden-orange hues that colored the evening sky and nodded. "Yes," she said with feeling. "It is."

"It must be a change from the city."

"Yes. A lot quieter, for one thing and I don't miss the daily commute, although the city has its advantages."

"Tell me," Chase murmured.

Josie made her way over to the loveseat and sat down beside him. Taking a sip from her glass, she drew in a breath and spoke.

"The city's alive with people. There's never a dull moment. Brisbane's not like Sydney or Melbourne, of course, but it has a charm all of its own. The river is busy with ferries and boats and yachts and all sorts of other watercraft and I love to go down to the port and watch the freighters coming in. They carry flags from all over the world and sometimes I wonder about the sailors on them: arriving in yet another foreign place, exploring another unfamiliar city."

She shrugged and smiled and felt a little foolish because she'd rambled on, but Chase only looked at her with gentle encouragement and she continued.

"I love the shopping, of course and all the things you can do in a city: the live shows, the musicals, the concerts. There's always something on. You're never bored there—at least, Chanel and I never were. She still lives there. She's finished her degree in medicine and is doing her internship at Royal Brisbane Hospital."

"I remember Chanel. She's a few years younger than you."

"Yes, she's three years younger. The last time you saw her was at my graduation and she was a gawky fifteen-year-old."

Chase smiled. "I recall she wore some kind of blue shiny dress that she complained long and loudly didn't fit. That's about all I remember. I had eyes only for you."

Josie's heart stopped completely and then thudded against her chest. She stared at Chase and remembered. Every word, every smile, every minute detail of that night was branded in her mind.

Chase was remembering, too, if the pool of emotion in his eyes was any indication. The light was fading fast, but he stared at her like he used to; like she was the only woman in the world. He moved closer until there was barely an inch between them.

"Josie," he croaked, his voice husky with need.

She wanted so much to kiss him, to take up where they'd left off, but this time, the purpose of his visit held her back. The mystery of the reason they were no longer together crashed into her consciousness and she eased herself away. He'd come there to tell her the truth, to give her the explanation she was owed.

She trembled at the thought of what he might say, but there could never be anything between them in the future until the past had been put to rest.

"Chase, we need to talk, remember? That's the reason that you came."

He blinked and then drew in a deep breath. Blowing it out in a rush, he nodded and then looked away.

"You're right. Yes, of course. Talk. We need to talk." He stood abruptly and gulped at the remains of his wine.

When it was empty, he set it on a low table that stood a short distance away and then ran his hands through his hair. Josie swallowed her nervousness and braced herself for what was to come.

"From the moment I spied you on the sidelines, sitting in the bleachers with that broken leg, I was in love with you. Your smile, your laughter, your presence—you lit up the stadium. I felt it clear across the other side of the football field." He shrugged and looked a little embarrassed, but the earnestness in his expression convinced her he was sincere.

"It sounds like some soppy crap from a terrible B grade movie, but it's the truth." He snagged her gaze and held it. "I still feel that way."

Josie's heart faltered and time stood still. She tried to look away, tried to break the spell, but couldn't.

With another sigh, Chase turned away. "The night of your graduation was the most magical night of my life. I couldn't wait to tell the world of our love. I couldn't wait to make you mine."

He shook his head sadly, caught up in the memories. Josie knew how he felt. She was remembering, too.

"What happened, Chase?" she asked softly. "Please, tell me."

His shoulders slumped and the light disappeared from his eyes. Slowly, like a man nearing the end of his time, he made his way back to her and sat down in the loveseat.

Now that the moment was upon her, Josie couldn't breathe. Panic clawed at her throat and all of a sudden, she didn't want to know. Surely, not knowing was better than hearing the awful truth—whatever that might be? And awful it must be or Chase would have told her a decade ago.

"Chase, you don't have to—"

"Yes, I do," he interrupted her and she saw the determination harden his face. "I do."

Josie eased out a breath between lips that were sand-dune dry and prayed for the strength to see this through. Chase's lips moved silently and she could only wonder if he was praying, too.

"The day after your graduation, the day after the most magical night of my life, my mother rushed me to a specialist at the hospital. I was poked and prodded and sent for a scan. A biopsy was done. Many hours later, after the results came back, the doctor told me I had cancer."

Josie gasped in shock and horror, never once suspecting this had been the reason for his abandonment. All the years when she'd cursed him for dumping her without a word rushed back to haunt her and she burned with shame. While she'd been thinking the worst of him, he'd been lying in pain on a hospital bed, hearing news of a devastating kind.

"W-was it malignant?" she stammered, already knowing the answer.

Chase nodded slowly. "Yes. In the rush to get to the hospital, I'd left my phone at home. I had no way to let you know."

"But what about after? You're here, alive and well. You got treatment. You got better. Why didn't you call me?" She tried hard not to sound accusatory, but the pain of his endless silence crept in. Chase moved a little closer and took both of her hands in his.

"I wanted to, believe me. There was nothing more that I wanted, but..." He shrugged helplessly.

"Don't shrug at me, Chase Barrington. I deserve better than that. I loved you with everything that I was. I wanted to be your wife!" Tears filled her eyes and she swiped at them with the back of one hand. She had to get a handle on herself. There was more to the story that Chase hadn't told her. She was sure of it.

"What kind of cancer did you have?" she demanded, suddenly realizing he hadn't told her.

He pulled his hand away from hers and leaned over to rest his elbows on his thighs. His head hung low.

She was right. There was something he hadn't told her. The certainty didn't make it any easier. Her heart pounded and she forced herself to ask again.

"Chase Barrington, you tell me *right* now. What kind of cancer did you have?"

She waited in silence with bated breath. It was the longest minute of her life. At last, he lifted his head.

"I had Stage Two testicular cancer. They removed all of one and most of the other and then I had chemo and radiotherapy to deal with the spread of it to the lymph nodes in my abdomen."

Josie gasped and tried to process what he'd told her. Before she had a chance, he spoke again.

"I was still trying to come to terms with the fact that I had cancer when the doctor started talking about infertility. I was nineteen and someone was telling me the treatment I needed to stay alive would make me infertile. I'd never father a child. I'd never know that joy. All the things we'd talked about, all the plans we'd made. They dissolved into ashes in front of me."

His voice hitched with emotion and Josie's tears fell unheeded down her cheeks. She couldn't believe what he'd told her, but knew it was the truth. It explained so much; it explained everything. Her heart weighed heavy with sadness for all that they'd lost, for all that could have been.

"Oh, Chase," she gasped and threw herself in his arms. Taking refuge against the strong wall of his chest, she cried and cried and cried. A long while later, the deluge subsided to the occasional sob and it was then that the guilt set in.

All through her crying jag, Chase had held her pressed tenderly against him, murmuring soothing noises against her hair, but it wasn't all about her. *He* had lost, too: perhaps even more so. He'd mourned the loss of their dream for a decade, believing everything was lost. She'd always maintained hope that one day, they'd find each other and everything would be all right once again.

"I'm so, so sorry, Chase. How could I have blubbered all over you like that? *You're* the one who had cancer. You're the one with the right to be devastated."

Chase stared at her, his green eyes a sea of desolation. "I was devastated. I *am* devastated. Every time I think about it, I have to try hard not to get angry at the hand I was dealt. It would have been okay if it had only affected me, but *your* dream was destroyed, too. It wasn't just me facing a very different future. The life you'd envisaged was also gone."

He shook his head slowly as if he were still unable to believe it. "We'd talked about the family we'd have. We'd even named our kids. You couldn't wait to be a mother. I couldn't tell you the dream was over. That it would never happen with me. I-I just couldn't do it." His voice cracked and he bit down on a sob.

Josie's heart broke at the anguish etched onto his handsome face. She wanted to erase it, to wipe away his pain, but she didn't know how.

"It's okay," she whispered and laid her palm tenderly against his cheek. The roughness of his five o'clock shadow brushed against her hand. "I understand. I wish you'd told me, but I understand why you didn't."

"Are you... Are you still mad at me for leaving without a word?" he uttered hoarsely.

She shook her head vehemently. "How can you even ask me that? I spent ten years being mad at you and loving you just the same. Now that I know the truth, the anger has disappeared. All I feel is love."

Chase's eyes widened in surprise and hope bloomed on his face. "Love? You still love me?"

Fresh tears sprang in Josie's eyes, but she nodded and smiled at him and tried to make him understand.

"Of course I still love you. It's never changed. A decade, a lifetime later and I love you as much as I always have. I love you with every fiber of my being. It's just the way it is. Even when I wanted to hate you, I couldn't stop loving you."

Chase leaned forward and held her head while he planted a hard kiss against her lips. "I love you, too. God, you'll never know how much." With that, he released her and stood and moved away. Josie frowned in confusion.

"What is it, Chase? What's the matter?"

He spun on his heel and faced her, his eyes bleak with despair. "Don't you see? This changes nothing. You love me. I love you. It doesn't cure my infertility. It doesn't give you a child."

Josie's jaw dropped open in shock. It was swiftly replaced with anger. No longer able to sit, she stood and advanced upon him.

"*You can't be serious?* You can't seriously expect me to believe you think your ability to provide me with a child is more important than spending my life with you?"

Chase's continued silence infuriated her.

"How can you think so little of me? How can you think me

so shallow? So selfish? So utterly self-absorbed? How can you think your worth to me is measured in your ability to father a child?" Her breath came fast and she made an effort to control her temper. In a slightly calmer voice, she continued.

"I love you, Chase. *You.* Not your body, not your bike, not your illustrious career. Love isn't about what you can give me. It's about how you make me feel. It's about me wanting to be the best person I can be—to make me worthy; to make you proud."

He shook his head, unconvinced. "But, you want to be a mother. It was all you used to talk about. You were born to be one. I saw you with the Logan boys and with Riley and Kate's twins. The yearning's still there. You can't tell me any different."

Frustration surged through her and she tried once again to make him see. "You're right, I wanted to be a mother. I still want to be a mother and yes, I wanted your babies. I won't deny it's true. I dreamed of the day I would hold our child in my arms. A little boy or girl with your emerald eyes and curls of golden brown. I couldn't wait for it to happen.

"Now, I find it's not possible, that a child of yours will never be, but it doesn't change the way I feel about you. You're so much more to me than a sperm donor and you know what? You're really starting to piss me off that you continue to think of me so poorly. Child or no child, I'll love you until I die. Get used to it."

A tiny glimmer of hope flickered in Chase's eyes. Josie stared at him and willed him to believe her. The death of her dream of one day carrying Chase's child was a blow, but she'd mourn the loss of that later. Right now, the question of Chase's fertility didn't matter. All that was important was that she convince him she was telling the truth.

A smile broke out across his face. He took a step toward her and then another. Within seconds, she was engulfed within his strong embrace and pressed so tightly against him, she could barely breathe. A moment later, he released her, but only to swing her up in his arms. He strode across the porch, with moonlight and the soft glow from the living room lighting the way. She hadn't even noticed the evening was fully upon them.

Bending his head, he took her mouth in a kiss so sweet and passionate, it almost brought tears to her eyes once again. His expression was one of love and tenderness as he gazed down at her. "I love you so much, Josie Munro."

Kicking the door closed behind them, he headed straight down the hall.

"What about the plumber?" she murmured against his neck, suddenly remembering.

Chase came to an abrupt halt and did an about-face. Striding back to the front door, he turned the lock. "The plumber can wait."

CHAPTER 21

Chase opened the door to Josie's bedroom and walked through the doorway. His arms tightened momentarily around her before he slid her purposefully down the length of his hard body. Her booted feet hit the floor and still he didn't release her.

His head dipped low and he captured her mouth, unable to get enough. She tasted so sweet and beautiful and familiar. She tasted like *his*. The thought sent a ray of wonder shooting through his heart. He still couldn't believe she loved him, had always loved him and that even though he couldn't give her a much-longed-for child, it didn't matter; her feelings for him were as strong as ever.

The miracle of it lit him up anew and his heart filled with the sheer joy of it. The feel of her in his arms was every bit as amazing as he remembered and he vowed silently to never again let her go.

With his arms still about her, he walked them to her bed and with one hand switched on the lamp on the nightstand. At once, the room was filled with a soft yellow glow and Chase sighed with pleasure. He wanted to capture every intake of breath, every expression on her beautiful face. He wanted to taste and touch and love every inch of her silky smooth skin. He'd lost ten years. He wasn't going to lose another second.

Drawing her back hard against him, he recalled from some distant memory how sensitive her ears were to the touch and gently nipped at her earlobe. He was rewarded with a moan and a shudder and she tipped her head back to give him greater access. He eagerly obliged.

His tongue snaked out and traced the intricate whorls and crevices over and over again.

"Oh, Chase, that feels so good. You've always known how to turn me on. I can't believe how many years we've wasted."

"Me neither," he responded between kisses, "and I'm going to do my best to make up for lost time. Starting right now."

She smiled and reached up and took his head between her hands and then forced it lower. On tiptoes, she pressed her mouth against his and kissed him until he was breathless. "You and me both," she murmured with a wicked glint in her eye.

The blood rushed from his head to his groin and his cock hardened almost painfully. He ground his hips against her, letting her feel how much he wanted her. He was rewarded by her sudden intake of breath and the darkening of her beautiful eyes.

"Make love to me, Chase," she whispered.

His heart pounded and his breath came fast. With hands that weren't quite steady, he reached for the ends of her T-shirt and eased it over her head. She wore a white lacy scrap of fabric that somehow passed for a bra. His fingers cupped her breasts.

The perfect mounds filled his hands and then spilled right over. Through the lace, he caressed the slightly darker nubs of her nipples with his thumbs until they were pebbled and hard.

Her heart beat hard beneath his palm and a pulse played a rapid staccato in her neck and yet, she stood still and silent and let him touch her and look his fill.

With gentle hands, he reached around behind her and worked at the clasp at her back. With a sigh of relief, he released it and her wondrous breasts sprang free. Hardly even aware of what he was doing, he flung the bra away and stared at her.

Her breasts were high and firm and perfectly

proportioned. Her nipples were a delicate shade of pink. He'd been with many women in the last few years and yet, he hadn't seen anyone so beautiful.

Of course, he was biased. Josie was the only woman he'd ever loved—but still, she looked like an artist's model, in perfect proportion.

"Why are you staring?" she whispered, a blush staining her cheeks. He lowered his gaze, but then looked back at her and told her the truth.

"I've never seen anyone more beautiful."

The stain on her cheeks grew darker, but she smiled and leaned up to kiss him. "Thank you. From you, that means a great deal."

Suddenly eager to see the rest of her, his hands went to her jeans. Making short work of the button and zipper, he slid them down her hips. He got to her feet and remembered her boots and pushed her gently back toward the bed. Smiling her understanding, she sat down and let him tug them off her feet.

Once the way was clear, he finished removing her jeans and tossed them aside. Her white lace panties quickly followed and all of a sudden she was naked. She lay back on the bed and again, he stared at her, unable to tear his gaze away.

She'd always been beautiful, but at eighteen, she'd been in the first blush of womanhood. Her hips had been almost straight, not rounded. Her waist, not quite defined. Ten years down the track and there was nothing girlish about her. Josie Munro was one hundred percent woman and he was going to die if he didn't have her.

Urgency now tore through him and he dragged his shirt off and threw it to the floor. Perching on the end of the bed, he likewise disposed of his boots. A minute later, his jeans came off and joined the growing pile on the floor. Within moments, he was naked and pressed up against her, skin to skin. With his heart still pounding, he drew in a deep breath and let out a deep sigh of satisfaction and relief.

He was home.

———————

Josie turned in Chase's arms and pressed her breasts against his skin, loving the feel of his muscled chest against her. The light scattering of dark hair that covered his pectorals tickled her. As far as she could recall, he hadn't had chest hair when he was younger. It was only one of the things that had changed since the night they were last together.

Reaching up, she tangled her fingers in the softness of his curls and tugged at them gently. Her hand slid down to cup his cheek and she stared into his eyes, hardly daring to believe he was there. For so many years she'd dreamed of this day, when he'd come back into her life and still love her. And here he was. In the flesh. In the very *firm* flesh.

Heat crept up her neck at the thought and feel of his erection. It pressed insistently against her stomach, demanding attention. Although she wasn't inexperienced when it came to men, she was far from confident and she could only hope Chase would take charge and show her what he wanted.

As if sensing her insecurity, he tilted her chin upward and kissed her tenderly on the lips. Warm and pliant, his mouth moved over hers, seeking, searching, giving. A surge of desire ignited deep inside her and she kissed him back a little frantically. Her tongue danced with his and at last found its way inside and she explored the warm recesses of his mouth.

He groaned against her lips and she couldn't help but feel a thrill of satisfaction. This beautiful man loved her and he wanted her for his own.

Chase moved until she was beneath him and his legs straddled hers. Her arms came around his neck and she drew him down for another mindless kiss. His erection pressed more insistently against her stomach and she yearned to have him inside her. Moving against him, she lifted her hips and tried wordlessly to tell him.

"Can you feel how much I want you?" he whispered against her lips.

She nodded and then replied, "I want you, too."

His arms tightened around her and he bent down to claim yet another fiery kiss. His knee nudged her thighs apart and he settled himself between them.

"Um... Do you want to use a condom?" she murmured and tried to ignore the flames that burned a path to her cheeks.

Chase stilled and then came up on one elbow and looked down at her with tenderness and love. One side of his mouth tilted in a little smile. "Well, we can if you want, but I'm pretty sure we don't have to worry about the pregnancy angle. We undergo regular medicals in the police force. I'm clean and disease free, but you don't have to take my word for it. What about you?"

The teasing glint in his eyes took the edge off his question and Josie smiled back at him. "No, all good for me, too."

"Then, I guess the answer's no," he said huskily and sealed it with a kiss.

Desire quickly built again and Josie's heart thumped in her chest. Her clit throbbed with need and she tingled and burned all over. She wanted him and she wanted him now. She told him as much in as few words as she could manage.

He didn't take much convincing. Within moments, his cock pressed against her entrance and she held her breath in anticipation. His hips flexed and his cock slid inside her, filling her, stretching her like no other.

She gasped and focused on the feel of him, way deep inside her. Slowly, slowly he withdrew and then plunged inside her again. Over and over, he loved her with his body.

"Oh, God, you feel so good. Oh, Jose, you feel like heaven."

His words glided over her and heated her desire to a fever pitch. She moved against him and met his thrusts, clinging to his broad shoulders. The feelings inside her continued to grow and the pressure in her core intensified. She tightened her hold on him, just as he tightened his hold on her.

With a cry, she reached her climax and toppled over the other side. A moment later, he joined her and together they found their release.

It seemed like a long while later, but it was probably only a few minutes, when Chase stirred and shifted his weight off her. He lay on his back beside her and gathered her close against him. She listened, sated and replete, as their breathing slowly returned to normal.

"I love you, Josie Munro," he whispered and pressed a soft kiss against her hair.

"I love you, too, Chase Barrington." She smiled, her heart alight with the sheer joy of it. This was the way it was meant to be. She and Chase. Together. United, as one. It may have been a decade later than it should have, but as someone far wiser than she had once said, it was better late than never.

Chase came awake with a start, frowning at the unfamiliar ceiling above him. Morning sun drifted in through the window. Josie stirred in her sleep and all at once, their night of lovemaking came back to him. He couldn't contain the smile or the surge of joy deep inside him when he thought of all that they'd said and all that they'd shared and all that was yet to come.

Unable to help himself, he reached for her and drew her into his arms. She sighed softly, still mostly asleep, and snuggled against him. Content to lie there all day with her in his arms, he resisted the urge to look at his watch. Five minutes. Ten. It was all he could last. With reluctance, he checked the time.

Five past eight. His heart sank. It was well past time to get up. His shift started at eight-thirty and he could hardly explain to Riley why he was late. Somehow, he didn't think his boss would take kindly to his explanation. As gently as he could manage, he shook Josie awake.

"Hey, Jose. Wake up, sweetheart. It's time to get up. We have to go to work." She mumbled something unintelligible under her breath and he smiled at her reluctance. He'd never slept with her until morning. It was a unique experience for both of them, but much as he wanted to savor the moment, they were both required at work. Knowing he had to wake her, he tried again.

"Josie, it's me. Chase. It's getting late, honey. It's already way past eight. I, for one, have to get going and I'm sure you probably do, too."

This time he got a response: A single eye came open. "Chase? It can't be morning already."

He smiled down at her, his heart filling with tenderness at the reluctance on her face. "I'm afraid it is, babe and what's more, if we don't get up and get going, we're both going to be late."

"What time is it?" she mumbled, burying her face in the pillow.

"It's well after eight. You need to get up and so do I." There was a full three seconds of delay and then his words seemed to find their mark. She sat up in such a hurry, the pillow went flying.

"Did you say it's already past eight? Oh, my goodness! I have a patient coming in at eight-thirty. Why didn't you wake me earlier? I need to shower and wash my hair. I need to—"

The last of her words were cut off when she closed the bathroom door. Chase bit back a chuckle and reached for his clothes. His shower would have to wait.

A shriek from the bathroom gave him pause and he frowned and walked over to the closed door.

"Jose, are you all right in there? What's the matter?"

"I forgot the toilet wasn't working in here. Darn, I'll have to use the one in the main bathroom." Wrapped in a towel, she emerged and made her way quickly across the room toward the door that led into the hall.

"You might need to re-book the plumber. I hope he didn't turn up last night and expect to come in," he said. She threw him a dark look and stalked through the doorway. Chase chuckled all over again. Damn, he loved that she wasn't a morning person. Neither was he.

As soon as Chase had a moment to spare at the station, he dialed Josie's office number and spoke to a woman who identified herself as Moira. As politely as he could manage, he asked to speak to Josie.

"I'm sorry, Detective Barrington, she has a patient with her. She doesn't like to be disturbed while she's with a patient."

Disappointment surged through him. It had been hours since he'd spoken to her. He needed to hear her voice. He tried again.

"Moira, I understand, but it's really important that I speak with her. It's... It's about a case she's been working on. Do you think you could interrupt her? I promise, it won't take long."

The woman sighed, but agreed to put him through. A moment later, Josie answered the phone.

"Detective Barrington, how nice of you to call, but I'm kind of busy right now."

"I know. The dragon lady told me."

"Moira's a sweetheart. I hope you weren't mean to her."

"Of course not, but she wasn't going to put me through and I really needed to speak with you."

Josie's tone sharpened with concern. "Is there something wrong? Are the Logan boys okay?"

"Yes, of course. At least, I assume so." He paused and then added softly, "I just wanted to hear your voice. I wanted to remind myself that it was real. That last night was real. That you and I..."

"It was real, Chase," she whispered, "and it was magical. I can't wait to do it all over again. And again. And again."

Chase groaned and his cock pulsed with blood. Stealing

a look around him, he became aware of the other officers in the room. A couple of them shot him curious looks. He held the phone closer to his mouth and lowered his voice.

"What time do you finish today?"

"My last appointment's at five. With a bit of luck, I'll be out of here a little after six."

"Dinner?"

"Sounds lovely." She sighed.

"How about we meet at The Bullet as soon as you finish?"

"But I'll still be in my work clothes."

"Why do you think I care what clothes you're wearing? I'm only going to take them off you the minute I get you alone."

She laughed softly and his heart filled with quiet joy. "You're a bad man, Chase Barrington."

"Yes, but you love me anyway."

"You're right," she said solemnly. "I do."

"See you at The Bullet."

"I'll be there."

A day had never dragged on for so long, but finally Josie closed the door on her last patient. She'd spent the day fighting hard to concentrate. All her mind wanted to do was to replay the previous night she'd spent with Chase and to look forward to many more nights to come.

She still couldn't believe the reason he'd disappeared a decade ago. Even now, after she'd had some time to process it, she was still a little stunned. He'd had cancer; surgery; chemo and radiation and he'd done it all alone. Well, his parents had probably been with him, but he'd done it without her by his side.

She couldn't imagine how shocked and scared he must have been. He'd been all of nineteen—barely an adult and facing such momentous, life changing news. And yet, he'd come through it. He'd gone on to complete his police training at the Academy. He'd returned to his hometown and carved out a successful career.

She could tell Riley respected him and that was no mean feat to achieve. Her brother was very demanding and had an uncanny ability to read a person like a book. It's what made him such a good commander. He and Kate both treated Chase like an equal and even more telling, like a friend.

She thought of the issues Chase had with his fertility and closed her eyes against the brief stab of pain. She couldn't remember the number of times she'd daydreamed about bearing his children: three girls and three boys. She'd had it all worked out. She'd even named them. They'd been miniatures of Chase: curly brown hair, green eyes, beautiful smiles. She'd fallen in love with them before they'd been born. Now they'd never be born. Never would she know the sheer joy of holding Chase's child in her arms.

The tears she'd managed to hold off last night now pressed behind her eyes. She bit her lip, but a sob escaped, slipping past her tightly held self-control. It was followed by another and then another. She cried quietly.

The loss of her dream of being a mother to Chase's children was a biggie. She owed it to herself to grieve. It was much healthier than keeping it locked up inside her and pretending it no longer mattered. Their love had stood the test of time. She was sure that together they would make it. While their past was gone and their future had yet to be written, they stood strong and sure in the present and that's what mattered.

She glanced at her watch and her heart skipped a beat. It was way past six. Chase would be wondering where she was. She swiped at the tears that had dried on her cheeks and collected her handbag from where she'd stowed it in the bottom drawer of her desk. Hurrying out of her office, she opened the door to the staff amenities.

Bending over the sink, she splashed a handful of water over her face and then patted it dry with paper towel. She pulled out a hairbrush and tugged at the band that held her hair back off her face and then quickly brushed it. Deciding to leave it loose, she tossed the band back into her handbag, along with the brush. A quick swipe of crimson lipstick and a toilet stop and she was ready to go.

She headed into a stall and then stopped short.

"Darn." She'd forgotten to call the plumber. The toilet in her bathroom was still blocked. It was probably lucky the Logan boys were no longer staying with her. Not that they couldn't survive with only one toilet for a few days. She'd grown up in a household of nine and for many years, they'd functioned without a second toilet. It was funny how quickly people got used to the extra conveniences in their lives.

With a wry smile, she finished her ablutions, washed her hands in the sink and headed out the door, her heart pulsing in excitement with every step that brought her closer to Chase.

The door to The Bullet swung open and brought with it a gust of cold air. A winter chill had set, reminding all of them it was late in the fall. Chase spun around on his barstool and then cursed under his breath when he realized it wasn't Josie. For the hundredth time, he looked at his watch.

She said she'd be finished a little after six. It was now going on for half-past. Surely she hadn't changed her mind? Why would she stand him up? They were good, weren't they? She'd assured him his revelations hadn't mattered; that she loved him anyway. Was she having second thoughts in the cold, harsh light of day?

He made an impatient sound in the back of his throat and took another sip from his beer. He was being stupid. Of course she hadn't changed her mind. She loved him. She'd be there. He was sure of it.

The door opened again and he steeled himself against turning around to face it yet again. Instead, he forced himself to relax and enjoy his drink. For a weeknight, The

Bullet was relatively lively. Most of the tables were filled with patrons enjoying dinner. Chase's stomach grumbled at the thought and he remembered it had been a long time since he'd chewed on the sandwich he'd bought from the corner deli.

Having skipped dinner the night before and breakfast that day, it was no wonder he was hungry.

"Is this seat taken?"

And there she was.

Hiding his relief, Chase smiled wide at Josie and then engulfed her in a hug. "Hey, you," he murmured, his voice husky with emotion. "I missed you."

Her arms tightened around his waist and her voice was muffled against his jacket. "I missed you, too."

He breathed in the scent of her hair and his heart filled with love. She smelled so familiar, so right, so *his*. A surge of protectiveness rushed through him and it was all he could do not to take her by the hand and haul her out of there and keep her safe from whatever lurked in the shadows.

Where had that idea come from?

Giving himself a mental shake, he relaxed his hold and eased her away from him. He was being ridiculous. Life was to be lived—the good, the bad and the downright ugly of it. He saw more than his fair share of the ugly, it was true, but it also made him appreciate that much more the good. Thrusting away his grim thoughts, he offered Josie a smile.

"Can I buy you a drink?"

She smiled back at him and shook her hair out of her face. She'd left it loose and it hung in soft golden waves around her shoulders. He remembered the silky feel of it in his fingers and ached to touch her again. But for now, it would have to wait.

"I'll have a vodka, lime and soda, thanks."

"Coming right up." Chase turned away and signaled the barman. After giving him their order, Chase turned back to Josie.

"Long day?"

She grimaced. "You can say that again. I had a full book

of appointments, but the day seemed to drag on forever. It must have had something to do with the fact I was meeting you at the end of it."

"I'm hearing you, babe. I couldn't tell you how many times I looked at the time. I think the blokes in the squad room thought there was something wrong with me. Even your brother was giving me strange looks."

She laughed. "I can't wait to see Riley's face when we tell him about us."

Chase's smile was a little more restrained. "How do you think he'll take it?"

"He'll be fine, don't worry. He likes you. I can tell. I'm sure he'll be happy for us."

"He likes me as a work colleague and friend. It's not quite the same thing as a brother-in-law."

Josie's eyes widened and her mouth fell open in shock. "Brother-in-law? Are you saying…? Do you want to…?"

"Get married? Of course I do. I've wanted to marry you from the moment I saw you. Nothing that's happened over the last ten years has changed that." He frowned and searched her face. "Has anything changed for you?"

Her smile lit up her face and took his breath away. She threw herself in his arms and kissed him soundly on the lips.

"Of course not. I told you last night. I'll love you until I die."

Chase picked her up and swung her around, happiness flooding through him. When he at last set her back down, he went down on one knee and took her hand in his. She gasped and a faint blush stained her cheeks, but her smile was soft and loving. He stared at her, giving the moment the solemnity it demanded.

"Josie Munro, will you do me the honor of becoming my wife?"

"Yes, Chase! Oh, yes!" Tears sparkled in her eyes. He stood and once again took her in his arms and held her close. Never again would he lose her. Never again would he let her go. He kissed her with all the love and hope in his heart.

The crowd in the bar erupted into spontaneous applause.

Sheepishly, Chase lifted his head and grinned. Josie broke into laughter and ducked her head.

"I hope you meant it, Chase because most of Watervale will hear about it before morning. I suppose I'd better call my brother."

"Do you want me to do it?"

Josie held his gaze, her eyes bright with emotion. "That's okay. I'll do it, but the fact that you want to is all I need to know. I do love you, Chase."

She leaned over and kissed him again and then slowly pulled away. A moment later, she tugged her phone from her handbag and held it up to her ear.

The barman arrived with their drinks and Chase fished a few bills from his wallet. Josie broke the news of their engagement to Riley and then spoke to Kate. Amidst laughter and tears, she finally ended the call.

"How did they take it?" Chase asked softly, already knowing from Josie's demeanor that the news had gone down well.

"Kate was a little surprised, but Riley wasn't surprised at all. They both asked me to pass on their congratulations. Kate wants to get together as soon as possible and begin making plans." She smiled a little shakily, as if still coming to terms with the speed of it. "You... You don't mind, do you?"

"Hell, no! Get to it, babe. The sooner the better. I've waited a decade for this. Now that I've finally found you again, I don't want to waste another minute until I can call you Doctor Barrington."

"I might want to keep being known as Doctor Munro? Or maybe even Doctor Munro-Barrington? That kind of has a ring to it, don't you think?"

Chase smiled. "I don't give a damn what you call yourself. As long as I can call you my wife, I'll be a very happy man."

"I guess I'd better call the rest of the family."

Chase groaned. "We could be here all night. I'm starving, woman. How about we go and order some food and you can call them while we're waiting?"

Josie tossed her phone back into her handbag and collected her drink. "That sounds like a very good idea."

———

In between phone calls, Josie finished her crab meat and sweet corn soup and shared the basket of garlic bread. Chase wolfed down a huge dish of pasta carbonara and then asked to see the dessert menu.

"How can you possibly fit anything else in?" she asked, aghast.

"Hey, I'm a growing boy," he protested with a smile. "Besides, I missed dinner last night and breakfast this morning. In the last thirty hours or so, I've had nothing more than a couple of sandwiches from the deli and a bottle of water. Yesterday I spent the day in court and today I didn't have time for anything more elaborate. I'm re-charging, that's all."

She rolled her eyes, but softened it with a grin. When she thought of the reason Chase had been in court, her smile slowly faded.

"You didn't tell me how Harton's expert witness fared yesterday."

Chase sighed. "Doctor Leonard Heather was everything you could hope for, which is great news for Daniel. Despite John Wall's rigorous cross examination, the guy came across as convincing and believable and he had a string of qualifications to back him up. Of course, he arrived at the conclusion that Daniel had no idea what he was doing and if he did, he didn't realize that it was criminally wrong."

"The exact opposite to the conclusion I drew," Josie murmured without rancor.

"Yes. Now, it's up to the judge to decide."

Josie drew in a deep breath and slowly nodded, her thoughts on the young boy whose future now hung in the balance. "How was Daniel? Did you speak with him?"

Chase shook his head. "He was with his lawyer and his

aunt was there. She seemed a little rattled by everything, as you'd expect. Being inside a courtroom for the first time can be intimidating for most people. But she was there, at least. That has to be a good sign."

Josie closed her eyes briefly and nodded, thankful that both boys had someone who cared looking out for them. "Yes, that's good. I'm glad."

Chase leaned over and took her hand. "Daniel will be okay, sweetheart. Both of them will get through this."

She grimaced and swiped at the tears that welled up in her eyes. "Yes, I know. I just wish I could be there for them, help them in some way. Daniel, especially. He's hurting so badly. I hope his aunt knows that."

"I'm sure she does. From what I could tell, she appears to be a decent person and she's Daniel's family. That has to help."

Josie sniffed. "Yes, you're right. I'm sure she'll love him—both of them—and take care of them like they need. I just wish—" She broke off, knowing to voice the words was futile. She wasn't kin to the Logan boys. She had no claim to them.

"Hey, how did your parents take our news?" Chase asked softly and she loved him for his attempt to change the subject.

"Good. Great. They're over the moon. Mom had convinced herself I was never going to get married. She's so pleased for us."

"Does she know about…?"

Josie shook her head. "No. It's no one else's business but ours. If and when we're ready to tell the rest of the family, we'll do it in our own time."

Chase frowned. "Um… There's only one thing. I… I might have mentioned something to Riley."

Josie looked up at him, confused. "Riley? When did you talk with Riley?"

Chase turned his face away and stared at the table. "Um…the other night. We kind of…got talking. I told him about us."

She stared at him, shocked. "You told him about us? You mean the 'us' of a decade ago?"

"Kind of. Not everything, but...enough. He knows about the cancer and my infertility."

Josie blinked and tried to take it in. She was surprised and a little taken aback, but she wasn't mad. How could she be mad? Chase had carried the secret around with him for ten years. She ought to be glad he'd found the courage to talk about it—even if it was with her brother.

"Okay," she said slowly.

"Are you sure it's okay? I mean, we promised not to tell anyone about the year we'd had together. I didn't mean to break your confidence. It was just that..."

"It's all right, Chase. I promise. I'm okay with it. I'm just a little surprised."

"Riley won't tell anyone if we don't want him too."

"I know."

Chase looked at her with searching eyes. "Are you sure you're okay?"

With a tender smile, she leaned across the table and gave him a soft kiss on the mouth.

"I'm sure."

———————

Scott Jones gritted his teeth and completed another push-up off the floor of his cell. Each time he came up on his arms, he lifted his head and stared at the calendar. One more day and he'd be out. One more day and he'd be free of this stink-hole; he'd be on the outside. One more day and he'd be free—free to put his plan into action. Revenge was so close he could taste it.

"This one's for you, Neil. Rest in peace, mate," he gasped and finished the last repetition. Every muscle in his body screamed for rest, but he wasn't finished yet. Flipping onto his back, he started in on the sit-ups. One down, one hundred and ninety-nine to go. Once again, on each upward lift, he pinned his gaze to the calendar.

He'd made some enquires about the town of Watervale. According to most sources, if he got out of prison early enough, he ought to make it to the town just after sunset. It would give him time to locate the woman the paper had identified as Doctor Josie Munro. She'd given evidence for the prosecution. He only hoped she'd done the right thing by Neil.

If she'd recommended the boy stand trial for murder and answer for his crimes, Scott might—just might—let her live. And once he was finished with her, he was going to track down Doctor Leonard Heather. That prick had been paid for by the defense. There was no way he'd given evidence that would support Scott's mate.

Scott grinned manically through his clenched teeth and forced himself up into another stomach crunch. The asshole who'd sided with the boy who'd murdered Neil had a number on his back. It was only a matter of time before he met his maker. Scott would make sure of it.

CHAPTER 22

Daniel kicked at the dirt with the toe of his battered sneaker and watched the puff of dust rise above it. The lunchbreak was almost over and soon he'd return to class. It had been two days since the judge had adjourned the case for deliberation and Daniel had chosen to return to school. His aunt told him it was his decision; that she'd understand if he wanted to stay at home. Daniel needed to do something normal because after tomorrow, being normal might never be his again.

He wasn't stupid. His barrister had made it clear if he went to trial and pleaded guilty, he'd be heading off to jail. The best they could hope for was a plea bargain that would reduce the charge of murder down to manslaughter. Even so, the likelihood of a custodial sentence was extraordinarily high.

Custodial sentence. That was a fancy way of saying jail. The ball of dread that had cemented itself way down deep inside him ever since that fateful night now shifted and swelled until he was choking from the weight of it. He gasped and clutched at his belly and bent low at the waist.

"Daniel, are you all right?"

He squinted through the pain and spied the kind face of the school counselor. Miss White was nice. She'd spoken to him when he'd returned to school after the shooting and again when his father was hospitalized.

He had his aunt, of course, and she'd been more than

kind, but she was way older than his parents and sometimes he wondered how much she really understood. It had been a long time since she was a kid. He suspected things were different now.

"Would you like to go to the infirmary? Perhaps I should call your aunt?"

He shook his head no, but agreed to go with her. He was fine. He didn't want to worry his aunt. She worried enough about him already. Besides, nothing and no one could fix him. It was way too late for that.

The best that he could hope for was that his dad would get better and come home and at least be there for Jason. Lately, it seemed his little brother had become a shadow— silent and barely moving. It was like the reality of what had happened, including Daniel's court case, had finally caught up with him and he was on a downward spiral. Daniel tried to remember the last time he'd heard his brother laugh or even smile and he came up empty.

He knew darn well laughter and even the thought of it had well and truly disappeared from *his* life. Probably for good, but he wanted to think Jason might find his way back there again.

The pain from his stomach subsided, but he let the counselor hand him over to the school nurse. The adults spoke in muted tones, but he understood the gist of their conversation. The concerned looks the two of them turned on him with predictable regularity said it all.

He'd only been back at school two days and already he didn't know how he was going to cope. The few friends he'd had before the nightmare started had slowly drifted away. They wanted to stick by him, he could tell, but it really was just too hard. Most kids now kept their distance; some of them were even scared of him.

His lawyer had warned him that even if the matter wasn't committed for trial, it could be weeks before he was sentenced. More psychiatric reports and assessments would be ordered and more statements would be prepared. Incarcerating a child wasn't done lightly, his lawyer assured him and the court wanted to make sure the punishment fit the crime. Until he came back to the court for sentencing, if that was how things panned out, he'd remain on bail and try to carry on as usual and forget about it.

Daniel scoffed quietly and shook his head. Forget about it. *As if.* There was as much likelihood of that happening as there was of his mother rising from the dead.

Josie finished typing up the notes on her last patient and saved the file. As they had done with predictable regularity since the night he'd arrived on his Fireblade, her thoughts drifted to Chase. They'd spent both nights since, catching up on old times and on things that had happened while they'd been apart. He'd cooked steaks on the barbeque at his place one night and last night, they'd eaten in at hers. The evenings and the nights spent with him had become the time she looked forward to most and she couldn't wait until one or the other of them didn't have to leave to go back home.

Home.

Home was where Chase was, wherever that might be. As much as she loved her cottage, she'd only taken a short-term lease. She wondered whether the owner would be willing to listen to an offer to purchase the place. She wondered what Chase would think.

His two-bedroom condo rubbed shoulders with a dozen other units housed together in a stark, red brick building reminiscent of apartment blocks that had been built in the early seventies. Whilst his unit had been comfortably decorated inside with modern pieces and bold splashes of color, the exterior of the building left a lot to be desired.

It was an understatement to say that style hadn't been at the top of the architect's list during the design brief. To add insult to injury, a garden made up mostly of weeds bordered the sidewalk that fronted a busy road. It couldn't compare to the peace and tranquillity of her little rural cottage.

The thought of putting in an offer on the place took root and began to grow. The surrounding acres could be put to good use. She'd always dreamed of a veggie patch and space for a few animals. A dog or two, maybe even a couple of sheep. And chickens. It would be fun to collect the eggs.

She smiled wryly at her wayward thoughts but couldn't quite get the idea out of her mind. She'd talk to Chase about it. Sound him out. Hopefully he wasn't too attached to his place.

The phone at her elbow rang and she picked it up. "Josie Munro."

"Josie," Moira replied. "I have Belinda Murphy from Family Services on the line."

Josie's heart skipped a beat and then she silently calmed herself. The Logan boys were fine. *Why wouldn't they be?*

"Thank you, Moira. Put her through." Josie took a deep breath and eased it out.

"Josie, it's Belinda. The Logan children are fine, but I-I'm afraid I need your help again."

"Really? What's happened?"

"Nothing to be worried about. Well, nothing directly affecting the boys. It's their aunt. Her elderly mother's taken quite ill. She's had a stroke and is in the hospital. It's rather serious, from what I can gather. Their aunt needs to return home immediately."

"Can't the boys go with her? I assume you're talking about their grandmother?"

"You're right, but from what I've been able to gather, the children have never met her. Kelly Logan was somewhat estranged from her family. I haven't had time to find out why. Besides, the children's aunt is going to be rather busy with her mother and has asked if the boys can stay here. We're hoping Trevor Logan might be released from the hospital soon but it's not going to be today."

"What do you need me to do, Belinda?"

"I was wondering... That is, would you mind having the

boys again for a day or two? I promise it won't be any longer than that. I spoke to the doctor treating their father only an hour ago. He's happy with Trevor's progress and expects to discharge him very soon. The boys will then be allowed to return home with him."

"Of course, I'm happy to help and don't worry about how long it takes for Trevor to return. I'm happy to have the boys for as long as they need me."

"Oh, thank you, Josie," the woman gushed with relief. "You're a real lifesaver. Again. You really should think about registering to be a foster carer."

Josie let the idea settle in her mind. It could be something she'd look into. Right now, she had to look after the Logans. "Maybe one day, I will," she answered and then added, "Where are the boys now?"

"They're still in school. Do you need directions?"

"No, I'm good, thanks. I collected them from there the other day."

"Of course you did. Well, if you need anything, please don't hesitate to let me know. I'm here to help."

Josie bit back a smile. "Thank you, Belinda. I will. Oh, have you called the schools? Do they need to be told I'll be collecting the boys?"

"I haven't yet. I wanted to check with you first. But I'm happy to call them now and let them know you'll be stopping by. I'll leave it up to them to tell Daniel and Jason."

"Okay, well, I guess I'll talk to you later."

"As soon as I know when Trevor's being released, I'll let you know."

"That would be great. The boys must be elated to know that their dad will soon be home."

"Actually, I haven't had a chance to tell them. I only spoke to the doctor an hour ago. The boys have been in school all day."

"Of course. Do you want me to mention it to them?" Josie asked.

"If you want to. It might lift their spirits to know things will soon be back to normal."

Josie refrained from commenting. She was sure when Belinda had a chance to think about what she'd said, she'd realize things would never be normal for the Logan family again.

After bidding each other farewell, Josie ended the call and then sat back in her chair with a sigh. Her last patient was due shortly. With a bit of luck, she'd be finished in time to collect the boys. She was filled with anticipation at the thought of spending a little more time with them, even for just a couple of nights.

———————————

Josie made the all-too-familiar walk to the principal's office of Watervale High School and waited for Daniel to appear. She'd finished with her client and had only minutes to spare to get to the school on time. She could have called Chase to see if he could collect the boys, but she didn't want to frighten them unnecessarily by having a police officer arrive at the school.

A few minutes later, Daniel came out of the principal's office and offered her a tiny smile and an even smaller wave.

"Hi, Daniel. I'm sorry to hear about your grandmother. I hope you don't mind coming home with me?"

He shrugged, but then said, "I don't even know her. She and Mom weren't close. Besides, I don't mind coming home with you. Thanks for coming to get me."

Josie offered to take his school bag and when he handed it over, she slung it over her shoulder.

"We're going to have to hurry so we can get to Jason's school before the bell. I don't want him to have to wait for us."

Daniel nodded and followed her out of the office. She was parked a short distance away in her father's Mustang.

"You own a really cool car," Daniel murmured and there was a ghost of a smile on his lips.

Josie smiled back at him. "You like it, huh? It belongs to my dad. He restored it from little more than a chassis. It took him like...forever." She rolled her eyes. "Men and their cars."

His grin widened and her heart flooded with gratitude. She was so thankful to see him smiling—even if it was only over a lame joke about her dad's car. It was a start and she hoped she'd helped to take his mind off the fact that the judge's decision was being handed down the next day.

Jason was already waiting for her just inside the primary school's front gate. He gave a ghost of a smile when he spotted them and Josie waved. She got out of the Mustang and flipped the seat forward so that he could climb into the back then tossed his school bag in after him.

"Would you like to go for an ice cream? We could go to McDonalds."

"Okay," Jason murmured from the back seat.

Josie glanced toward Daniel beside her. "How about you, Daniel? Would you like to go to McDonalds?"

He shrugged. "I guess so."

Josie noted their reluctance but forced a smile. "Good. McDonalds it is then."

While the boys were enjoying ice creams, Josie called Chase and quietly brought him up to speed.

"Thanks for letting me know. I actually called the hospital earlier. I wanted to find out the likelihood of Trevor Logan being discharged in time to be at the court house with Daniel tomorrow. I think Daniel would appreciate having his father there. Thankfully, the doctors are pleased with his progress. He should be discharged in the morning."

Josie nodded and swallowed the lump that had lodged itself in her throat. "You're a good man, Chase Barrington. Don't ever let anyone tell you different."

He muttered a response that Josie didn't hear, but she could tell that he was pleased. He promised to stop by later. She ended the call with a soft smile on her face and then called out to the boys.

"There's something I want to tell you both. It's about your dad."

Their faces immediately sobered and she hastened to reassure them that everything was all right.

"In fact, your dad's doing great. The doctor's hoping he'll be well enough to come home tomorrow. That will be great, won't it?"

Both boys nodded solemnly and then Jason broke out in a grin. It had been so long since she'd seen him smile, she was a little taken aback.

"Dad's coming home? Is it true?" he asked with more life in his eyes than she'd seen all afternoon.

Josie nodded. "Yes, hopefully he'll be discharged from the hospital in the morning."

"I have to be back in court in the morning," Daniel stated flatly.

"Yes," Josie said carefully. "And Detective Barrington and I are hoping your dad will be there with you."

A tiny light of hope glinted deep within Daniel's eyes. "Dad will be there? At the court house? He'll be there when the judge makes his decision?"

"Yes, sweetheart, I believe he will."

"So, he's all better? He's well enough to come home?"

Josie's heart filled with sadness at the anguish and hope that warred on Daniel's young face. He'd been through more than most adults and he was only twelve years old.

"Yes, darling. I believe the doctors have agreed that he's well enough to come home. I'm sure he's eager to see you again."

Daniel nodded and bit his lip and Josie could see he was trying hard to hold back tears. Unable to help herself, she stood and put her arms around both boys and hugged them close. Daniel sniffed and then the tears began to fall: big, quiet tears that slid soundlessly down his cheeks. Jason buried his face in her clothes and clung to her.

After a little while, both boys pulled away. Daniel swiped at his eyes with the back of his hand. Jason's expression remained sober. Josie almost wished the younger boy would break down, too. Bottling up his emotions wasn't healthy.

She made a mental note to speak with his school counselor about it.

"Let's go home," she suggested softly and was rewarded with nods from both of them. Gathering her handbag and keys, they left the restaurant and headed toward the car.

———————

Scott Jones floored the accelerator pedal. The cheap second-hand car fishtailed down the highway and he shouted with jubilation. He was finally free of the shithole that had taken six years of his life. The guards had processed him early and he was making good time. He calculated he'd arrive in Watervale late in the afternoon, with plenty of time to scope out the town and locate Doctor Josie Munro.

He'd been fortunate the photographs of her in the newspapers had been of good quality. Her image was seared into his brain. He was sure someone would know her and would tell him where he could find her, particularly when he told them he was a friend of the family and needed to contact her urgently. The ruse had worked for him in the past. There was no reason to suspect it wouldn't work again.

Most people only saw what they wanted to see. He'd tidied himself up a bit; bought some cheap, new clothes. No one would ever know that less than twelve hours earlier he'd been an inmate in Sydney's notorious Long Bay jail. No one would connect him with Neil. From what he'd been able to gather from the newspaper articles, Neil had been murdered before he'd even entered the town limits.

Scott licked his dry lips and scrubbed a scarred hand over his stubbled chin. What he wouldn't give for a shot of whiskey—or even a cheap bottle of gin. It had been six long years since he'd tasted alcohol and the thought of being able to pull into a bar and order a drink had him salivating.

He spied the indistinct shapes of the houses of another town a little bit up ahead and thought longingly of doing just that, but then he remembered the reason he was driving like a man possessed, straight through the middle of nowhere, and he bit down hard on the urge. He was on a mission to avenge the only man who'd ever shown him kindness.

Over the course of Scott's twenty-five years, he'd spent more time in prison than out. His latest stint had been drug-related—just like the majority of prisoners doing time. He'd barely been nineteen when he'd been convicted and sentenced to a non-parole period of six years.

He'd been stunned at the severity of the sentence. *Fuck, it had only been marijuana.* So what if he'd been growing his own crop? So what if he'd been supplying towns up and down the coast? It wasn't like he was dealing in cocaine or crystal meth. They were the hard-core drugs.

His first night in Long Bay had been a nightmare. He'd been bashed while taking a shower. It was kind of a traditional way of saying hello to the newcomers, so he learned later. The pricks would probably have raped him too, if it hadn't been for Neil.

At the time, he had no idea why Neil Whitcomb befriended him. He only found out months later that he reminded Neil of his brother. The truth of it was, Scott didn't give a fuck about the reason: Neil Whitcomb had been his savior.

From that very first time in the shower, Scott stayed close to Neil's side. It didn't take him long to realize he couldn't have found a better buddy to look out for him.

Neil was an old hand and had spent more years in prison than out. There was no one in the system who didn't know him—inmate and guard alike. Neil had power in the prison that Scott hadn't even known existed and it was only the very brave or stupid who took Scott's protector on.

Occasionally, it happened and that's when Scott got to earn his keep. He might have been young, but he was fit and strong and the years of his childhood spent living on the streets had taught him how to fight. He was only too happy to show the idiots a lesson. Anyone who threatened Neil found out the hard way that it wasn't a good idea.

He'd put one bloke in the infirmary for the best part of a fortnight. He'd been a little stressed the asshole might die. But then, the fucker had pulled through and had returned to the cells, silent and suitably chastened.

The beatings served as a warning to others and for most of the time, he and Neil were left alone. It helped the time pass tolerably and until Neil had been paroled early, Scott's stint in Long Bay had been done in relative ease.

And then Weasel had brought him the news. Weasel had told him that the man who'd been brother and father to him had been murdered by some stupid kid.

He shook his head again at the memory and cursed aloud at the injustice. Neil had done his time; he'd repaid his debt to society and look how he'd been treated? Shot dead with a bullet to the back of the head. The kid had been too gutless to face him. It was an ignoble end to a warrior and Scott was determined to set things right.

Or die trying.

––––––––

Josie parked the Mustang outside the gate that led to the front door and climbed out. The boys had left the clothes she'd bought earlier in the week in the spare room, so there was little to bring inside, apart from their school bags. Jason had also taken the news of his grandmother's illness with surprising calm and seemed content to spend another night or two with Josie. Once again, she worried about his resilience and vowed silently to make time to talk to him.

As soon as they got inside, Daniel disappeared down the hall and Jason asked if he could watch TV. Josie nodded and walked into the kitchen. With a little sigh, she went about gathering supplies for dinner from of the pantry. She didn't know if Chase would stay and eat with them, but she hoped he might. Over the past few days, she'd gotten used to sharing the evening meal with him and now she made provision for him at the table.

After putting together a tossed green salad and setting out steaks to thaw, she remembered she still hadn't called the plumber and tugged her phone out of her handbag. She scrolled through her contacts and found the number and dialed. To her relief, it was answered on the third ring.

"Pete's Plumbing."

"Oh, it's Josie Munro. I had a job booked in with you earlier this week. Someone was supposed to come out and fix my blocked toilet. I'm not sure what happened, but no one arrived. I just wanted to make sure I'm still on the list."

"You out on Whiskey Creek Road?"

"Yes, I'm staying at the cottage on the Holloway farm."

"Yeah, I remember. Sorry, I got caught up with a broken sewer line. It took longer than I expected and by the time I was finished, I was stinking to high heaven. I wasn't fit for company. If you'd seen me, you'd understand what I'm saying."

"Okay, that's fine, but when can you come out? It's already nearly five."

"Oh, don't worry about that. I don't work to a clock. Do you have a second toilet?"

"Yes, I do, but I'd really like this one fixed."

"Oh, I'll get it fixed for you, love. I might not get out there until dark, but I'll do my best to get out today. How's that sound?"

"Well, I guess if it's the best you can do, then it will have to do."

"Like I said, I'll do my best. If I'm lucky, I might even get out there before six."

Josie thanked him and ended the call. She could hear the low murmur of the television coming from the adjoining room and wandered down the hall in search of Daniel. No doubt the knowledge that the judge was handing down his decision the next day was playing on his mind. She found him lying on his bed, staring at the ceiling.

Easing down, she perched on the side of the bed. "How was school?" she asked quietly.

His only response was a half-hearted shrug.

"You've had a lot to deal with these past couple of months. It's okay if you're feeling a little overwhelmed. In fact, most people would be feeling that way. Tomorrow's a big day. I want you to know that, no matter what happens, I'll still be here for you."

He nodded, the movement of his head stiff and jerky. "My lawyer said unless the judge decides I'm not old enough to know what I was doing, I'll be going to jail."

Josie bit her lip against the instinctive denial that rose to her lips. There was no point in giving him false hope. The reality was exactly as his lawyer had stated.

"You think I'm old enough to face up to my actions, don't you? That's what you told the judge."

"Yes, Daniel, I did, but I didn't say it because I want to see you punished. I was asked to provide my professional opinion and I did that."

"It's all right. You did what you had to do. You told the truth." He drew in a ragged breath and kept his face averted. "When I saw what that man was doing to my mom, at first I froze. It took me a moment to realize what was happening. Then I just went into action. It was like a switch had been turned on inside me. All I could think of was getting to the shed, getting the gun and blowing his head off."

Josie tried not to let his words affect her. It wasn't as if she didn't know how it had all gone down. Somehow, though, hearing Daniel talk about it in such a matter-of-fact way, made it all the more real.

"I made sure I loaded the clip with ten bullets—the most it could take. I wanted to make certain I did the job properly. The last thing Dad said to me before he left to go on the road was to look after my mom and my brother. And that night, my mom was being hurt. I had to make it stop."

Josie suppressed a shiver, hating that a child had been handed that responsibility, and had such an experience, such a horrific memory—a memory he'd carry around with him for the rest of his life. She leaned toward him and held out her arms. He turned and threw himself against her and buried his head in her lap.

She expected tears, but he didn't cry. For long moments, his body remained tense and then on a heavy sigh that sounded like the weight of the world was on his shoulders, he shuddered and went limp. A minute later, he pulled away from her and sat up with his back resting against the headboard. His expression was resolute.

"Thank you for everything you've done—for me and for my brother. I-I really appreciate it. I don't know what we would have done if you hadn't been willing to take us in."

"Honey, you're so very welcome. I'm more than happy to do anything I can to help you—both of you. You're such great boys. Neither of you deserve the turmoil and tragedy that has recently beset your lives. I wish I could take the pain away, but I can't. If I can help in even a small way, I'm more than willing to do it."

Daniel nodded and then compressed his lips and closed his eyes, as if staving off a surge of emotion. A deep sadness flooded his face. A moment later, he opened his eyes and she almost gasped at the raw emotion that pooled in their depths.

"I'm ready to face the judge tomorrow; I'm ready for whatever might happen. I killed a man and I meant to do it. No matter how many times I see his brain exploding against the wall behind my mom's head, I'd do exactly the same thing again if I had to."

He bowed his head and his voice lowered to a harsh whisper. "I must be punished. It's only right. I'm ready for whatever will happen."

"Daniel, you don't—"

"No. Please, don't say anything. I-I'd like to be alone."

Josie stared at him a moment longer, wanting to help, needing to ease his pain, but he kept his head lowered and his face turned away. Although it went against every one of her professional and motherly instincts, she swallowed a sigh and stood and quietly left the room.

––––––––

Scott Jones unfolded the piece of paper he'd tucked away in his pocket after the kindly old lady in the post office had provided the information he sought. Doctor Josie Munro was renting an old farmhouse on the outskirts of town. The nearest neighbor was apparently more than four miles away.

A surge of excitement went through him. It sounded perfect. He could have a lot of fun on the outskirts of town with the nearest neighbor more than four miles away. Everything was falling into place. Even now, it was like Neil was looking out for him.

"This is for you mate," he whispered, looking up toward the roof of his cheap rust box of a car. Leaning forward, he punched the address the woman had given him into the GPS and waited for it to load.

CHAPTER 23

Chase glanced at his watch and his pulse picked up its pace. His shift was almost over. He wanted to head over to Josie's straight after work. Every moment he spent with her was a moment to be treasured and stored away in his memory. It was soppy, romantic crap, but it was exactly how he felt. He knew what it was like to live without her. He also knew he didn't want to do it again.

He saw Riley heading out of his office. His boss was halfway across the squad room before he spied Chase at his desk. He changed direction and Chase braced himself, not sure what might be forthcoming. Riley hadn't spoken to him alone about Chase's relationship with Josie since the night Chase had spilled his guts to him at The Bullet.

"Chase, how's it going?"

Chase acknowledged Riley's question with a nod. "It's been a fairly routine day, boss. I interviewed Deleece Boney about the assault inflicted upon her by her boyfriend. She's sporting the biggest shiner you've ever seen, but now that it's daylight, she's decided she doesn't want to press charges. She's sure he only did it because she got a little mouthy when he came home drunk—again." Chase shook his head. "Without her statement, we have shit. He's gonna walk."

Riley grimaced. "How can we help these women find the courage to stand up for themselves if they keep going back? We need to do a better job helping them understand they have options."

Chase's fists tightened in remembered angst. It frustrated him no end the number of times they were called to a domestic disturbance only to have the offender walk free when the victim refused to press charges in the cold, harsh light of day. Of course, everything was so much more complicated than that, but it still didn't make the end result any more palatable. He doubted anyone had a quick fix solution, but it didn't mean he'd ever give up trying.

"About Josie, I take it you told her about the cancer?"

Riley's question jolted Chase's thoughts back into focus. "Of course. I told her everything."

Riley nodded. "Good. That's the way it has to be. You can't build a relationship on lies. Trust is everything. If you don't have it, you don't have anything."

"What about love? You won't make me believe you don't think the world of Kate."

"Of course, I do. I love her with my life. She *is* my life. But love's the easy part. Love can withstand more of a battering than you can imagine. You won't believe me now, but one day you'll discover what I say is true. It's been ten years since you and Josie were together and yet, I bet you love her more than ever now. I bet you never stopped loving her, right?"

"Right."

"See? That's what I'm talking about. That's how strong love can be. It's withstood a decade of neglect. Trust, on the other hand, is not so impregnable. Once trust has been breached, there's no going back. Not time, not forgiveness, not even love can restore that unshakable faith and belief we all have in the person we love before that trust is lost."

Riley stared at him. "People will try and tell you differently—that if you both want it badly enough and try hard enough, trust will be regained and things between you can be as good and as strong as it was before, but they're lying—or totally misguided. It can't happen. It won't happen."

His gaze intensified on Chase's, holding him captive. "I love my sister as much as any brother can. I accept that you love her, too. I can live with that. You're a good guy. But if you ever hurt her, if you ever give her reason to doubt you, you'll answer to me. Understand?"

"Yes, sir. I understand."

"I have four brothers. They're all in law enforcement. They're all older than Josie and they're all as big as me. Do you understand?"

Chase's gaze didn't flinch away from Riley's hard stare. "Yes, sir, I understand."

Riley's narrowed gaze held his for another long moment. As if satisfied with what he saw, he nodded briskly and then moved away.

"Take care of her. Make her happy."

"I will. I give you my word."

When Riley turned and walked away, Chase blew out his breath in relief. He stood behind every word he'd said, but it was a small comfort to have some physical distance between him and Josie's very protective, older brother. He glanced at the clock and noticed his shift was officially over and then looked down at his rumpled clothes.

Apart from his visit to Deleece Boney's squat on the less than desirable side of town, he'd also helped locate a child who'd run away from his mother at the shopping mall, followed up routine enquires on a well-known local drug dealer and dealt with a stealing incident at Watervale High School.

His once-crisp white business shirt looked decidedly worse for wear. He needed a shower and probably a shave and a set of fresh clothes wouldn't be a bad idea. Even though the Logan boys were there, he lived in hope Josie might let him spend the night, or at least part of it, in her bed. The least he could do was make an effort on his appearance.

With his mind made up, Chase logged off and gathered his things. At the thought of being with Josie again soon, his heart lightened and he left the office with a skip in his step.

Josie slipped into the living room where Jason lay curled up on the sofa. The TV was tuned to an afternoon game show, but his expression showed very little interest in what was playing out on the screen. He'd kicked off his tattered sneakers and socks and his feet were pale in the late afternoon light. Night would soon be upon them. The sun faded quickly in the fall.

She thought of Pete the Plumber and hoped he'd still make it out. Having a second toilet was convenient, especially with the boys. She glanced again at Jason's forlorn features and resolved to talk to him. She wondered if he was still receiving counseling from Phoebe.

Taking a seat beside him, she looked across at him and offered him the same encouraging smile she gave to all of her new patients. Most of them looked like him: uncertain, scared, but trying oh so hard not to show it. Like she had with his brother, she started out with a non-confrontational topic.

"How was school today?" And just like his brother, he replied with a shrug. Josie suppressed a sad smile.

"I spoke with your principal right before I collected you. He's a little worried about you."

Another slight shrug.

Unperturbed, Josie continued. "He's concerned you might not be getting all the help you need. There's been an awful lot going on in your life and a lot of people would be feeling overwhelmed. I know if it were me, I'd be going completely bonkers. I don't know whether I'd want to talk about it, but you know what? Between you and me, sometimes talking about it is the best thing you can do."

Jason remained silent, but she could tell he was listening. The glazed indifference had left his eyes and his expression was keen. He turned away from her, toward the television, but she didn't mind. The fact that he was listening was what mattered.

"Once, when I was a kid in high school, I tripped up and broke my leg. I had no great story to tell about how I'd done it—no glorified tale. I hadn't fallen off while galloping my horse; I hadn't come off my skateboard or my BMX bike attempting a death-defying stunt. Nothing as impressive or heroic as that.

"No, I fell over my own big feet while practising a cheerleading move I'd done hundreds of times before. To make matters worse, I did it in front of not only the rest of the cheerleaders, but the whole football team. They were on the field practising game moves. I'd never felt so humiliated."

A tiny grin tugged at the corners of Jason's mouth and Josie's heart swelled with emotion. At last, she'd gotten a smile out of him. With a deep breath, she continued.

"I broke both of the bones in my leg and pretty badly, too. I had plates and pins and screws put in my leg to hold the bones together. I was in a cast for eight weeks and then spent another four on crutches. I missed the entire cheerleading season. I watched it from the sidelines, unable to do anything else.

"Now, I don't know if you know anything about cheerleading, but it's pretty important to a teenage girl. I was so mad about breaking my leg, I was in a bad mood for more than a month. But I was also embarrassed about how it had happened and so I kept quiet about it for most of that time. Inside, I was furious I was missing the season; outside, I did my best to smile.

"My mom, of course, knew I was angry and upset and disappointed. She could tell without me saying a thing. Moms have special abilities like that. I think God made them that way."

A single tear welled up in Jason's eye and silently rolled down his cheek. Josie cursed beneath her breath. She'd forgotten for a second that he no longer had a mom. With nothing to do but to continue, she forged on, hoping he'd stay focused on her story and not on his recent loss.

"Mom told me it was okay to be mad. She told me to voice my anger. She encouraged me to shout and cry and yell out my disappointment and so, I did. Afterwards, I felt so much better."

She reached out and brushed a lock of unruly hair off his forehead. "Sometimes we need to voice our feelings, to give in to our temper; to shout out our hurt, to express our disappointment. All of those emotions are real and normal and need to be given their due. And afterwards, it's like all of those feelings we'd bottled up inside us have floated away in the air to dissolve and disappear like bubbles."

Jason's lower lip wobbled and he blinked as if to hold back more tears. Sliding closer, Josie drew him up against her and was quietly relieved when he leaned into her. She could feel the tension in his body and hoped he'd heed her advice. He was wound up tighter than a piano string. His pain was tangible.

"It's okay, Jason. Let it go, sweetheart. Let that anger and hurt and disbelief... Let that disappointment and confusion go. Talk to me about it and let's see if we can't make it disappear. I promise you'll feel better. I can assure you, I did.

"After I yelled and cried out my frustration and disappointment that I couldn't be a cheerleader that season, it felt like a weight had lifted, like I was ready to accept what had happened and move on."

She smiled down at him and ruffled his hair. "From that day, my attitude changed and I was okay about my broken leg. I did the exercises like the physical therapist told me and over time, I healed. I also made new friends that year—other kids who for one reason or another, spent their time on the sidelines. It never would have happened if I hadn't broken my leg."

He pulled back a little and looked up at her with wide, dark eyes. She was gratified to see the tears had dried and a little of the sadness had gone.

"Sometimes things happen that are so bad, we can't for the life of us understand why they happened: Why was God so angry? Why did he let it happen? Why me?" she whispered, her voice low and hoarse. "But later, after we've had a chance to think it through or yell it out or do whatever it takes to feel better about the hand we've been dealt, we often see a higher purpose, a reason for the ill that has come our way."

"But I don't understand why God had to take my mom away!" Jason shouted. "Why did she have to leave? I miss her so much. I want her back."

The last of his words were thrown at her on a howl of pain and Josie's heart broke with the sadness of it. Jason buried his head against her side and cried his heart out.

She put an arm around his thin shoulders and drew him in closer against her. His tears continued to fall, soaking into her blouse, and she made soothing noises against his hair. As much as it pained her to listen to his sorrow, she knew it was the best thing for him. She bet he hadn't cried much since it had happened, if at all. He needed the release that the crying bout would give him, even if he didn't know it.

After awhile, his sobs quietened to the occasional sniffle and shudder. At last, he raised his tear-stained face. He looked at her with such dejection, she almost cried out.

"Talk to me, Jason. Tell me about your pain. I want to help, honey. I want to help any way I can."

"You can't help," he burst out. "Nobody can. My mom's gone. She's never coming back. I'm never going to see her again."

"One day you will," she offered, hesitating a guess that he'd been raised a Christian. "You'll see her up in heaven."

"I don't want to wait that long," he sniffled. "I want to see her now. I miss her so much. Ever since she's been gone, everyone in my family's been sad. My dad's so sad he had to be put in the hospital. Daniel hasn't laughed once since it happened. I don't think he's ever going to laugh again. I miss my family—the way we used to be. I want things to go back the way they were before, but then I remember it's never going to happen."

"You're right, sweetheart. Things are never going to be the same again, but that doesn't mean you can't be happy, that you can't be a family again. It won't be the same without your mom, but your dad and Daniel love you as much as they always did. Nothing's changed about the way they feel about you, just like nothing's changed about the way you feel about them."

She tightened her arms around him and sent a short prayer heavenwards to help her find the right words that might help him understand.

"Sometimes bad things happen for no good reason—at least, not for any reason we can see. It makes us angry and we feel cheated. If things happen, we want to know why and we want to know that the reason is one that's worthwhile. Losing your mom is none of those things and it's normal to feel mad."

She reached down and tilted his chin up until he was facing her. "So, be mad. Scream and shout. Just like I did when I broke my leg. Somehow, it helps us to feel better, or at least, a little less mad. Sometimes, it helps us to heal."

"I don't want to forget her," he whispered in a tiny, sad voice.

Josie's heart tripped over with emotion and she blinked back tears. "No one said anything about forgetting, darling. Healing doesn't mean forgetting. Do you think I've forgotten the weeks and months I spent in the bleachers waiting for my leg to heal?"

He shook his head with the slightest of movements.

"That's right, I didn't. More than ten years later, I still remember every second of it and every minute of the pain. But, eventually it lessened and it got easier to live with. Eventually, I was able to look at it as a time in my life when things weren't bright and cheery, but neither was I without hope. My leg would eventually heal; there would be other football seasons. Your family will also heal and there will be other happy times. You won't believe me right now and that's perfectly okay, but honey, please do me a favor?"

He stared up at her. "What?" he croaked.

"I want you to call me. Whenever you're feeling sad or angry or frustrated or hurt or disappointed, or anything at all. Call me and tell me about it and I promise I'll help you feel better."

"Can you make my dad feel better? It makes me upset knowing he's too sad to be with us."

"Oh, honey. He wants to be with you! He wants that more

than anything, but you're right. He is sad, but he's talking about it to someone like me and they're going to help him through it. In fact, remember what I was talking about earlier, in the car? Did you hear me telling Daniel your dad's hoping to be at the court house tomorrow? If you like, I can arrange for you to see him. Would you like that?"

"If he's coming out of the hospital, maybe we can go home with him tomorrow? Do you think we can do that?"

Tears burned behind Josie's eyes at the hope and eagerness in the boy's eyes. At the same time, she tried not to feel disappointed that she might only get the night with them.

"Maybe. Who knows? We'll have to find out tomorrow, but if he's allowed out of the hospital, there's a good chance he'll be allowed to take you home."

Jason nodded, a contented smile on his face. With a sigh, he snuggled up beside her. He was silent for so long, she thought he might have fallen asleep but then he whispered in the dusk, "Thank you, Josie. You're right. I do feel better."

***

Scott Jones killed the ignition about half a mile from where the GPS told him the farmhouse rented by Doctor Josie Munro was located. He'd taken care to pull off onto the shoulder of the road and drive a distance into a thick stand of pine trees. The dense foliage hid his vehicle from the casual observer traveling along the road and he was confident if anyone did come along before he returned, they wouldn't notice it.

Flipping open the trunk, he pulled out the length of rope, duct tape and the knife he'd managed to procure from an ex con before he'd left Sydney. He would have preferred a gun. Somehow, it would have been fitting. But guns were expensive and not as easy to come by in a hurry and he'd had to settle for the six-inch Bowie. The woman hadn't looked hefty in the newspaper picture. It should be enough.

Stowing the items in his belt and the pocket of his jeans, he shut the trunk. With a last look around him, he headed in the direction of the Holloway place.

It didn't take him long to find it; it was exactly as the old girl had said. More of a cottage than the farmhouse he'd imagined, but it sat out in the middle of a field and apart from a few lights in some of the windows, there were no other signs of life. There wasn't another house in sight and he was filled with anticipation at what was to come.

Taking cover behind the occasional tree and otherwise crawling on his belly, he made his way up to the house. A shiny green Mustang stood in the drive, right outside the front gate. He looked for the keys through the window and found them in the ignition. Country people were so trusting. The Mustang would be an additional reward.

Night had fallen softly around him, but his eyes adjusted to the dark. Up close, the lights from the cottage were warm and welcoming and beckoned him forward with their soft yellow glow. The faint noise of a television could be heard over the chirping of the crickets. A moment later, the silhouette of a woman passed the window and he smiled. It looked like she was in.

Creeping up closer to the porch, he took the time to circle the perimeter. There was a queen-sized bed in one bedroom and two single beds in the other. In the dimness, both rooms appeared to be empty.

From what he could tell, it was just her and a young kid— a boy who was asleep on the couch. There was certainly no sign of a man. Perhaps she was a single mom, like his mother had been?

His lip curled up in disgust at the memories. His childhood had been far from happy. A surge of anticipation went through him. Just a woman and a child: His job was going to be even easier than he imagined. He couldn't wait for it to begin.

Daniel rolled onto his side and stared up at the sliver of moon just visible from his position on the bed. It was nearly dinner time. Any minute, he expected Josie to call him. She'd been so kind to him and his brother when she didn't have to be. She didn't even know them.

She'd been paid by the prosecution to provide them with a report on his mental state. He wasn't stupid. He knew they were debating about whether or not, when he pulled that damn trigger, he knew that it was wrong. Of course he knew it was wrong, but what was he supposed to do? Stand there like an idiot and watch the man hurt his mom?

His dad had left him in charge: 'Take care of your mother and little brother, okay? You're the man about the house when I'm not home.'

He'd taken his responsibilities seriously. Had acted before thinking. But like he'd told Josie, it wouldn't have mattered if he'd known he'd be facing jail. He would have reacted and acted exactly the same.

His mind turned to what might happen after the judge made his decision. The thought of going to jail frightened him. He didn't know anyone who'd been sent to jail, but on TV it looked like a scary place to be. The meanness, the cruel jokes, an underlying threat of violence: Even the thought of it terrified him.

If his barrister was right, Daniel could be sentenced to at least two years of juvenile detention—and that was if the judge was in a good mood. *Two years*. He'd be fifteen before he got out and that was if he were lucky. He couldn't help but wonder what things would be like when he was released.

Would he look the same? Feel the same? Would people treat him differently? It was bad enough now at school, with most of the kids unsure how to talk to him. Some of them thought he was a hero, but just as many more stayed out of his way, like they were scared of him.

Scared. Of him. He shook his head. Life sucked. There was nothing surer.

A shadow passed by his window and Daniel froze. His heart thumped hard against the wall of his chest. He hardly dared to breathe. Someone was out there. It was happening all over again. *Or was it?* Maybe he'd imagined it. He'd imagined a lot of things since the night of the attack.

He strained to listen for any sound, but there was nothing. Gradually, his heartbeat returned to normal and he relaxed. He told himself he was being silly. What were the chances of someone breaking in? It was stupid to even think like that.

They wouldn't be attacked again. Stuff like that only happened in the movies. Everyone knew that. He was being a baby, hiding away in the dark. Jumping at shadows.

The faint murmur of the television reassured him. He was in Josie's home. He was safe.

CHAPTER 24

Chase ran a brush through his wet curls and attempted to restore his hair to some kind of order. He'd taken longer at home than he wanted to, but the thought of a hot shower and fresh clothes was too tempting to resist. He shampooed his hair, had a shave and just finished brushing his teeth. A spray of his favorite cologne completed the job.

His grin in the bathroom mirror was rueful. The last time he'd taken so much care over his appearance, he'd been about to go on a date with Josie. He'd been all of eighteen and he was just as worked up in his gut then as he was now. He couldn't wait to see her again.

Striding out of the bathroom he switched lights off as he went and collected his wallet, cell phone and keys off the table in the hall. He snatched a jacket off the coat rack near the front door and was reaching for the door knob when the phone in the kitchen rang.

He stopped. His home number was private. The only people who had it were his family and very close friends. With his parents both dead, he counted his father's brother and his wife as his next of kin and took the time to stay in contact with them as often as time allowed.

With a sigh, he did an about-turn and headed toward the kitchen. If it was his aunt or uncle calling, it could be important. He hoped he wasn't about to hear bad news.

He picked up the phone on the fourth ring and answered it. "Chase Barrington."

"Chase, old mate. How are you doing?"

Chase smiled at the sound of his cousin's voice. With no brothers or sisters, Beau Barrington was the closest thing Chase had to a sibling. They were the same age and had spent many a school summer break together, getting into mischief.

They'd grown up miles apart, with Beau having been born and bred in Sydney, but their fathers had always been close until Chase's had died. Since then, both Chase and Beau made a conscious effort to stay in touch.

"Beau, I'm good. In fact, I couldn't be better. I'm feeling on top of the world."

"I see." There was a pause that lasted a heartbeat. "So, what's her name?"

Chase sighed in mock confusion. "I have no idea what you're talking about."

"Bullshit," Beau replied, laughter in his voice. "I haven't heard you sound this happy since your folks were alive. There has to be a girl involved."

Chase quickly capitulated, eager to fill Beau in on all the details. "You're right. Her name's Josie."

"I knew it, you sly old dog!" He paused and then added softly, "This one's really special, isn't she?"

"How can you tell?"

"Your voice went all soft and mushy when you mentioned her name. You're not the soft and mushy type."

Chase smiled. "You're right again—on both counts. She *is* really special. I've been in love with her for over a decade. I've finally been able to claim her as mine."

Beau whistled low in Chase's ear. "Wow, mate, that's...that's pretty special. Why did it take so long?"

"It's a long story, cuz and one I might fill you in on one day, but right now, I have to run. She's waiting on me for dinner."

"She sounds like a keeper, mate. Take good care, okay, and call me when you have time to chat. I'd love to hear how it took Chase Barrington, legendary Romeo of Watervale, a whole ten years to steal the heart of the woman he loved."

Chase chuckled. "You're so full of shit, Beau."

Beau laughed. "You love me for it, cuz. You know you do."

"Yeah, yeah, yeah. You'd better get back to the hospital. I'm sure there's someone that needs to be saved."

"You're right. That's what I do. I save people's lives. Some days I get it more right than others."

"You're a great doctor, Beau. Sydney Hospital's lucky to have you."

"Yeah, yeah, yeah. That's what everyone says. Didn't you hear? I made employee of the month the other day. Got my face up on the wall of honor and everything."

"As I said, you're full of shit, Beau."

Beau laughed again. "Say hello to your Josie for me."

"Yes and give my regards to... What's her name again?"

"Jennifer. We split up last week."

"Oh, I'm sorry to hear it."

"Don't be. We've been drifting apart for a long while now. Heading in different directions. She started talking marriage and kids. All of a sudden, I felt like I was suffocating."

"You haven't found the right one; that's all it is. When you do, running away will be the last thing on your mind. You won't be able to get her down the aisle quick enough."

"Speaking from experience, I take it?"

"Absolutely." Chase's voice rang with truth. He couldn't wait to call Josie his wife.

"I'll keep an eye out for the wedding invitation," Beau joked.

"Watch your mailbox."

———————

Scott crept up onto the front porch. A floorboard creaked

under his foot and he winced. Taking care to keep close to the shadows, he held his knife at the ready. Through the window, he saw a woman come out of the kitchen, wiping her hands on a cloth. She called to the boy on the couch.

Scott's gaze traveled over the woman's body, curvy in all the right places. Blood flowed to his cock. Within moments, his erection strained against his jeans. It had been far too long since he'd had a woman and this one was as fine a specimen as any. The light-colored blouse molded to her big tits and he could imagine them filling his hands. Her dark skirt skimmed her slender hips and ended just above her knees. Her calves were slim and shapely; her feet were bare.

All up, she was a very tidy package and he was going to enjoy her before they were finished. There was nothing surer. With the rope and duct tape firmly in his pocket, he reached for the screen door.

Josie tossed the towel she'd wiped her hands with, onto the kitchen counter and went out into the hall. She called out to Jason to wash up for dinner. Chase still hadn't arrived, but he couldn't be far away. His shift ended at six. She was sure he'd be there by the time she was ready to serve. Daniel still lay on his bed, now surrounded by the darkness. Josie sat down beside him.

"Are you okay?" she said quietly.

"Yeah. I'm okay."

"Dinner's nearly ready. Would you like something to eat?"

"Yes. Thanks, that sounds great."

"I've invited Chase over, too. Are you all right with that?"

"Yes. He's nice. I like him."

"Good. I like him, too." She offered Daniel a shy smile and was pleased when he returned it. In a lot of ways, he seemed way older than his nearly-thirteen years.

"How about you go and wash up? I'm going to put the steaks on."

"Sure. I'll come out in a minute and help."

Josie flashed him another smile. "Take your time. There's not much left to do. Come out when you're ready."

She left him and continued down the hall to her bedroom. Walking into her bathroom, she glanced at the toilet and remembered the plumber still hadn't shown. She swallowed a sigh. It looked like she'd have to wait until tomorrow.

She picked up the brush that lay on the vanity and ran it through her hair. She'd left it long and loose and it hung in soft waves around her face. Opening the top drawer, she pulled out a lipstick and swiped a generous coat over her lips. With a spritz of perfume, she left the room.

A sound near the front door caught her attention and her heart skipped a beat. Chase had arrived. Or maybe the plumber? She would be happy to see either one of them. She hurried down the hall and opened the door.

An unfamiliar man, small and indistinct in the darkness, already had the screen door open. Josie frowned momentarily and then comprehension flooded through her. She smiled and extended her hand.

"Hi, you must be Pete the Plumber. Thanks for coming out so late. I must admit, I'd almost given up on you."

The man appeared a little confused, but quickly recovered. A moment later, he stepped into the entryway. Josie closed the door behind him and wondered briefly where his tools were. *Perhaps he was coming in to diagnose the problem first?*

The thought had no sooner formed when she felt something cold and hard and sharp at her neck. The plumber's forearm came around her from behind and pinned her by the throat. Fear, acute and icy, raced through her veins and settled like concrete in her belly.

What the hell was happening?

She tried to cry out, but all that she could manage was a croak. Her windpipe was slowly being crushed beneath the strength and weight of his ropy forearm and it was all she could do to snatch enough breath to stay alive.

Her frantic thoughts flew to the boys and she prayed they would be spared. Another traumatic incident coming so soon after the two they'd already endured might be enough to tip them over the edge. Then she latched onto another thought: *Chase*. He was on his way out. He couldn't be far away. All of a sudden she was torn between wanting him there and praying that something would keep him away, keep him safe.

If he stumbled onto the scene unawares, heaven knows what would ensue. He'd immediately go into cop mode, but whether the outcome would be good or bad, only God knew. She found herself silently, desperately praying that he'd arrive and all would be okay, but the fear in her belly eroded any confidence that her prayers would be answered.

The man pushed her roughly down the hall, past Daniel's darkened room and into her own.

"One word and you're dead. Got it?" the man growled low in her ear. The knife pressed more tightly against her skin until she wanted to cry out, but she bit her lip until she tasted blood and tried to focus on the pain. It would take her mind off what was surely to come. She could feel the man's erection through his jeans. He was pressed up close behind her and there was no doubt about his intentions.

With the knife still held against the soft skin of her neck, he slowly eased his arm away from her throat until she could gasp and wheeze and suck in air.

"Not a word, you understand?"

Manhandling her over to the bed, he pushed her back, hard, and followed her down. The knife hovered in his hand, inches away from her face. He reached over her and with his free hand, switched on the nightstand lamp.

"I want to watch you while I fuck you. I want you to remember me in your dreams."

She shuddered with fear and revulsion and swallowed down the bile that rose in her throat. While she fought the urge to vomit, all she could think of was Chase and keeping the boys safe. If she stayed quiet, maybe he'd leave right after he'd finished and the boys would never know what happened.

One-handed, he pushed up her skirt and tugged down her panties; his hands were rough with haste. She heard the snap of his jeans and the slide of his zipper and bit down once again on her lip.

She moaned softly in fear and pain and tears rolled down her cheeks. She tensed. Any moment he'd be inside her, violating her, making her worst nightmares a reality she could never escape.

———————

Daniel heard a slight commotion at the front door and ducked out for a look. A lithe, well-built man held a knife to Josie's throat. His muscles bulged beneath his cheap cotton shirt and he pressed his beard-roughened face against her ear. In an instant, visions of that night at his house, of his mother, struck him with an intensity that left him trembling with terror. It was happening all over again.

He spun on his heel and ducked back into his bedroom, his heart pounding so hard it felt like it was going to leap right out of his chest. His thoughts were fast and panicked and he tried frantically to think of a plan. He had to do something to help her, but this time he had to think first.

She'd mentioned something about the detective coming over, but what if he got there too late? Daniel was already going to jail for one murder. What was another one, if it meant keeping Josie safe?

He looked around the room, his gaze glancing off the furniture. Along with the beds, there was a dresser in one corner and a closet on the far wall. He raced to it and tore open one of the doors and waited for his eyes to adjust to the dark.

The hanging space was empty, as was the area below it. He blinked rapidly, becoming increasingly agitated and then he saw it. Standing in the shadows, deep in the closet was a baseball bat, perhaps left there by the previous occupants.

His mind skittered over the thought, but he didn't have time to think. Right now, he needed a weapon and it was the closest thing he could find. He snatched it up and held it tight and crept back into the hall. The man had shoved Josie past Daniel's bedroom. He could only guess she was in hers. It was the only thing that made sense. Apart from the main bathroom, it was the only other room at that end of the house. With silent steps and a pounding heart, he closed the distance between them and prayed he wasn't too late.

Chase turned into Josie's driveway and his heart skipped a beat at the sight of the Mustang. The front rooms of the cottage were lit up with soft lights that filled the windows with a warm yellow glow. He couldn't believe how right it felt, coming home to her. Well, not exactly home, but he wasn't going to quibble. Soon it would be home. *Their home.* Maybe not this cottage, but somewhere.

He climbed out of his vehicle and reached into the backseat for the bottle of wine he'd stowed there. He'd remembered her penchant for Prosecco from the last time, and had stopped at the liquor store on his way out of town. With anticipation in his heart and a smile on his lips, he jogged up the front steps that led onto the porch.

The screen door was open. He frowned and went to knock on the front door. It opened under his hand. He frowned again.

"Josie?" he called out and then spied Jason in the living room. He was asleep on the couch. The television droned in the background. Chase left the room and went into the kitchen. A freshly made salad sat on the counter, along with a tray of steaks. The table was set for four. Everything was ready. But where were Josie and Daniel?

More cautiously now, Chase returned to the hall and trod

carefully toward the bedrooms. The first one he came to was the boys'. It was empty. His heart kicked up a gear and he told himself not to be stupid. They had to be in the house. It was dark outside. *Where else would they be?* Jason was asleep on the sofa. There was no reason to suspect anything was wrong.

Still, as he crept closer, toward Josie's bedroom, his cop instincts hummed louder and he strained to hear anything out of the ordinary. *Nothing.* And then it hit him: It was the silence that was amiss. There should have been the murmur of conversation or the sound of the running shower. Something. Anything.

And then he heard it. A gasp and a cry and then someone yelling, "Stop!"

"Stop it! Stop it, or I swear I'll kill you."

It was Daniel and his voice was ragged with fear. Chase bolted down the hall and came to a halt outside Josie's room. The door was closed. He put his ear to the panel, but could hear nothing over his racing heart. Reaching for his gun, he cursed under his breath when he came up empty.

Of course he was unarmed. He was off duty. He'd left his gun locked in the safe at work, like he always did. Forcibly calming his frantic thoughts, he tried to come up with a plan.

"Don't come near me. I swear to God, I'll knock your head clean off your shoulders." It was Daniel's voice again, but this time, Chase heard the answering murmur of a man. His blood ran cold at the implication, but he refused to ponder what might be happening behind the closed door.

Unarmed, he felt useless, but there no time for thoughts that were anything but helpful. He wasn't going to waste another second searching for a weapon—and calling for back-up wasn't an option. By the time he made the call and his colleagues arrived there, it could be too late. He had to go in and hope for the best. It was the only possible way. He drew in a deep breath and shoulder-barged his way into the room.

His heart stopped dead when he saw her, lying

spreadeagled across the bed. A man leaned over her with a knife to her throat, his gaze darting between Chase and Daniel. Josie saw him and her eyes widened with relief. It was quickly replaced by fear. The knowledge that she was scared for him registered way down deep inside, but Chase refused to allow her concern to distract him from the deadly situation.

"*Police!* Put the knife down."

The man stared back at him, his lip curled upwards with contempt. "I'm not finished yet."

"Put the knife down now and step away from the bed." Chase inched closer to Daniel, who seemed to be frozen to the spot. Chase noticed the baseball bat in the boy's hand and tried to catch his attention. Right now, the bat was the best option Chase had.

As if suddenly registering his presence, Daniel jerked toward him. Chase reached out and prised the bat out of the child's hands. Daniel's hands tightened momentarily and then he seemed to realize this was best and he released it without a word.

Chase took the bat and wielded it with purpose in the direction of the intruder's head. He advanced on the man and something in his expression must have given the other man pause. He looked from Chase to Josie and then back to Chase and with a curse, climbed off her. With the knife still in his hand, he half turned away from them and spat on the carpet.

"Put the knife down. *Now!*" Chase yelled and waited and counted the seconds, praying the man would comply. The two of them stared at each other for long moments, before the intruder appeared to give in.

An instant later, the man feinted to the left and then to the right, all the time slashing with the deadly blade. Chase kept his gaze narrowed on him and did his best to dodge the glint of steel. He caught movement out of the corner of his eye and prayed that both Josie and Daniel had the sense to run. He didn't dare turn his head and find out if his prayer had been answered.

The man came at him again, a glimmer of triumph in his eye. It was obvious he knew how to use the blade and either didn't care or didn't believe that Chase was a police officer. Chase sidestepped another vicious swipe, but not quite quickly enough. Fire seared through his left bicep and he gritted his teeth against the pain.

Glancing down, he saw blood quickly well up in the cut and drip down onto the floor. Dripping, not pulsing. *That was good.* It meant the prick hadn't sliced through an artery. With fresh anger burning through him, he advanced on his attacker with icy determination. With deadly accuracy, he swung the bat and landed a hefty blow across the other man's forearm.

The intruder screamed in agony at the same time Chase heard the distinct sound of breaking bone. The knife fell to the floor from useless fingers. For good measure, Chase swung the bat again and caught the man across the shoulders. The intruder went down in another moan of pain, cradling his injured limb close to his chest. Immediately, Chase advanced upon him and grabbed his uninjured arm. He hauled him to his feet.

Finding rope and duct tape in the man's pocket, the realization of what he'd planned came rushing at Chase and the implications made him almost lightheaded. With gritted teeth, he thrust the terrifying thoughts aside and secured the man's good arm to the steel frame of Josie's bed.

Leaving him there, Chase pulled out his phone and called for the police and the ambulance and then turned his attention to Josie. She stood just outside the doorway with her arms tight around Daniel. Tears streamed down both of their faces. It was hard to know who was doing the comforting.

Dark purple and red bruises lined her throat. The sight of them infuriated Chase, but he swallowed his anger. He'd save it for the scum on the bed.

He closed the distance between them. He pulled them both into his arms and hugged them hard. His chest tightened and he was so choked up on emotion, that for long moments, he couldn't speak. They stood in a silence that was only broken by the occasional quiet hicuppy-sob.

"I-I-I…"

Chase pressed a kiss against Josie's hair and tried to offer her comfort. *"Shh.* Don't talk. It's all over. You're safe. I'm here and so is Daniel. We're fine. Everyone's fine. No one's ever going to hurt you again."

She lifted her head and the expression of utter devastation in her eyes shook him to the quick. She turned to gaze at the boy by her side.

"Daniel," she croaked.

He ducked his head. "I-I'm sorry I didn't get here sooner, before—"

"But you…you did. You *did.* You stopped him. You're my hero, my very, very brave boy." Her voice caught on the last words and fresh tears coursed down her cheeks.

Chase could see Daniel was trying hard not to cry again. The tears welled up in his eyes and his breath hitched on a sob. With a sigh, the boy seemed to give up the fight and buried his face against Josie's chest.

Chase took a moment to check the wound on his arm and was relieved to discover the bleeding had almost stopped. He tightened his arms about Josie and Daniel like they were a life raft on a stormy ocean. It wasn't until he heard the faint sound of sirens in the distance that he loosened his grip.

CHAPTER 25

Despite the hot air that blew from the courtroom vents, Daniel shivered. The day outside was cold and dreary, mirroring the day of his mother's funeral. The feelings that weighed him down inside were just as dreadful, and a deep cold penetrated his bones. In a few short minutes, the judge would hand down his sentence and the final scene of the tragedy that had become his life would play out for all to see.

Despite the excellent representation provided by Blake Harton Jr nearly a month earlier, and the expert evidence given by Doctor Leonard Heather, the judge had found Daniel competent to stand trial.

When the announcement was made, he'd sucked in a breath, the judge's words pounding in his gut. While the decision wasn't entirely unexpected and his lawyer had warned him it was a real possibility, the totality of the judge's had words hit him like a ton of bricks.

When he finally could breathe again, he'd snuck a look at Josie who sat close by and wanted nothing more than to reach out and offer her comfort. Her expression was one of utmost sadness and desolation and tears sparkled in her eyes. Her reaction set off one of his own and he blinked hard in an effort to hold his tears. Now, the day of reckoning had arrived. In a few short moments, his sentencing hearing would begin.

He glanced around the courtroom. Despite the fact his

case had made national headlines, the public gallery was sparsely filled. He guessed it had a lot to do with the fact he was a minor and the judge had ordered a closed courtroom, keeping all but family and approved spectators outside.

Josie and Chase sat side by side with their hands entwined, seeming to take strength from one another. Daniel's lawyer had inadvertently told him Chase was footing Daniel's legal bill. He'd been nearly overwhelmed with surprise and gratitude. His father, while always being a good provider and hard worker, could never afford to pay for the likes of a Blake Harton Jr. It was just another thing he was grateful to Chase for. Over time, since the attack on Josie, the three of them had cemented a bond and Daniel was pathetically pleased to see them here.

His aunt sat near the back, on her own. He wondered, distractedly, how his grandmother was faring. His gaze drifted to the chairs directly behind him and he was overwhelmed to see his father and little brother there, their presence a reminder that he was loved and despite today's outcome, he'd always have a place in their hearts. His father offered him an encouraging smile that wobbled at the edges, but that wasn't what choked him up. The fact that his father was there was all that mattered.

Daniel's gaze shifted to Jason and he gave his little brother a wink. Jason's expression remained solemn and Daniel understood. There was nothing funny about the likelihood he'd be sent to jail. It was just that he didn't know of any other way to cope. If he didn't make light of it, he'd likely fall apart, right there, in front of everyone. He had to stay strong and make out it didn't matter. It was the only way he could survive what was to come.

The rap on the door behind the bench signaled the arrival of the judge, and the clerk asked everyone to rise. Daniel stood on shaky legs, glad that at least half of his body remained hidden behind the high wooden enclosure of the dock. His lawyer shot him a sympathetic glance and Daniel gave him a nod of reassurance. He was fine. He'd get through this. If he thought that often enough, it might just turn out to be true...

The judge took his place at the bench and everyone took their seats. To Daniel's surprise, the judge then looked across at Blake Harton Jr and asked him to call his first witness.

Daniel frowned and glanced around him to ascertain whether anyone else found this turn of events odd. He thought the giving of evidence was over. *What was this all about?* When Harton Jr called his father, Daniel was even more confused. He leaned forward and called out to his lawyer in a loud whisper.

"Mr Harton, what's going on?"

Harton turned to face him and then bent his head low. "I'm sorry, Daniel. I forgot to tell you. We're allowed to call witnesses at your sentencing hearing. The prosecution's entitled to call them too, but in this case, they've declined."

"What are the witnesses for?"

"To assist the judge in making his decision, insofar as punishment is concerned. I'm hoping once he hears from your dad, your counselor and Doctor Munro, he'll be more inclined to listen to my pleas for clemency."

"You mean, I might not get sent to jail?" Daniel did his best to keep the hope from flooding his voice. The possibility was nothing short of the feeling he got when he thought of winning the state cross country championship.

Harton shook his head and lowered his gaze. "You pleaded guilty to manslaughter. Like I said before, I don't have any real hope the judge won't impose a custodial sentence, but I'm going to do my best to ensure you're given the absolute minimum."

Daniel nodded and then sat back in his seat, prepared to face whatever came next. He'd pleaded guilty against his lawyer's advice, but it had been the right thing to do. He couldn't imagine pretending otherwise, despite the fact he now faced going to jail.

The sound of his father taking the oath and informing the court of his name and place of abode, snagged Daniel's attention and he fixed his gaze on the only parent he had left. Harton got to his feet and methodically began to ask his questions, with a command that would make anyone pay attention.

After covering his childhood and the times when they'd go hunting and shooting and fishing, Harton asked what Daniel's father thought about the events that led them there this day. Daniel sucked in a deep breath and held it, almost too nervous to breathe.

"I've never been more proud of my son," Trevor Logan stated, his voice firm and clear. He stared directly at Daniel. Daniel swallowed the lump in his throat and blinked back a surge of tears.

"What do you mean by that, Mr Logan?" Harton asked.

"I mean that he did what any man would do in the circumstances, only he wasn't a man. He's just a boy. Not yet thirteen. How can we hold him accountable? He did what he could to protect his mom. He was only following instructions."

"Would you like to clarify that, Mr Logan?" the lawyer asked.

"I was a line haul truck driver. I spent a lot of time away from home. Away from my wife and kids. Whenever I was leaving for my next run, I'd kiss my wife and my boys and tell them good-bye and then I'd turn to Daniel, and I'd tell him to take care of his mother and brother. 'You're the man of the house while I'm away. Look after them.' I said it every single time."

His father's breath hitched on a sob and then his shoulders began to shake. Daniel's chest was gripped so tight, he could barely squeeze through a breath. Hot tears burned his eyes and no matter how hard he tried, there was no holding them back. They slid down his cheeks in a watery path of pain and there was nothing he could do.

"Are you saying Daniel acted the way he did because he thought that's what you meant when you told him to take care of his mother?" This time, the judge made the enquiry.

Daniel's father lifted his head from where he'd lowered it

to his chest and eyed the judge through his tears. Grief ravaged his face.

"Yes, that's exactly what I'm saying. It wasn't Daniel who killed that man, it was me. Daniel might have been the one who pulled the trigger, but I'm the one who taught him how to shoot. I'm the one who applied for his gun license and though I never told him the combination to the gun safe, I knew he was there beside me every time I went to open it.

"Did I ever imagine he'd one day take a gun and shoot a man who was raping his mother? Not once. Not ever. But I can't say I'm sorry. He did what I would have done and now he's being punished."

Trevor lifted his arms and then lowered them back down in a helpless shrug. "The law is the law, or so I've been told. It's just the way it is. He shot and killed a man. I've been told he has to be punished, but I feel my son's been punished enough. His mother..."

When his dad turned to stare at him, Daniel couldn't drag his gaze away. His heart pounded so hard he could barely hear what his dad said.

"I want you to know son, no matter what happens, I'll never stop feeling proud of you and you'll never know how grateful I am that you did what you did." His dad's tears came faster and Daniel bit down hard on a sob.

"I love you, son. I'm so darn sorry it's come to this." He gestured toward the courtroom and its occupants. "The police, the lawyers—everyone tells me punishing you for shooting the man is the right thing to do, but it feels so fucking wrong. I'm sorry, son. I'm sorry. There's nothing else I can say."

Daniel's tears streamed down his face until he was openly sobbing, but he was way beyond caring. He pushed away from his seat in the dock and opened the gate that led out into the courtroom. The corrections officers guarding him made a half-hearted protest, but Daniel wouldn't be deterred. His dad stepped down from the witness box and closed the distance between them at a jog.

"Dad!" Daniel gasped and was enveloped in a hug so

hard it stole his breath.

"Son! Christ! I'm sorry. I'm so, so sorry. I love you, son. I love you."

His father's pain-filled words were murmured over and over again, like a recording that had no end. Daniel clung to his dad like a mountain climber who, at any moment, could slip and fall over the edge. His heart pounded, his breath came fast, but still he didn't let go. It was Josie and Chase whose softly uttered words finally penetrated his head.

"Daniel, honey, let's come back and sit down," she murmured and gently prised him away.

"Come on, mate, let me help you back to your seat," Chase said and took hold of Trevor's arm.

The rest of the hearing passed in a blur. Daniel listened to his counselor, Phoebe, explain to the court how he hadn't been thinking in terms of killing the man in his mom's bedroom. His only thought had been to protect her and for that, no one could blame him.

Josie backed up what Phoebe had said and also talked about the heroic way he'd saved her from a certain sexual assault. The reminder of that night sent a shudder running through him and he had to concentrate hard to remember that this time, it had turned out all right.

His lawyer pleaded for leniency and cited various case law as precedents. The judge seemed to absorb all that was said and after a short adjournment, came back with his decision.

While he accepted the prisoner was only twelve and had merely acted on instinct, it was also necessary to send a message to other members of the public that laws were there for a reason and had to be obeyed. Taking into account all of the evidence, and weighing up the need for deterrence against the need to be truly fair, the judge handed down a two-year custodial sentence with a non-parole period of six months.

Daniel's legs gave out underneath him and he collapsed down on his seat. *Six months non-parole period.* It was better than he'd hoped. Much better. And from the look on the face of his lawyer, Harton was happy with the outcome, too.

He leaned over and gave Daniel's shoulder reassuring squeeze. "It's a good result, Daniel. In six months, you'll be out of there."

Daniel could do little but nod. A moment later, Josie was beside him, enveloping him in warmth and love. She hugged him close.

"I'll come by and visit as often as they'll let me and I'll bring Jason with me. I'll make sure Phoebe is allowed to continue to meet with you and we'll keep up to date with your school work. We'll talk on the phone and email and before you know it, you'll be back home where you belong."

He stayed silent and buried his face in her chest and breathed in her sweet Josie scent. He had no more words and none were necessary: Nothing was going to change the judge's decision. He'd stay out of trouble and do his time and count down the day to his release.

He felt the weight of his father's reassuring hand, heavy on his shoulder, and blinked back a sudden rush of fresh tears. Knowing he had people who loved and cared for him waiting for his return would make the long days and nights ahead of him bearable. There would be life after the detention center. He was determined to make sure of it.

CHAPTER 26

Josie let herself into Chase's condo and set the sacks of groceries on the kitchen counter. She hadn't been able to bring herself to return to the house on Whiskey Creek Road and was grateful that Chase had invited her to stay with him. She thought of her early musings about the little cottage and was saddened to know that her dreams of buying the place and living there had come to such an awful, abrupt end, because after what had happened there, she'd never be able to live there again.

She shuddered at the thought of what might have happened if Daniel hadn't barged into the room, brandishing the baseball bat. His intrusion had been enough to startle the man who'd been intent on doing her harm and she'd never be able to express the depth of her gratitude.

Only that morning she'd visited Daniel in the detention center a couple of hours away and had been pleased to discover he was doing well. His school grades were up and he'd mentioned the names of a couple of other inmates who were fast becoming friends. At the end of their visit, he'd even given her a slight smile. It was a start.

Now, she emptied the grocery sacks of their contents and tamped down on a surge of excitement. She was cooking Chase dinner and she'd gone to great pains to make it special. Ever since the night of her attack, he'd treated her with kid gloves. At first, she'd been far too traumatized to do more than allow him to hold her close, but the assault had been more than a month ago and it was time to wrestle her life back.

She'd been receiving intensive counseling ever since it happened and had attended another therapy session earlier that day. She thanked God and Daniel for saving her the horror of a rape, but it had still taken exhaustive therapy and regular self-acclamations to convince her none of it had been her fault. She had been a victim of circumstance; a pawn in an evil man's plan. She hadn't asked for it, she hadn't deserved it and she owed it to her, Doctor Josie Marguerite Munro, to forgive herself.

Today, inspired by Daniel's progress, she'd made some progress of her own. She'd said the words aloud. Not only to herself, but in the presence of her therapist. And she'd meant them. She refused to be a victim for a second longer. She refused to let Scott Jones win.

She'd learned the name of her attacker through Chase after Jones' arrest. She shuddered again and whispered a prayer of heartfelt gratitude that it was over and he was safely locked back up in jail. His trial would come much later and she'd have to cope with the ordeal of giving evidence and re-living the memories that would inevitably resurface. For now, she'd focus on the present and that very much included Chase.

Chase Barrington. The love of her life: her moon, her stars, her everything. Despite the horror of the preceding events, whenever she thought of him, her heart swelled with happiness. So much, she didn't think she could contain it and she didn't want to. She wanted to cling to the feeling forever and die with a smile on her face.

The sound of her cell phone ringing interrupted her thoughts and she tugged it out of her handbag. Glancing at the screen, she smiled.

"Hello, Chase. I was just thinking about you."

"Nice thoughts, I hope. I'm always thinking nice thoughts about you." His voice was low and suggestive and she giggled. Heat stole up her cheeks.

"I was just calling to let you know I'm going to be home a

little earlier tonight. We've had a quiet day at the station and Riley told me to go home. Sometimes I really like that brother of yours."

Josie laughed quietly again and her heart rate picked up its pace at the thought Chase might soon be there.

"I'm just preparing dinner. Come home as soon as you can. I love you."

"I love you, too."

Josie ended the call and continued with her preparations. She'd bought fresh seafood from the deli and was making garlic prawns and rice. It was Chase's favorite dish, along with pecan pie. She'd ordered the pie from the bakery. All she had to do was whip up some cream.

She thought of other uses for whipped cream and the heat in her cheeks burned hotter. Though she'd spent every night since the attack wrapped up in Chase's strong arms, he'd done nothing more than kiss her softly and lovingly on the lips and hold her through the night.

Not that she was complaining. She loved being held close against his chest. She felt safe and secure and protected. But, she wanted more, she needed more and tonight, she was going to try her hardest to get it.

The thought of seducing Chase sent a flutter of nerves dancing around inside her and she flushed with heat again. They hadn't made love since the night before Scott Jones' attack and her body craved intimacy with him again.

Hurrying, she stored the rest of the groceries and put the prawns away in the fridge. They wouldn't take long to cook. Right now, she had more important things to attend to.

Rushing down the hall, tugging clothing off as she went, she hurried into the bathroom and turned on the faucets in the shower. When the water was hot, she stepped inside the cubicle and quickly lathered her hair. She shaved under her arms and shaved her legs and rinsed out the conditioner until her hair was squeaky clean.

Knowing it wouldn't take him long to reach his condo, she turned off the water and quickly toweled herself dry. Striding naked into the bedroom, she opened Chase's closet and took out the shopping bag she'd stowed in there a couple of days earlier, after she'd been browsing through the women's section in a department store.

The black satin and lace negligee had snagged her attention from right across the room. It had been displayed on a shapely mannequin that filled it out in all the right places. She'd wandered over for a closer look, checking over her shoulder to make sure no one else had noticed her interest.

The fabric was soft and shiny and felt like a river of silk beneath her fingers. The low V-neck and corresponding thigh-high slits up either side were more daring than anything she'd ever imagined wearing.

She turned away from it more than once, but each time, she'd been drawn back. The third time she returned to the display, she snatched one in her size off the rack and hurried to the cashier.

Thankfully, she was served by a young girl who was more interested in picking the polish off her fingernails than taking any notice of Josie's purchase. She'd brought it back to Chase's unit and had hidden it in the back of his closet, hoping there would come a time when she'd be brave enough to wear it.

Now, she pulled the flimsy excuse for a nightie from the department store bag and shook it out. It felt as soft and silky as it had in the store and it flowed across her fingers like warm caramel. She imagined Chase seeing her in it and desire and anticipation coursed through her.

Working quickly now, she pulled the nightdress over her head and shimmied it down her body. It fit just as snugly as the one on the model in the store. She didn't have time to blow-dry her hair, but combed the wet strands and quickly twisted them into a loose knot. She spritzed herself with perfume and had just disposed of the store bag when she heard Chase's key in the door.

Her heart stuttered with excitement and then, a second later, took off at a flat-out gallop. She heard him call her name and swallowed against a mouth that had suddenly gone dry. It was one thing to think about seducing him, but now that the moment was upon her, it was like it was their very first time. She stood frozen with indecision in the middle of the bedroom.

Chase appeared in the doorway and the look of shock, followed immediately by excitement, shattered all of her fears. As if in a trance, he shrugged out of his jacket and tossed it on the floor, his gaze riveted to hers.

"Jesus, Mary and Joseph, are you real?" he muttered and closed the distance between them.

A moment later, she was crushed against him and his hot mouth was over hers. He kissed her until she was gasping for breath and then he kissed her a little more. His hands roved over her back and caressed the satin-covered softness of her hips. His hand cupped her bottom and pressed her against his erection.

The feel of his hard cock pressing against her belly sent fire shooting all the way down to her core. She burned for the feel of him inside her and craved the relief only he could give. It couldn't come soon enough.

She squirmed against him and let him know with her mouth just how desperate for him she felt. In case he didn't get the message, she told him.

"I want you. I need you. Make love to me, Chase."

Emotion flared in his eyes and he dragged her back against him for another mind-blowing kiss. She threaded her arms up around his neck and clung to him. Suddenly impatient for the feel of his skin, she loosened his tie and struggled with the buttons of his shirt. Within minutes, she'd accomplished her task and sighed in satisfaction when she placed her palms flat against the firm muscles of his chest. They bunched beneath her fingers.

She bent her head and swiped her tongue over one of his nipples and was rewarded by his sudden intake of breath. With a surge of purely feminine power, she bit back a smile and laved the other one.

Chase threw back his head and groaned. "You're killing me, Jose."

"Can you think of a better way to go?" she murmured, her voice low and husky with desire.

His eyes flared hotly. Without warning, he bent and picked her up. In two long strides, he reached the bed and deposited her gently across its breadth. A moment later, he joined her.

Toeing off his boots, he kicked off his socks and then loosened the belt around his waist. Her hands went to his and stilled them.

"Here, let me."

His hands fell away and he lay back against the pillows. His eyes closed on a taut sigh. Josie knelt beside him and went to work on his pants. Within moments, the hindrance of his belt, button and zipper were removed and she slid her hand into his boxers. His cock was hard and hot and throbbing and she marveled at its size. Her fingers tightened around him and once again, she was rewarded with a gasp.

She released him and tugged at his suit pants and he assisted by lifting his hips. She pushed the clothing down his legs and he kicked it off the rest of the way. Her gaze roved over him and came to a rest on his erection. It strained against the fabric of his underwear and it was all she could do not to climb astride him.

But she wanted this time to be special. She wanted it to be all about him. He'd been so patient and gentle and understanding. She wanted him to know how much his compassion and his love meant to her.

She eased the boxers down his hips and once again, he accommodated her by aiding her in her task. They went the way of his other clothes. He stared at her through eyes shadowed with need and eyelids heavy with desire. Yet again, she closed her hand around his cock and this time, bent low and took him in her mouth. She swirled her tongue around his head and dipped it into his slit.

It was warm and salty and wet and she tamped down on her own need. Opening her lips over him, she took him all the way back in her mouth and sucked like she'd never get enough.

"Oh, Christ, Jose. That feels so good. Babe, you need to stop though. It's been awhile and if you keep that up, it will be over before it's begun."

She listened to his words and was once again filled with satisfaction. That she could make him feel so desperate sent a shaft of pleasure racing through her. The heat of it centered in her core and her clit tingled with need.

Chase gently tugged her upwards and she released him with a soft sigh. His cock scraped across her belly. She lay stretched out on top of him, her breasts crushed against his chest. The satin and silk lay between them and all of a sudden, even that thin barrier was too much.

She sat up and straddled him and then worked the negligee over her head. He stared at her with his mouth slightly open, as if he couldn't drag his gaze away. With a flick of her wrist, she sent the nightie to the floor and then slid down the length of his hard body, making sure she stopped when his cock slipped against her cleft.

Her lips were warm and wet and throbbing. She needed him inside her. Reaching down, she manoeuvred his erection until the tip of his cock pressed against her entrance. A wiggle of her hips and he slipped inside her and they both breathed sighs of relief.

"You feel so good," she whispered.

"I'm hearing you, babe." Chase groaned and surged up inside her.

Josie moaned at the feel of him stretching her wide, and began to move her hips. Fire and need built deep inside her and her movements became more frantic. She leaned over him and clung to his shoulders and cried aloud when he reached up and squeezed her nipples.

The action catapulted her over the edge, and this time, she cried out in relief. Her muscles contracted around his thick cock and she gloried in the feel of it. Slowly, she returned to earth and smiled down at him.

"Now, it's your turn."

He didn't need any more encouragement. In one quick movement, he flipped her over onto her back, his cock still buried deep inside her. Surging into her, he thrust once, twice, three times. The fourth time, he groaned and collapsed against her, spent.

It took awhile for their breathing to ease. Chase rolled off her and gathered her close in his arms.

"Wow, I'll take that homecoming any day. What brought that on?" he asked softly.

Heat rushed up Josie's neck and buried her face in his side. Now that the moment was over, she was shocked at her forward behavior.

Chase moved slightly and tilted her chin up so that she was forced to meet his gaze. "I'm not complaining, babe. Anything but, believe me. I guess I'm just…a little surprised."

"I met with Daniel this morning. He's doing so great. He… He told me you were responsible for engaging the services of Blake Harton Jr and that you footed the bill."

She stared at him and loved him even more when he blushed and looked away. The fact that his kindness and generosity embarrassed him only served to reinforce how wonderful he was.

"Is that what brought this on?" he murmured, indicating the rumpled bed where they lay.

She smiled and shook her head. "No, but I just wanted to tell you it was an incredibly generous thing for you to do and the knowledge makes me love you even more. I also had another counseling session. I think Daniel's quiet strength made me realize it was time. I need to put the whole thing with Jones behind me. I need to reclaim my life. My life includes you. There's no me without you. It's just the way it is."

Chase's arms tightened around her and he pressed a hard kiss against her hair. "I love you so much, Josie Munro. I'm never *ever* going to let you go again."

"I love you, too and for the record, I'm not going anywhere." She lifted her head and kissed him softly on the lips.

They lay in companionable silence until Chase spoke. "I want to talk to you again about babies."

Josie tensed and then eased out her breath. "I've already told you. It doesn't matter. I'm not going to lie and tell you I wasn't disappointed when I learned that you were more than likely sterile, but like I said before, I don't care. I don't love you only because I'd like you to father my child. You're so much more to me than that."

Chase squeezed her arm. "I love that you love me, despite my lack of fathering ability, but you know, all might not be lost. At least, that's what the doctors told me a decade ago."

He said it so quietly that for a moment, she wasn't quite sure she'd heard right. She pulled away from him and sat up. "What did you say?"

Chase sighed softly. "When the doctors started talking about removing my testicles and words like chemo and radiotherapy were bandied about, the word infertility also crept into my vocabulary. The doctors talked to me about the effects of the drugs I'd be taking and they urged me to have some of my sperm cryogenically frozen."

He shrugged. "I was nineteen. I'd just been diagnosed with Stage Two testicular cancer. I couldn't even think past the looming surgery with all its possible pitfalls and complications. The last thing I could focus on was fatherhood, despite all the dreams we'd shared. Lucky for me, my mother was more clearheaded."

"What did she do?"

"Mom was with me the whole time and it was she who insisted I do what the doctors suggested. And so I did."

Josie frowned and shook her head. "You froze your sperm?"

"Yes."

"Where are they?"

"I don't know. In a lab somewhere in Sydney. I have the paperwork in my office."

The implications began to leak into Josie's consciousness. "Do you think they might still...work?"

Chase shrugged again. "Who knows? They told me it was my best chance if I ever wanted to be a father."

At first, Josie's smile was hesitant, but the more she thought about what he'd just told her, the wider it grew.

"I'm not going to pretend your news doesn't thrill me. Even the possibility of having your baby makes me go warm and soft inside. It would be amazing and so unbelievably lucky—a miracle, even—but I still stand by what I told you earlier. The truth is, baby or no baby, I love you. I always have and I always will."

Epilogue

Four months later

Josie hung up another framed picture on the wall of her new living room. They'd purchased the house on the edge of town a day after their whirlwind wedding. The purchase had been completed just days ago, but already she was decorating.

Chase was still at work, but she'd completed her clinic early. She wanted to get home and finish what she'd started in their living room. A new leather couch, big enough to seat three, stood against one wall, in front of the widescreen TV. Matching reclining armchairs stood on either side. Cushions in hues of orange and red complemented the butter-colored leather and gave the overall room a warm and sunny feel. On one armchair, Josie had set a calico cushion that was very dear to her heart.

While she hadn't been able to bring herself to return to the cottage on Whiskey Creek Road, her longing for a little land outside of town hadn't diminished. The house they'd managed to find was perfect.

On the opposite side of town, it was still far enough away from the town limits that they weren't bothered by noise and traffic. Their five acres was also large enough for the coveted veggie patch. They were even planning to run a handful of chickens.

Josie hung the final picture—her favorite one taken at

their wedding—and stood back to admire her handiwork. It looked good—no, it looked great. Just liked she'd imagined. She couldn't wait to show Chase. And that wasn't the only thing she couldn't wait to show him. Although their first attempt at IVF a month ago hadn't been successful, she was still excited about her news.

As if conjuring him up, she heard his vehicle pull into the drive. Hurrying into the kitchen, she riffled through her handbag and pulled out the envelope she'd stowed there. Hiding it behind her back, she rushed to meet her new husband at the door.

He stepped up on the porch and greeted her with a soft kiss.

"Happy birthday, darling. I'm sorry I couldn't get away earlier. There was a car accident out on the highway and it tied us all up for hours. You probably heard it mentioned on the news. If you give me a few moments, I'll shower and change and then take you out to dinner, like I promised."

She smiled. "Take all the time you need. It sounds like you've had a hard day. But just before you go, I want to show you something." Keeping the envelope concealed behind her back, she took him by the hand and led him into the living room. "*Voila!* What do you think?"

His gaze traveled around the room, taking in the new curtains and pictures. She'd also added a walnut-colored coffee table and sideboard, their hominess completing the room. His gaze paused on the photos of their wedding and then dropped to the solitary cushion on the armchair. His eyes darkened with emotion. He drew her in close against his side. When he spoke, his voice was husky.

"You kept our cushion."

She smiled and nodded, too choked up to speak.

"It looks beautiful, sweetheart. All of it. It feels like home already."

She stood on tiptoe and planted a kiss on his mouth and wondered how she'd gotten so lucky.

"There's something else I want to show you."

He quirked an eyebrow upward in silent question. "*Mm?*"

With a deep breath, she drew her hand out from behind her back. In silence, she handed him the envelope.

He stared at it for a moment and then tugged out the letter inside. He scanned its contents. She knew the instant he comprehended its meaning.

"Foster parents? We've been *approved*? How did they process it so quickly?" His voice was full of wonder, his eyes wide with disbelief.

Josie beamed and nodded. "I don't know, but they did. I suspect Belinda Murphy might have had something to do with it."

Chase whooped and hollered and swung her around in the air, lifting her feet off the floor. His laughter rumbled through his chest.

"I don't believe it! When we talked about it, I was so excited at the possibility but I didn't want to get my hopes up. In fact, I tried not to think about it at all, especially after our attempt at IVF." He shook his head and laughed again. "Who'd have guessed we'd be approved the first time we applied?"

He spun her around again with a smile wider than the Mississippi and then set her back on the floor. His lips met hers in a loving kiss.

"I have so much to be thankful for and I owe it all to you," he murmured.

Josie gazed at him and her eyes filled with tears. She thought of Daniel and hope filled her heart. He had a month of his sentence to go. He would get through this, she knew he would and when he came out, she and Chase would be waiting to help him in any way they could.

Chase drew her close and pressed his lips gently against her tears. "Don't cry, sweetheart."

"They're happy tears. I can't believe we're now qualified foster parents. We can help other kids in need."

Chase hugged her hard. Josie sighed with happiness and contentment. "I can't think of a better way to celebrate my birthday."

Questions For Bookclub

1. In Australia, a child aged between twelve and eighteen is entitled to apply for a minor's gun license to be used in conjunction with the supervision of a licensed adult. Do you think twelve is too young for such a responsibility?

2. When Daniel came upon the scene with his mother and Neil Whitcomb, his first instinct is to get a gun. Do you think this reflex was a result of the fact he was familiar with firearms from a young age, or would anyone have reacted this way?

3. As a teenager, when Chase makes the decision to turn away from Josie without explaining why, he did it for her benefit. Do you think he made the right decision? If not, why not?

4. Daniel is charged with murder. Do you think this was the right thing for the police to do? What other choices did they have?

5. Daniel decides to plead guilty to manslaughter against the advice of his lawyer. Do you think he made the right decision?

6. Daniel was sentenced to a two-year custodial sentence. Do you think this was fair? Why or why not?

Note to Readers

I do hope you have enjoyed reading Chase and Josie's story. Please feel free to leave a review for The Defendant. Every review is very much appreciated and I thank you for taking the time to leave one.

The Shooting—Book Nine in the Munro Family Series is the next book in the Munro Family Series and is Tom and Lily's story.

Here's a sneak peek:

All that glitters is not gold...

Tom and Lily Munro have been married for sixteen years. They love each other and are happy in their respective, successful careers. With a cute teenage daughter and a son who has never caused them any grief, their life is just about perfect.

Then Lily becomes a victim of a school shooting and is left fighting for her life. Tom's beside himself with fear. What will he do if she dies? How will he live without her? And what about the suspicious lump he's found in his breast? Does he have the courage to find out if it's serious?

In the midst of his fear and panic and indecision, his daughter begins acting out. With Lily still gravely ill in hospital, Tom's at a loss what to do. He has so much more going on right now. Finding time to sit with Cassie and delve into the reasons for her behavior are almost beyond him. He wants to believe it's nothing more than normal teenage rebellion, but his heart is telling him it's so much more...

His once-perfect life is falling apart—shattering before his very eyes.

Can he stop the carnage before it's too late? Will this Munro family ever be able to pick up the pieces?

The Shooting will be released on 20 May, 2015 and is AVAILABLE NOW for pre-order from iBooks, Kobo and Amazon.

If you would like to subscribe to my newsletter to receive news on upcoming Munro Family stories, release dates, book launches and other snippets, please go to my website at www.christaylorauthor.com.au and follow the link. I love to hear from my readers. Please feel free to contact me at christaylor@antmail.com.au Let me know who your favorite Munro family member is.

About the Author

Chris Taylor grew up on a farm in north-west New South Wales, Australia. She always had a thirst for stories and recalls writing her first book at the ripe old age of eight. Always a lover of romance and happily-ever-afters, a career in criminal law sparked her interest in intrigue and suspense. For Chris to be able to combine romance with suspense in her books is a dream come true.

Chris is married to Linden and is the mother of five children. If not behind her computer, you can find her doing the school run, taxiing children to swimming lessons, football, ballet and cricket. In her spare time, Chris loves to read her favorite authors who include Richard North Patterson, Sandra Brown, Kathleen E Woodiwiss and Jude Devereaux.

You can find out more about Chris and sign up for her newsletter at her website:

http://www.christaylorauthor.com.au